SIMPLY *Anna*

OTHER BOOKS AND AUDIO BOOKS

BY JENNIFER MOORE

Becoming Lady Lockwood

Lady Emma's Campaign

Miss Burton Unmasks a Prince

JENNIFER
MOORE

Covenant Communications, Inc.

Cover image: *Jamaica Kingston Devon House* by Eye Ubiquitous; Robert Harding. Reference Photography; Figure photography by McKenzie Deakins, http://mckenziedeakins.com.

Published by Covenant Communications, Inc.
American Fork, Utah

Printed in the United States of America
First Printing: September 2015

21 20 19 18 17 16   10 9 8 7 6 5 4 3 2

ISBN-13: 978-1-68047-364-3

To Marmé and Par
For all the late nights teaching me to sew,
Wendy's picnics at our special place in the park,
And slipping me wilds when we play UNO.

Acknowledgments

I AM SO VERY GRATEFUL to all who make it possible for me to follow my dreams.

My husband and sons support me every day, understanding when I forget to make dinner or need to rearrange their schedules to fit with mine. They are the foundation of all that I do, cheering me when I'm down and cheering *for* me when things are great.

The writerly friends who have taken me into their fold, offering a shoulder to cry on or a brilliant bit of advice. I could never do it without all of you: Josi, Nancy, Becki, Ronda, Jody, Marion, Jeanette, Christy, Margot, Ken, Cory, Chris, The Bear Lake Monsters, and Carla. Your encouragement means the world to me.

Jolene Perry, Margot Hovley, Lisa Schwebach, Mandy Kimball, and Melissa Fugazza, thanks for reading this when it was the roughest of rough drafts. Your input is a treasure.

And the team at Covenant. I am so lucky to work with you. Stacey Owen is the world's best editor. Stephanie Lacy's a marketing whiz, and Christina Marcano designs the most beautiful covers. Kathy Gordon, Robbie Nichols, and so many others work behind the scenes to make me look good. My name is the only one that ends up on the cover, but all of you deserve to be right there too.

You all bless my life on a professional as well as a personal level in ways you don't even realize. Thank you, thank you, thank you.

Prologue

Anna Wheeler paused, clutching the doorframe as the boat pitched. Once the vessel righted itself, she smoothed down her skirts and entered the ship's dining room. She curtsied, even though only one of the four adults noticed her.

Amelia—Lady Lockwood, Anna's mistress—caught her eye and smiled briefly before turning her attention back to the others seated at the dining table. The small table seemed abnormally large in the cramped space.

Anna pressed her book to her chest as she walked around the edge of the room as close to the wall as possible. If life had placed her in another role, would she still make it her habit to blend into the background? Would she be the center of attention—causing people to laugh, engaging in interesting conversation? There was so much she wanted to say, so many observations she wanted to share . . . But it was insensible to indulge in fantasies. She was not a member of high society.

She was simply Anna.

Her occupation relegated her to the position of bystander. She felt as though she was permanently on the outside looking in, watching others live their lives. A lady's maid must be content to observe, she reminded herself.

Anna had worked for Lady Lockwood since Amelia had rescued her from a cruel employer three years earlier. She'd been very fortunate to enjoy her new employer and situation, bidding farewell to her chambermaid uniform and dressing in Amelia's older gowns as she accompanied her mistress on errands and helped with her wardrobe. Although the countess hardly needed a lady's maid at sea, Amelia wouldn't hear of leaving her behind when they embarked on this voyage.

Lord and Lady Lockwood were the owners of the ship, captained by Sidney Fletcher, who was married to the earl's sister. Sidney also sat at the table with his wife, Emma, and their adopted five-year-old son, Nico.

Once she had overcome her initial bout of seasickness, Anna had assumed the role of a nanny aboard the ship, caring for Nico and Lady Lockwood's infant daughter, Lottie. Sidney and Emma had discovered Nico in Spain after his parents were killed by French soldiers. She'd rarely seen more loving parents. But Nico was a five-year-old possessing all the curiosity and recklessness of a young boy, and Anna had to watch him constantly on the ship.

In the first week of their voyage, a man had fallen from the rigging into the water, and though the crew had immediately reefed the sails and sent a lifeboat to search for him, they'd found nothing. After that, Anna refused to allow herself to be lulled into a false sense of safety, especially where Nico was concerned.

Anna walked to the cabinet on the wall, but before she opened it, the captain stood and rounded the wooden table to approach her. Anna dipped in a curtsy, an action she continued to perform in spite of the captain's assurance that such courtesy was not necessary on the voyage. "Is there something I can do for you, sir?"

"Quite the contrary, Anna. I'd hoped to thank you for your brilliant idea of rigging the canvas over one of the dinghies to create a play area for Nico. Who would have thought a small boy's imagination could make a lifeboat into a pirate ship?" The captain smiled affectionately as he spoke about the boy. "A six-week voyage is tedious for a child, and I cannot recall my son being happier—nor so well behaved. Though I do wish you had come to me with the suggestion instead of persuading my wife to act as though the idea were her own." He raised his brows kindly to show that he was not reprimanding her.

Anna glanced toward Lady Emma and then lowered her face. "I did not think it my place, sir, to advise a captain on the management of his ship."

He shook his head, opening his arms as he spoke. "Nonsense, in this case it is the management of a child. I fear it is my tendency to assign duties instead of remembering what it is to be a young boy. I appreciate any such help, especially while my wife is . . . in her present state."

Anna blushed at the mention of Lady Emma's delicate condition. If all went well, when the family sailed home to England after Christmas, they would have a new member.

The ship pitched, and Anna grabbed the back of a chair for support. The brass lanterns on the ceiling swayed, their pools of light moving back and forth across the room. The waves had grown rougher, even in the smooth water of the Caribbean. She had overheard the captain mention to the earl that afternoon that they were likely in for a tropical squall.

"Mrs. Fletcher indicated that the particular choice of companion for Nico was your idea as well—Mr. Harvey," Captain Fletcher continued, clasping his hands behind his back. "I admit I'd have never considered him for such a position."

Anna glanced up at him and looked down at her hands. "He seemed a gentle sort of person. Mr. Harvey mentioned once that he had a son near to Nico's age." She gripped the chair harder as the deck rolled. She hoped the captain didn't intend to scold her for such a bold suggestion. "I believe he has been despondent, possibly pining for his family. I only thought when I am occupied with helping the women or tending to the baby . . ."

"The pairing has been perfect." The captain leaned to the side, without seeming to notice, as the deck tipped. "Mr. Harvey has seemed in better spirits, his performance has improved, and Nico has taken on an air of calm as he's spent time with such a subdued man. You are an excellent judge of character, Anna, a talent I'm afraid is too often for naught in your profession." The captain spoke lightly, his smile broad, and Anna wondered if he was teasing her. One could never be quite sure with Captain Sidney Fletcher.

Sidney inclined his head slightly. "But I have disturbed your solitary time, and I know how precious such a thing is aboard a small ship."

"I have come to put the book away and fetch Nico for bed." Anna reached to unlatch the cabinet of the bookcase, but the ship pitched again, and the book fell from her hands.

It hit the deck, and Captain Fletcher scooped it up. "Edward Long's *History of Jamaica*. Third volume." He raised he brows and tipped his head to the side. "You have no doubt completed the other two."

Anna nodded and held onto the chair with both hands. She'd thought learning about the island would help dispel some of her anxiety when it came to traveling to such an exotic locale. "Yes, sir, and I hope to finish this last one before we arrive."

He opened the cabinet and slid the book next to the others. "I estimate you have a day, perhaps two. Though I predict we will spot the island before midday tomorrow."

"And will it take so long to arrive once the island is in sight, Captain?"

"The current will bring us to the windward side of the island, but as there is no harbor on the north shore, it will take another half day to reach Kingston on the leeward side."

Anna nodded. Although she'd heard the crew telling each other they were near to their journey's end, she'd not realized it could be her last night aboard.

"But you have no doubt learned all about the favorable trade winds in the Caribbean and Columbus's disastrous landing on the north shore in your exhaustive study." Sidney pointed to the bookshelf.

"Yes, sir, though I admit, I was far more interested in the tales of pirates and bands of escaped slaves." She fingered the pendant on her necklace and glanced up at him. "Are we in much danger from such men?" Anna felt a mixture of nervousness and excitement as she'd read the stories of the untamed Caribbean. She'd never expected to travel the world.

"I find myself more concerned about the French." Sidney lifted a shoulder. "We're still at war, after all. However, I assure you, this ship can outrun anything Napoleon should send after us. As for buccaneers, and Maroons—"

"*Any* of the three groups are equally likely to hold us for ransom and deliver us for a handsome profit," Amelia said as she joined them.

Anna curtsied, and Captain Fletcher inclined his head toward the countess.

Amelia pointed toward the books. "Even the buccaneers, or the Brethren as they prefer to be called, have become sadly practical." Her eyes sparkled as they usually did when she spoke of her island home and the oddities that awaited them there. "They do enjoy their reputation as bloodthirsty villains and foster it carefully, as it is to their advantage to be feared. But the truth is they are businessmen seeking a living. Not that their methods are honest by any means. They live by their own rules, bound to one another by oaths. Most islanders consider them more of an annoyance to be tolerated than anything, though it would not be wise to cross them."

Anna had a hundred questions on the tip of her tongue, but she knew her place and instead closed her mouth and smiled politely, hoping Amelia would expound on the topic without prodding. She wondered how Amelia could remain so cheerful while she spoke of murderous outlaws. "It sounds very . . . interesting, my lady."

"And you shall love Jamaica." Amelia clasped Anna's hand in her excitement. "The warm air, the flowers in the trees, the colorful birds. It is like no place on earth. I cannot wait for all of you to see the plantation. William and Sidney, of course, have seen it already." She turned toward her husband.

He nodded from his chair, where he held their sleeping infant in his arms.

The ship tipped, and the three of them shifted their positions to maintain their balance.

Emma approached and slid her hand in the crook of her husband's elbow. "Good evening, Anna." She rested her other hand on her round belly.

"Lady Emma." Anna dipped again. "Is Nico ready to retire?"

Emma smiled and looked back at her curly haired son. "He and I have quite different opinions on the matter." She motioned for Nico to join them.

But the boy shook his head. He folded his arms and scooted farther back into his chair.

Sidney sighed and raised his eyes to the heavens.

Anna approached Nico and knelt so they were at eye level. She set her hands on the arms of the chair and leaned toward him as if to share a confidence. "Nico, the captain tells me we shall be able to see Jamaica tomorrow morning. How will you be the first to cry 'Land ho!' if you are too tired to awaken early?"

Nico looked from Anna to his father.

Sidney nodded. "It is true, Nico. I wondered if you might be responsible for the management of my spyglass. I need a crew member with excellent eyesight."

"*Tengo—*"

"In English," Sidney reminded him.

"I have very good eyesight," Nico said. He opened his eyes wide as if to illustrate his point.

"You may be the perfect man for the job," Anna told him. "But if you do not get enough rest . . ."

Nico slid off the chair and took Anna's hand, pulling her toward the door. "Come, Anna. It is time for sleep."

Lady Emma and Anna exchanged a smile. Sidney and Emma kissed their son and bid him goodnight.

Anna glanced at Amelia and Lord Lockwood whispering together and admiring their beautiful daughter, Lottie. The familiar pang of loneliness swelled in Anna's chest. She touched the pendant at her neck. How she wished she had a family of her own, someone to kiss her good night. She brushed the thought away. It would do no good to dwell upon what could not be. A lady's maid was not destined to become a wife or a mother. She was bound to the family she served.

There was a time when her life had run a different course. If only things hadn't changed, she would have been presented at court, danced with handsome gentlemen, maybe even had a husband and a baby of her own by now. But the sudden deaths of her parents had ended Anna's dreams for her future. She was fortunate to have a position with a kind family and would do well to remember it.

Nico clasped Anna's hand again. Anna closed the door behind them, unfastened a lantern from the wall, then led him down the narrow passageway to the quarters they shared.

She helped Nico change into his nightclothes and told him a story, watching his eyes grow heavy. She lowered her voice, convinced he was nearly asleep when he sat up in the berth.

"Anna, *mi espada.*"

"Your sword?"

"I cannot go to sleep without *mi espada.*" Nico began to cry.

Anna knew from experience that he would only become more agitated if his toy was not found, and it would be virtually impossible to convince him to sleep at all. She brushed his curls off his forehead, laying him back down. "Do you remember where you left it?"

"*Sí.* In the pirate ship."

She remembered precisely where Nico had placed the toy sword in the lifeboat when they'd been called to supper. "Then I shall fetch it," she said. "But only if you stay in your berth and close your eyes."

"*Gracias*, Anna," Nico said in a sleepy voice.

Anna lifted the lantern and stood. The choppy waves had not calmed, but if she did not hurry, they would only become rougher. She stepped into the hall and hesitated, glancing to where the light still shone beneath the dining room door. Then she hurried to the companionway at the other end.

Anna ran a finger over the pendant on her necklace as she did whenever she needed confidence. It had been eight years since her parents died of measles. The necklace, a gold disc engraved with her name, had been a christening gift. It was all she had to remember them by. *Not all.* She chided herself. She had memories of their laughter and smiles, an assurance that they loved her. That was more than most could claim.

Focusing her mind on the task at hand, Anna held onto the rails and climbed the steps of the companionway, ignoring the creaking of the ship as it rocked on the building waves. Raindrops pattered on the sails and decks.

The deck tilted, and she held onto the railing to wait as the ship righted itself. She stepped from beneath the overhang, wishing she had a cloak to pull over her head against the rain.

The lifeboats were stored above the deckhouse. Mr. Harvey had fashioned a rope ladder that could be rolled up and stored with the dinghy to keep the deck clear. Nico was much quicker than Anna at scaling the ladder, but over the past few days, she'd joined him in his private "pirate ship" often enough that she knew she could make quick work of climbing up and fetching the boy's missing sword, even encumbered with the lantern.

She reached with one arm to release the ladder from its coil. The wind blew it from her grasp, and she clutched the gunwale railing to keep her balance. She gasped at the cold as a spray of seawater soaked her. Little streams of water flowed over her face and dripped down her back. Luckily the flame remained lit.

Since there was nowhere to set the lantern, she continued to hold it with one hand and released her grasp on the rail to catch the flapping rope ladder. Once she had a firm grip and placed her foot on the bottom rung, it would be only a matter of working her way up to the deck. The sails flapped noisily overhead, and the wind moaned. She looked upward at the blackness, grateful for the lantern. From this distance, the running lights at the stern were merely smudges. A wave of fear washed over her, and she started to question her decision to go after the sword. She hadn't wanted to bother anyone, but now . . .

The ladder swayed, and she pressed herself against the ropes as tightly as she could. A strong gust pulled her hair from its fastenings, and for a moment she couldn't see at all.

She shook the soaked curls out of her face. Irritation began to replace fear. This circumstance was of her own making. She'd been foolish to go above decks in a storm when she could have simply told Captain Fletcher or another crew member where to find the toy. She was ridiculous to think she was the person to retrieve it. Why could she not simply follow directions? Why did she feel it her duty to solve every problem? Her need to delve into matters that were beyond her and find a solution was her greatest shortcoming. She gritted her teeth. To turn back without the sword when she'd come this far was pointless.

Hurry, Anna. She climbed the last rungs of the ladder and knelt on the roof of the deckhouse as she worked to loosen the wet cords that fastened the canvas cover over the lifeboat. Once she was able to pull back a portion of the canvas, she shone the lantern inside, spotting the toy sword immediately.

She clutched the canvas with her free hand and swung her legs over the side, dropping down into the dinghy. A wave tilted the ship, and Anna crouched in the bottom of the lifeboat, holding tightly to a bench to keep from falling. The flapping canvas over her head gave a small bit of shelter from the rain and the spray of the sea that pounded like a drum. For a moment she contemplated remaining inside, warm and dry, until the storm passed. But she knew if she was gone much longer, someone might put themselves in danger to come searching for her.

Anna climbed back out of the lifeboat with the sword and lantern in one hand. She hurried to refasten the covering on the boat and turned around to descend the ladder. When she moved the lantern, the light shone upon an oar lying on the other side of the deckhouse roof. Nico or Mr. Harvey must have taken it out of the boat and forgotten to return it. Captain Fletcher had warned Anna and Nico numerous times about losing the oars. Without a way to propel the lifeboats, they could be helplessly tossed at the whim of the sea.

She again unfastened the canvas, moved to the other side of the dinghy, squatted down, and pulled the heavy oar toward her, but she couldn't lift it with one hand. The wind swept rain over her. She pushed her wet hair out of her eyes and set the lantern upon the roof, holding it in place with her feet. She wedged the sword beneath the hull of the lifeboat to keep it from being lost. When she lifted the oar, a wave rocked the boat, and the weight of the oar pulled her forward. She released it as she tried to maintain her footing and keep the lantern from tipping over.

The oar clattered to the roof and slid with the incline of the ship. She was certain it wouldn't land upon the main deck but would fall into the sea. Anna pulled the lantern's rope over her wrist to free her hands and fell to her knees, stretching across the wet deck to catch the oar.

She clasped the polished wood just as another wave hit the ship. The impact knocked Anna from the deckhouse roof. The oar she was clutching jerked her arms as it struck a line of rigging and rebounded, throwing Anna into the churning sea.

Chapter 1

A HORN BLARED, AND LORD Philip Hamilton, second son of the Marquess of Leavenworth, awoke with a jolt in an unfamiliar bed. His heart raced as he batted aside the netting that hung from the canopy above him and jumped to his feet. An instant later, his mind cleared. He recognized his portmanteau on the floor and his shaving implements upon the dressing table. He studied the room. He'd only seen it by candlelight the night before when a servant had shown him to the master's bedchambers. The walls were whitewashed, the ceilings high with exposed wooden beams. Gauzy curtains billowed in front of open windows. Some type of tropical fern grew from a large pot in the corner. Letting out a deep breath, he ran a hand through his hair and willed his heart to calm.

He walked barefoot across the polished wooden floor and stepped out onto the balcony, which ran the entire length of the upper story. A surge of unfamiliar smells assaulted him: rotting vegetation, heady flowers, and the unmistakable odor of farm animals. Exotic bird calls sounded through the trees. Insects hummed and chirped. The chuckles of poultry and the grunts of what he thought might be pigs came from the yard below. He squinted, but the grounds were shadowed. The light purple of the sky told him it was nearly dawn. The sound that had jerked him from his slumber must have been the trumpet of the conch shell calling the slaves to the sugarcane fields.

Since his ship had arrived in Kingston two days earlier, every sight, smell, and sound was new. Even the air felt different—heavy and damp and unbelievably hot. Philip had felt as if he'd stared at every exotic and unfamiliar sight with eyes as wide as a green girl at her first debutante ball.

Stepping back into the room, he searched about for a rope to pull or a bell to ring—something to call for a servant. He could not recall a time in his twenty-nine years that he'd arisen without a servant nearby to assist him—or at least the means to summon one. Even on the passage from England, a ship's steward had dressed and shaved him and, at Philip's bidding, delivered a warm breakfast. Philip curled his lip, irritated at the prospects of acquiring a valet and instructing the other servants in the proper way to perform their duties. But such was to be expected from his new life, he thought, in the uncivilized wilds of Jamaica.

He located his trunk in the dressing room next to his bedchamber. At least someone had delivered his luggage, although they hadn't bothered to launder and press his clothing, which was wrinkled and still stank of the sea. Philip gritted his teeth and shook out a pair of trousers and a shirt, dressing hurriedly and resigning himself to the fact that he would have to forego a shave as he was eager to inspect his newly obtained holdings. Six weeks sitting idle aboard a ship had tried his patience, and with all the unoccupied hours, his mind had done little besides dwell on his misery, his humiliation, and his heartbreak.

After his fiancée had jilted him and become engaged to his elder brother, Philip had seized his father's offer of the Jamaica plantation, and within two weeks he had boarded a vessel bound for the West Indies. He suspected that the marquess's own embarrassment at the scandal, as well as pity for his younger son, had dictated his proposal.

Philip would receive the sugar plantation as his inheritance. His father would continue to support the venture for a year until Philip acquired an understanding of the agricultural estate, after which the holdings would be in Philip's name and the success or failure of Oakely Park would be fully dependent on him. The plantation had turned a profit over the years, though not a large one. After studying the correspondence and his father's ledgers, Philip was certain that he could increase the earnings. He looked forward to the challenge. He would impress his father with his accomplishments and capability. And once he found a wealthy woman to marry, his assets would grow that much faster. Now that he had felt the bitter sting of love, he had no use for it and would therefore approach marriage in the way he believed it would best serve him—as a business transaction.

A working plantation in a savage land was a far cry from the grand estate in Kent where he and Jacqueline had planned to settle, raise children, and live out their lives happily together. But in actuality, the dreams had been his alone, and Philip's stomach clenched as it always did when he thought of *her*. He shook his head. She was no longer *his* dearest Jacqueline but, by now, his brother's wife, Lady Rothwell. The very idea of encountering the pair, not to mention the pity and gossip of the *ton*, had been enough to keep Philip inside his London town house for weeks.

Apparently many of his friends had known of the affair all along. The *Times* had even printed a caricature which portrayed Philip playing at cards, oblivious to the couple embracing behind him. In the end, Philip was the only one dumbfounded when he'd discovered her betrayal.

The awareness that she had merely toyed with him, batting her eyes and whispering promises, all the while scheming to ensnare the future marquess, made his face and stomach burn. Throwing himself wholeheartedly into running the plantation was his own sort of penance for allowing himself to be duped so completely.

Philip glanced at the mirror above the dressing table. His waistcoat was wrinkled. He hadn't tied his own cravat since his days at Eton, and the unsightly knot he managed to produce would have elicited scoffs and ridicule from his friends in London. He threw the limp strip of fabric to the ground and snatched up another. The result was not much improved nor was his disposition when he strode into the dining room a few moments later.

He sat at the head of the bare table and waited, his temper rising. Was he expected to prepare and serve his own breakfast? This entire situation was completely unacceptable.

"Hello?" he called but heard only his own voice echoing back through the rooms. Smacking his hands upon the dining table, he pushed his chair over the boards of the floor, as noisily as possible, and stood. If the servants were not going to appear, he would have to find them. If he had to rouse them from their slumber, they would be sorry.

He swept from the room and stormed down the wide hallway, peering into each doorway he passed. Was there truly no kitchen?

Where were the servants' quarters located? And how was it so blasted hot this early in the day?

When he reached the end of the hallway, he turned and marched back the way he'd come, but he found no one in that direction either. In the dining room, he paced back and forth in front of the windows and finally opened an outside door.

He stepped onto the patio at the back of the house. A wooden shack with a chimney emitting gray smoke stood before him, silhouetted against the brightening sky. Light glowed from the window, and a shadow moved inside the open doorway. The mixture of outdoor smells was now joined by one that he recognized—food. Strange-smelling food, but food nonetheless. Philip's stomach rumbled.

He crossed the distance and stepped to the door, rapping on it before pushing inward. A wave of heat floated into the already hot air.

A tall, dark-skinned woman turned from the stove, where she was prodding some sizzling brown strips of something in a large pan. She was the same woman who had shown him to his chambers the night before. *Betty*, if he remembered correctly. Rather presumptuous of a servant to expect to be addressed by her Christian name, but he would tend to matters of propriety later.

"Good mornin', my lord." Betty curtsied and tipped her head forward. She was dressed colorfully with a scarf binding her hair, and with a regal bearing completely unsuited to a servant. "If you be so kind to wait in de dining room; breakfast is nearly ready." She spoke with an accent he couldn't identify.

Philip was taken aback by her manner, which lacked the submissiveness he was accustomed to. He almost felt as though he were being reprimanded. "I *have* waited. For the better part of an hour." He raised his brows and leaned his head toward her to signify how completely intolerable this was. "I expect my meal to be ready when I sit down to eat."

"You rise at de same time every mornin', my lord?" Betty turned back to the sizzling shapes and scooped them into a bowl. She did not seem at all disturbed by his admonishment. "Or how will I know when you are hungry?"

Philip opened his mouth to answer and then closed it. Her question was not insubordinate, simply curious, and he had no answer. He'd never stopped to consider how the domestics knew when to serve a meal. It had just appeared, warm and ready, whenever he'd entered the dining room. But figuring out the routines of the household staff was not his responsibility.

"I do not intend to awaken on a schedule to accommodate the cook. The housekeeper should instruct you in the timing of meal service."

"My lord," Betty lifted her chin, "*I* am de housekeeper, and in de years I tend to Oakely Park, you are de first owner to visit de property. I follow directions, but I cannot read yo' mind." With a cloth, she pulled a covered pan from the coals. She lifted the lid, and a waft of steam carried the smell of some sort of sweet cakes to his nose.

Philip did not reprimand her for her lack of respect; he was too distracted by the noise of his stomach as she tipped the warm cakes onto a plate. And besides, he had already determined a solution to the problem.

"It appears the household is dreadfully understaffed. Search the servant registries or employment agencies and engage a cook. And while you are at it, find me a decent valet." Philip folded his arms. He was becoming decidedly uncomfortable standing in the doorway of this kitchen building speaking to a servant in her domain.

"I manage de kitchen perfectly well. Yo' meal will be served when it is ready." Her eyes narrowed the slightest bit. "Ezekiel will be yo' valet." Betty nodded her head toward a point behind Philip.

He turned as a dark-skinned boy hurried past him into the kitchen. The boy moved with an uneven gait; though in the gloom, Philip couldn't see what caused his limp.

"I hardly think the boy knows the proper way to tie a cravat or press a jacket." Philip tried not to scoff at the idea. This was bordering on the ridiculous.

"He learn fast. Once you teach him, he'll not need to be shown again."

Philip opened his eyes wide. The very idea of demonstrating the care and presentation of his wardrobe was beyond absurd. He struggled to control the irritation in his voice. "*I* do not know how to perform such tasks. These services are not done by gentlemen, which is why I need a valet."

The slightest tick of Betty's brow was all it took for him to feel like a child whose ignorance was just being tolerated. His unease had brought out a pouty quality to his voice that was humiliating. Not to mention it was completely beneath him to argue with the housekeeper. "I will await my meal in the dining room." Philip spun on his heel and hurried back into the house. He had never been so discomposed by an encounter with a servant, and he resolved to regain the upper hand the next time he spoke to Betty. But first he needed something to eat.

He drummed his fingers on the table while he waited, and presently the boy arrived with a pitcher of juice. Betty followed, carrying the remainder of the meal.

The brown strips, Betty told him, were plantains, a typical island fruit cooked in oil. The cakes were cassava bread filled with a sweet fruit sauce.

He lifted his glass and tasted the sweet drink but couldn't distinguish the individual flavors.

"Dis is boiled sugar, lime juice, an' coconut milk," Betty said. "In de mornings, men mix it wit' rum." She opened a cupboard door and removed a dark glass bottle, offering it to him.

He wrinkled his nose and shook his head at the vulgar idea of imbibing so early in the day, but truthfully, if he had not considered himself a gentleman, he would admit to being sorely tempted due to his growing irritation.

He studied Betty in the light of the dining room as she served his meal. It was impossible to guess her age. The skin of her face was smooth, but her eyes held the wisdom of experience. That and the poise with which she carried herself led him to believe she was likely ten years his senior, at least.

Once she had ensured that Philip had all he needed, Betty left him to his meal. The boy—*Ezekiel*, Philip reminded himself—stood patiently while Philip ate his odd but delicious breakfast. Philip wished he had a newspaper or something to distract him from the large brown eyes watching him. It was disconcerting. Philip wondered for a moment why it seemed different for a boy to stand at attention in the dining room than a liveried servant whom Philip would hardly have noticed unless he needed his glass refilled.

When he was nearly finished with his meal, a knock sounded at the door. The boy hurried away and returned a moment later.

"Mr. Braithwaite is here, my lord." Ezekiel spoke in a soft voice, low for his age.

Was the boy his footman as well? Philip closed his eyes and let out a breath. "Very well. Please show him in."

He put the annoyances of household affairs from his mind as he waited to meet his overseer. Before leaving London and on the ship, he'd read correspondence between Mr. Braithwaite and his father. Philip had not been impressed by the man's prose, but the plantation was consistently turning a profit, albeit a small one, so he determined that Horace Braithwaite's expertise simply tended toward business affairs and not written language.

Philip breathed deeply, anticipating the start of his responsibilities as a plantation owner. He was anxious to immerse himself in the dealings of the plantation, increase his holdings, and be an independent man. He would make his father proud, and finally Philip would be the commander of his own destiny, answering to no one and certainly not allowing anyone close enough to distract him. His heart was closed.

He lifted the drink to his lips again, and his eagerness wavered. He knew he could learn quickly and work hard, but a quiver of trepidation slid up his spine as he realized just how unprepared he was to start such a venture and to do it alone. He would have to depend heavily on the counsel and experience of his overseer. He hoped his confidence was not misplaced.

Chapter 2

At the sound of approaching footsteps in the hall outside the dining room, Philip brushed his napkin over his mouth and stood.

When Horace Braithwaite entered the room, Philip found that the overseer was not at all as he had expected. The man's clothing was slovenly. He wore no jacket or waistcoat but simply a tattered shirt, partially untucked and rolled up at the sleeves. His cheeks and nose bore the telltale red splotches of one who drank heavily, and his blood-shot eyes darted around, giving the appearance of a person who was naturally suspicious. His shoulders were broad, but his stomach was soft and protruded over his waistband.

"Mr. Braithwaite." Philip offered his hand, determined to act professional, even though the man had not presented himself thusly. "It is a pleasure to meet you in person, sir."

"Eh, so ya arrived, did ya?" Horace said with a broad accent. Philip hadn't expected his overseer to speak with the cultured tones of a gentleman, but he was surprised by the coarseness of his words and presentation. He gripped Philip's hand in his meaty one. "Yer younger than I thought."

Philip chose to overlook the man's faux pas in neglecting to refer to him by his title. By rights, he should be called Lord Philip, but this was not London, he reminded himself. He clasped his hands behind his back. "Yes. It is my intention to inspect and assess firsthand the workings of the plantation. You will find, sir, that I shall be much more involved in the management of the property than was my father. I intend to make my home here for some time."

Horace sniffed loudly and let out a heavy breath which smelled of rum. "Admire yer determination, lad, but if ya don't mind my sayin' so, a soft-handed dandy like ye'll not last the week." He obviously wasn't pleased with the idea of a supervisor.

Philip felt his neck heat in a combination of offense at the man's audacity and apprehension that his words would prove true. But it wasn't up to the overseer to deem whether or not his superior was equal to the task. "That remains to be seen." Philip bit off his words, attempting to keep his temper in check. "I wish to become acquainted with the plantation."

The overseer sneered. "As you like. It'll be hot as blazes soon; we should have started earlier." He turned to leave the room, and his gaze lit on Ezekiel, who looked at the floor and moved closer to the wall.

Philip followed Horace into the main hall but stopped as he tried to remember what he had done with his hat and gloves the night before. He'd been exhausted at the end of his journey, but he must have handed them to someone. Come to think of it, who should he speak to about readying his horse?

"If you please, my lord." Ezekiel held out Philip's top hat and leather gloves. His gaze was fixed on the ground. "I'll fetch yo' horse right away." He scurried out the front door with his awkward rising and falling gait.

Philip was surprised and a bit impressed that the boy so readily anticipated his needs.

When Ezekiel passed Horace, the man swatted him on the back of the head, nearly sending the boy tumbling down the front steps. The overseer yelled after him in the pidgin language Philip had overheard people speaking when he'd arrived on the island.

Philip was surprised at the man's behavior but refrained from commenting on it. He did not know the history, and it would not be appropriate to question his overseer in front of the servants.

He put on his top hat, strode down the front steps, and then turned to get a view of the house in the daylight. It was situated perfectly among shady palmettos. The impressive two-story white building showcased a balcony held up by white pillars. The style was so different than the heavy stone manor house where he'd spent his childhood. An explosion of colorful flowers surrounded the building and flowed from pots on the balcony. Slender palm trees with their large swaying heads lined the road leading to the front of the mansion. A swell of pride grew in his chest. He couldn't believe Oakely Park was his own.

Philip was still admiring the house when Ezekiel led the horse around the corner.

Horace walked to the shade of a small grove on the side of the house to fetch his own mount.

The horse Philip had purchased when he'd arrived in Kingston was saddled, and Philip could tell he'd been brushed down after the journey. He wondered briefly who cared for the animals. He would have to make sure the stable was one of his stops as he toured the plantation today.

Philip inspected the girth straps, adjusted the stirrups, and swung himself into the saddle. He allowed himself a smile. He had chosen to ride in the carriage for the last two days, owing to the fact that he'd not been in the saddle for months. But today, in the sunlight, he could not help the warm contentment that spread from his chest as he sat astride the horse.

The boy handed up a riding crop.

"Thank you, Ezekiel." Philip spoke absentmindedly as he took the crop in his hand, inspecting it before laying it across the saddle.

"Yo' welcome, my lord," the boy said, and when Philip glanced at him, Ezekiel beamed. His teeth were remarkably white contrasted with his dark skin. "Will dere be anything else, my lord?"

"No, that is all for now." Philip noted a softening in his heart at the boy's earnestness and hurried to squelch it. He'd obviously been out of society for too long and needed to take care to maintain the necessary distance between master and servant.

"Do not dally, boy," he said in a sharp voice, flicking his wrist in an indication that Ezekiel should move out of his path. The light in the boy's eyes dimmed as he limped backward, but his smile remained. Philip felt a tinge of guilt. He'd never known a servant so eager to please. Most were content to do their duty and remain as invisible as possible. He thought many took deliberate pains to stay out of his way. When he glanced back, Ezekiel waved his hand.

Philip turned his eyes quickly forward. He followed Horace at a gentle trot down the yellow dirt lane and up a steep hill nearly half mile from the house. They reined in, and the overseer told him that from this vista, he could view the entirety of his plantation, from the sea in the northeast to the Blue Mountains in the southwest.

"And how long have you been at Oakely Park, sir?" Philip asked.

"Going on seventeen years. Ye'll not find another what can manage the place as well as me." He wrinkled his nose and made a slurping sound as he sucked at something in his teeth.

"I certainly don't intend to take your position from you."

"As if a whelp like you could do this job." Horace dug his fingernail into the gap between his teeth and then studied closely whatever it was that he removed.

Philip tightened his jaw but did not acknowledge the insult. He turned his gaze to the fields below separated from one another by thorny hedges. The vivid green stalks in various stages of growth swayed back and forth in the wind. Oxen and mules pulled creaking carts heaped with loads of sugarcane toward a collection of buildings whose stone chimneys discharged gray smoke. Horace explained that these were the sugar works. Above them, latticework frames covered in canvas sail cloth rotated slowly atop the windmills.

"I did not see any windmills as I passed other plantations. Are they typical for sugar manufacture?" Philip asked.

"'Ere on the north side o' the island we've a steady wind. Most others use animals or manpower to turn the crushers."

The overseer pointed as he identified the various areas of the property. Past the main house was a small collection of buildings. Among these were the overseer's house, bookkeepers' offices and apartments, workshops, livestock barns, storage buildings, and a hospital. Even farther down the hill was a village of huts surrounded by greenery—the slaves' quarters.

"'Ave ya 'ad enough then?" Horace said, turning his horse and starting back down the hill toward the Great House.

"I should like to view it all firsthand," Philip said.

Horace shrugged his shoulders and nudged his horse back up the hill. Philip didn't miss the way the man blew out his cheeks.

Horace led him first to the sugar works. They dismounted and stepped beneath the thatched roof. Inside, huge rollers rotated, powered by the windmills. Dark-skinned men and women scurried about in an orderly sort of chaos, some unloading the cane, some feeding it into the rollers, some removing the crushed chaff.

Philip strode around the building, marveling at the immense machinery and the manpower required to run such an operation. When he watched the large rollers smash the sugarcane and squeeze out the juice into a waiting trough, he widened his eyes and leaned forward then quickly put himself in check, not wanting to appear too inexperienced in front of his workers.

Philip took a half step back, and as he did an immense man turned to face him. Not only was the man incredibly tall, his arms and neck were corded in muscle beneath his shiny black skin. His short hair was peppered with gray at the temples, and small wrinkles pulled at the sides of his eyes. Lines of raised scars ran along the ridges of his cheekbones, around his eyes, and over his forehead. Philip tried not to stare.

"Tribal marks," Horace said, pointing to the man's face. "Brutes damage their skin on purpose in Africa."

Philip had never seen anything like it. The marks were both fascinating and fearsome.

"This here's Malachi. 'E's the headman of this gang." Horace explained how different gangs performed various jobs on the plantation. Today, Malachi's gang ran the sugar works.

Philip assumed Malachi's age to be around forty—likely one of the oldest workers in the mill and certainly the strongest. Unlike the other slaves who moved around the building, Malachi met Philip's gaze with confidence instead of ducking his head.

The largest man Philip had ever laid eyes on, Malachi possessed a calm manner, a sureness unexpected from a slave. In the few moments Philip observed, he saw that the others looked to Malachi, a natural leader. Philip was reminded of stories of slave revolts on the islands that he'd read about in the newspapers. The idea of having Malachi for an enemy was terrifying. He hoped he would earn Malachi's loyalty.

Horace spoke to the large man in the pidgin language. Although Philip couldn't understand his words, the tone and gestures were unmistakable. Horace was berating Malachi. He held up a horsewhip, shaking it as he spoke, as if to emphasize his words.

The sight of the whip made Philip twitch uncomfortably. He did not think Horace actually had need for physical discipline at the moment. But perhaps there was something he did not understand about the way the mill was being managed.

The large man simply nodded and returned to work, pointing and speaking in a low voice to the other members of his gang.

"What did he do wrong?" Philip asked when they stepped back outside.

Horace shook his head. "Naught." He snorted lustily and swallowed. "Need to remind 'em who's in charge is all." He tucked the whip into his waistband and lifted his shirt, revealing a pistol. "Ye'd do well to remember, it's up to us, the *backra*—white men—to keep the lazy Negroes in line."

Philip was becoming even less impressed with his overseer as the moments passed. The workers seemed hardworking and capable, but when he and Horace had approached, he noticed a decided tension in the air. Philip wondered if it was just a natural reaction to the presence of a supervisor, but something about it seemed off.

As they toured the different buildings in the sugar works, it seemed as if the overseer watched the slaves, hoping for a chance to rebuke them instead of supervising their production.

The men led their horses down the hill, following the Roman-style aqueduct where the sweet-smelling cane juice flowed into large copper pots. Some men and women, but mainly older children, tended fires in the brick furnaces beneath the pots and stirred the boiling cane juice. The long-handled spoons they used to remove the foam from the liquid's surface were nearly as tall as the children using them.

As midday approached the heat was nearly unbearable. Philip eyed the workers' light clothing with something close to jealousy as beads of sweat rolled down his spine. His woolen jacket and waistcoat were damp and heavy in the island humidity. He couldn't imagine how hot it must be standing near the fires. Thank goodness for the breeze.

Horace was explaining that after the impurities were removed from the syrup, Barbados white clay was used to color the sugar crystals in the curing house in order make the white sugar used in baking and tea. Philip listened with one ear. His mind raced, and he felt completely overwhelmed. How would he ever learn all he needed to in order to manage the plantation?

While Horace droned on, Philip watched a group of women use poles to remove a pot from a fire. One of the women lost her footing and dropped her pole. The pot tipped, dumping boiling cane juice over her leg.

She screamed in agony, clutching her leg as other workers pulled her out of the way and righted the hot copper pot.

A child cried out, "Mama! Mama!"

Philip started in her direction, but Horace pushed him aside, rushing toward her. Assuming Horace was in a hurry to offer assistance, Philip was horrified to see the man instead seize the injured woman by the hair and beat her across the neck and back with his horse whip.

The woman cowered beneath the blows. The other women trembled.

The child screamed but was held back by a young girl.

A man ran forward, standing between Horace and the woman. He held his hands up. "No. Doctor! She needs doctor!" He turned to inspect her scalded legs.

"How dare you!" Horace snapped the whip on the man's back.

Revulsion flooded Philip. He was appalled by such cruelty. He rushed forward and grasped the overseer's arm. "Stop that immediately!" He wrenched the whip from the overseer's hand, his muscles quivering with anger. "I will not tolerate such brutality, Mr. Braithwaite."

The overseer's eyes bulged, and his face was red. "Need to keep 'em in their place. Ye show one bit o' tolerance for bad behavior, and they'll walk all over ya."

Philip glared at Horace as he pushed past, shoving the whip at him. "Step away, sir." He instructed one of the women to fetch a doctor and another to bring water to the injured woman. He knelt beside her and lifted her face. Her eyes were wide with pain and fear. The child ran to her, weeping. His stomach sickened at the overseer's behavior to the young mother. Philip would not even treat an *animal* so poorly.

The woman returned with water, and Philip left the injured woman to her care after being assured the doctor was on his way.

Philip marched his overseer out of range of the workers' hearing and turned to him. "Mr. Braithwaite." Philip fought to keep his voice calm. He stood close to the overseer, looking him directly in the eye. "I forbid any such beatings or floggings at Oakely Park. This woman did nothing wrong. She simply tripped."

Horace narrowed his eyes. "You've no idea what schemes the Negroes will invent to get outta work. Can't allow 'em to dupe ya. They're cunning."

The overseer's rashness and disregard for his authority heated Philip's blood further. "I will not allow such a thing, Mr. Braithwaite. If you cannot abide by my rules—"

"Rules?" Horace sneered. "The only rule is that the white man is in charge and must maintain order." His eyes narrowed as he lifted his whip again. "Negroes are easy to replace. 'Ere's no need to worry about punishing 'em too harshly." He snapped his whip in the direction of the man and young woman on the ground to make his point.

Philip held up his hand. "That is enough, sir," he said in a quiet voice. "If you cannot abide by these rules, I am prepared to terminate your employment immediately." The man's words and actions disgusted him.

"Blasted rich brat!" Horace yelled. "Ya think ye can waltz in and steal Oakely away from under me? After all I've done?" He reached beneath his shirt and withdrew the pistol from his belt.

Philip stumbled backward in shock. His heart pounded so forcefully he thought it might explode in his chest. What kind of place had he come to? He looked around wildly, his senses heightened to the point that his fingers hurt.

Instead of aiming the pistol at Philip, the overseer pointed it at the young woman sitting on the ground holding her child and the man crouching next to her.

Horace sneered at Philip. "You'll learn. You gotta keep 'em afraid. 'Is here's the only way to control 'em." He pulled back the hammer with his thumb at the same moment Philip—fueled by hot rage—leapt at him, pushing his arm upwards.

The blast from the gunshot tore through the air, and Philip's ears rang. He wrestled the weapon from Horace's hand and pushed him to the ground. "Leave Oakely Park immediately, sir. I do not want to see your face on this property again, or I will report you to the constable in Port Antonio." Philip was shaking so badly he didn't even know if his words were clear. He towered above the overseer, holding his gaze without blinking.

Horace stood slowly; his small eyes were dark bits of flint. "Ye'll regret this day," he said in a snarling voice that sent a chill skittering down Philip's spine. He turned his gaze to the workers, waving his arm around. "All of ye!"

Philip and the servants watched Horace mount his horse and ride toward the overseer's house. His ears continued to ring, and his trembles turned violent. He sat heavily upon a large rock to calm himself. The excitement over, his limbs became heavy with exhaustion. What on earth would he do without an overseer?

A group of men ran up the hill toward them, and Philip stood, knowing he needed to take control of the situation. One man introduced himself as the plantation surgeon, Dr. Bevan, and Philip set him to tending to the woman's injury. The other men were bookkeepers who had heard the gunshot and come to see what had happened.

Philip sent them to ensure that Horace Braithwaite indeed left the property, and he turned down any offers of assistance. He would meet with the bookkeepers tomorrow. He mounted his horse, wanting nothing more than a cold drink and a long nap. He turned the horse toward the Great House but paused and glanced up the hill behind him.

Malachi stood in the doorway of the crushing house. The large man held his gaze, bending his head forward solemnly, then returned inside.

Chapter 3

"My lord, there is something on the beach—over there on the rocks."

Philip glanced from Tom Norton toward the jagged shoreline. There was indeed something on the rocks, partially submerged. It resembled a bundle of linen. Whatever it was must have washed ashore, perhaps from the storm two nights earlier. He did not allow the lump to concern him; the rising tide would wash it away soon enough. A mass of textiles hardly registered among the cares tumbling about in his mind—not the least of which was a dinner invitation for that evening with his new neighbor John Stapleton and John's daughter, Clarissa.

Tom dismounted and walked closer to the beach, his hand shading his eyes.

If nothing else, Philip would acknowledge Tom Norton to be observant, another reason he was pleased with his decision to promote the bookkeeper to the position of overseer, in spite of the man's age. He was only a few years older than Philip.

Philip nodded. He had made a good choice, even though the man seemed abnormally interested in flotsam washed ashore by the sea. But Philip could overlook Tom's quirks, as long as they didn't impede his ability to manage the plantation.

From the reports he'd heard in the two weeks since dismissing Horace Braithwaite, Philip had gathered that the former overseer had been generally feared and resented. Dr. Bevan had told him lashings were a routine occurrence and described other, more brutal punishments that turned Philip's stomach. He had no idea such things were taking place on the plantation. Or anywhere for that matter. With no one to regulate the man's behavior, the slaves were deprived while Horace's pockets grew fatter as he appropriated the funds he should have used for their rations.

Philip didn't know where the man had gone after being dismissed, and truthfully, he didn't care one whit. He was glad to be rid of such a despicable person.

Philip gazed at the view of the ocean. The prospect was breathtaking. The water was so clear that even from this distance he could see the sandy bottom, colorful fish, and ragged coral. The shoreline was occasionally occupied by enormous sea turtles laying eggs or basking in the warm sun. White-crested waves crashed into the rocky shore and pulled back in a mesmerizing presentation. He closed his eyes for a moment just to listen to the relaxing sound.

He'd accompanied Tom this afternoon on an excursion to a part of his property the new overseer thought would be suitable for a coffee farm. Philip was skeptical. He didn't believe coffee could ever be as profitable as sugar. But he wanted to inspect every bit of his holdings and had agreed to accompany Tom. In order to reach the location, they followed the island road along the margins of the sea. The route led along the beach in order to skirt around the borders of another plantation.

Philip glanced at his pocket watch. It was nearly three o'clock, and the sun was blasted hot. He looked to where Tom was picking his way through the rocks and rolled his eyes to the heavens. Moving to the shade next to Tom's horse, he dismounted, giving the animal a respite as he started to pick his way through stalky grass to the beach.

"I think it is a person, my lord," Tom called over his shoulder.

Philip grimaced at the unexpected nuisance. If a body was discovered on his property, he should undoubtedly investigate. They would need to alert the constable as well. Mr. Norton's curiosity was going to prove a disruption to their schedule.

Philip stepped over the sand and jagged rocks, wondering if salt water would permanently damage his Hessian boots. He reached Tom and could see that the bundle was indeed a person, a person with a mass of blonde hair and—a gown. A *woman*. He squatted down, and the two of them carefully turned her over.

His stomach twisted when he saw her face.

The woman's head lolled to the side. Her hair was matted with blood. The skin of her face and arms were a deep red, swollen and covered in blisters. Her lips were cracked.

The sight made him ill, and he breathed heavily. Aside from his grandfather's wake, he'd never seen a corpse. He could not for the life of him judge her age, not in her disturbing condition. He noted her gown was not one of a servant.

Tom pressed his fingers beneath her jaw.

"You don't think she could possibly be alive, do you?" Philip asked. "Not looking like . . ."

"I do not feel a pulse, my lord."

For some reason the declaration brought a weight to Philip's throat. "From where did she come?" he murmured. It didn't seem respectful to speak loudly.

"I do not know." Tom stood and scanned the beach. "I assume by the severity of her burns, she has been exposed to the sun for quite some time." His gaze moved out over the water. "Perhaps she was shipwrecked?"

Philip looked back at the woman, trying to imagine how she'd possibly gotten to his beach. Had she indeed been shipwrecked? Were there others? The fear of his ship sinking had plagued him during the entire passage from England. He could not imagine the horror of floating in the massive waves of the sea and wondered at what this woman must have endured.

"My lord." Tom carried a wooden oar toward him. Ribbons and bindings of the same color as the woman's gown were wrapped around it. "I think this is how she came ashore. She must have tied herself to the oar to keep from drowning."

Philip leaned his head to see the back of the woman's dress. He did not want to touch the body again. The laces were indeed missing from her stays. A pity that she'd gone to such effort only to . . .

"And look at her hands." Tom lifted one of her red arms, pointing to a scraped palm. "She must have made it to shore, only to fall. Or a wave could have dashed her into the rocks."

Philip considered the scenario. Tom's deduction seemed realistic. And tragic. She had come so far. Survived the sea only to die when she was so close to safety. "So what do we do now, Mr. Norton?"

"Well, I suppose we—" Tom's head snapped around as the woman emitted a soft moan.

She was alive! The men stared at each other for an instant before they jerked into action.

"I'll fetch some water." Tom scrambled over the rocks to his horse.

Philip removed his jacket and used it to cover the woman's burned arms. He pulled her completely from the water and off the rocks, moving her into what he thought to be a more comfortable position on the sand. All feelings of revulsion were replaced by a frantic need to save her—and the frustration that he had no idea what to do. "Madam, can you hear me?" He reached to pat her face but thought better of it when he saw the swollen red skin and blisters. He clasped her shoulder instead and shook her gently. "Madam?"

Tom returned with his water skin and poured a trickle between her lips.

Philip lifted her head to help her swallow.

The woman didn't respond, and the water flowed from the corners of her mouth over her chin.

"She needs medical care immediately," Philip said. "Help me to get her onto my horse, then you must ride ahead to alert the doctor." He reached beneath her knees, lifting her easily, and walked up the beach toward the road.

"My lord, I will carry her."

Philip shook his head. "My horse is the stronger mount." He lifted the woman onto his saddle. Tom kept her in place while Philip climbed on behind.

Tom handed him the reins, mounted his own horse, and galloped off ahead.

Philip set a quick pace toward the Great House. He figured speed to be more beneficial than comfort to the poor woman. He held onto her as tightly as he dared to prevent her from slipping off. She was utterly limp. Philip couldn't help but notice how small and frail she was in his arms. Her head bounced with the horse's movements, and he carefully held it against his chest to keep her still. He glanced down at her mess of bloodied curls and was reminded again how far he was from London in this wild place.

When he rode up the lane to the Great House an hour later, he saw Dr. Bevan, Tom, Betty, and Ezekiel assembled on the front steps. He brought the horse to a halt and handed the reins to Ezekiel then climbed down as carefully as possible, keeping hold of the poor woman. Once he stepped to the ground, he slid her off the saddle and into his arms.

Dr. Bevan raised his brows when he saw the wound on her head.

"Shall I carry her, my lord?" Tom asked.

Philip shook his head, not wanting to jostle her more than necessary by shifting her to Tom.

"Bring her to de guest chamber," Betty said. She walked up the stairs with her typical regal grace. Philip wondered how she maintained her calm when there was a dying woman in his arms.

Philip and the doctor followed Betty through the house and up the stairs to a guest chamber a few doors away from the master's rooms. Philip laid the woman on the bed. When he pulled his arm from beneath her shoulders, something metallic caught his eye. He untangled it from her hair and stepped back to study it. A gold chain with a pendant. Tipping it toward to the window, he read the engraving on the disc. "Anna," he murmured. For some reason it was disconcerting for such a wretched-looking person to have such a pleasant name.

Dr. Bevan pinched her wrist between his fingers to feel for a pulse. He lifted her hair, studying the gash on her head. "She's lucky you found her," he muttered. He didn't look up but continued speaking calmly as he pulled up the woman's eyelids. "Betty, I shall require bandages from my bag." He waved his hand toward the black satchel on the floor behind him.

Betty retrieved the items. She glanced at Philip then raised her chin toward the door.

Philip knew a dismissive gesture when he saw one. He took a step backward, his gaze still on the woman lying on the bed.

"Dis is no de place for you. De doctor and I will help her." Betty glanced over his clothing and pursed her lips. "And you change and wash befo' dinner wit' de Stapletons." She shooed him out of the room and closed the door.

Philip looked down at his clothing, surprised to see his cravat, waistcoat, and jacket soiled with blood, salt, and sand. He lifted his gaze to the closed door in front of him then turned toward his bedchamber, wondering if he would ever feel like the master of this house.

Philip washed, taking extra time to scrub the dried blood from beneath his fingernails. It was sobering to see another person's blood covering his clothing. His stomach tightened as he pictured the wound on her—*Anna's*—head and her dark swollen lips.

He stepped out of his dressing room and was buttoning his shirt when the sound of a voice in his bedchamber caused him to start.

"Would you like me to tie yo' cravat, my lord?" Ezekiel said.

Philip closed his eyes for a moment, waiting for the burst of alarm to subside. He turned and found the boy holding out a wrinkled pair of trousers and a lint-covered jacket. Philip was suddenly exhausted. The troubles of managing a plantation and the discovery of a nearly dead woman had strained his nerves to the breaking point, and now he would attend his first social engagement since he'd arrived on the island looking disheveled and inelegant. He definitely needed a proper valet.

"Thank you, Ezekiel." Philip tried to keep his irritation from showing on his face. "I will dress myself this evening."

"Very well, my lord." Ezekiel dropped the clothing into a pile on the bed. "I will ready yo' horse, my lord." He flashed his teeth in a cheerful smile and hurried out the door.

Philip lifted his crumpled trousers. If it were not for the boy's merry grin, he'd have relieved him of his valet duties the first day, but for some reason he couldn't bring himself to do it. Perhaps it was because the boy tried so hard. He looked at his ruined boots and blew out a breath. The hopeful glow in Ezekiel's eyes reminded him of himself as a child, seeking but rarely finding approval from his father. The disappointment when the marquess had been too occupied or unimpressed with Philip's efforts still stung.

It would not for long, and his dinner appointment was the next step in achieving the esteem he'd searched for his entire life.

A few moments later, after surrendering the fight to form a fashionable knot out of a limp cravat, Lord Philip strode down the stairs.

Tom stood in the main hall. When Philip arrived, he stepped closer and handed him a wooden case. "You'll be needing this, my lord."

Philip took the heavy box and lifted the lid. "A pistol?" He raised his gaze to the overseer.

"You've not traveled alone at night. Crocodiles, highwaymen . . ." His voice tapered off. "You could take a servant."

"Kensington Estate is only a little over a mile away." He was not a child and, come to think of it, his only domestic manservant *was* a child. He was definitely not going to ask for an escort to ride such a short distance down the road.

Tom shrugged. "Night comes fast in the tropics as I'm sure you've noticed. And it's best to be prepared in any case."

Philip thanked the overseer and bid him farewell. He removed the weapon from its box. It was not a gentleman's weapon—not a well-designed blunderbuss with silver fittings on polished walnut—but a sturdy, long-barreled, battered horse pistol. He measured the weight in his hand. The bulky firearm would not fit into his pocket, and he didn't want to stuff it into his waistband and ruin the effect of his tailored jacket. In the end, he decided to hold it in one hand and guide the horse with the other.

He glanced back up at the window to his guest chamber, wondering if Anna would still be alive when he returned.

As the horse made its way toward the main road, Philip was struck by the absurdity of his day. If someone had told him three months earlier that he would be riding through a tropical jungle in disheveled clothing with a cumbersome weapon after pulling a mortally wounded woman out of the sea, he would have thought them destined for Bedlam.

Chapter 4

WITHIN AN HOUR, PHILIP SAT at a polished mahogany table in the Stapletons' dining room, eating a meal of stewed fish, sea turtle, and fruit. The house was decorated much like Oakely Park, with bare wooden floors and high ceilings. In the corners of the room, slave children waved large fans to move the warm air. They seemed much too small for the duty. Philip wondered how long they would be able to perform the task before their arms tired.

To his left, at the head of the table, sat John Stapleton, a large mustachioed man with straw-colored hair. John's daughter, Clarissa, was seated directly across from Philip.

Clarissa's face was round, her eyes large. Dark ringlets bounced around her head when she moved. Her appearance reminded Philip of a porcelain doll. "How do you like Jamaica, Lord Philip?" she asked.

Philip pressed his napkin to his lips and considered her for a moment. What kind of answer did her question warrant? Did she want to hear his true opinion? That the two weeks he'd spent as master of Oakely Park made him feel both overwhelmed and immensely contented? That he'd never been so lonely without his friends and family, and yet a hard day's work on the plantation brought satisfaction of which he'd never dreamed? He did not think she sought to understand his inner emotions, and instead he settled for a trite reply. "I have never seen a more beautiful land. The deep blue of the sea, bright flowers in every color—I should be happy to remain at Oakely Park forever." His response was truthful but vastly incomplete. How did one describe the conflicting emotions that every moment in this strange land produced?

The answer seemed to please her. Clarissa nodded, and her curls bounced as if they had a mind of their own. "I am happy to hear that, my lord. And do you know the society is very pleasant as well? We regularly travel to Port Antonio to attend balls and assemblies. There is no theater, but we do dine with the officers and their wives from time to time. Perhaps you would join us?" She puckered her lips and blinked her eyes while she watched him.

"I should be delighted to." Her wide eyes were slightly unnerving, and Philip dropped his gaze to his plate. "I thank you for the invitation." He took a drink of fruit juice and turned to her father. "From what I saw as I arrived, Kensington Estate seems a splendid plantation."

"You'll not find any better—the largest and most prosperous on this side of the island." John's voice boomed through the room. He puffed out his chest. "I'm even looking to expand, and at this very moment, my agent is very near to coming to an agreement about purchasing Landon Grove—the property next to yours. It's mostly jungle and mountains, but there's some good cane land, and the river runs right through. The absentee owner's run the place into the ground, and my man tells me he believes we shall secure the plantation for a song." He lifted his chin, obviously believing this to be an accomplishment Philip should appreciate. "And with her mother buried these five years, my Clarissa is to inherit the entirety of my holdings. Lucky is the man who marries her. He'll be rich as Croesus." John caught Philip's eye and raised his brow, nodding his head forward.

Philip didn't need to be hit over the head to take the man's insinuation, though it was extremely vulgar to discuss in front of Miss Stapleton. He felt a flush creep over the back of his neck and decided to change the subject—again.

He placed his fork and knife on his plate. "There was a strange occurrence at Oakely Park today, and I would ask your advice on how to handle the matter."

"Didn't fire another overseer, did ya?" John chuckled. He stabbed his fork into a piece of meat. "Heard you had a bit of a weak stomach for corporal punishment." He bit into the meat and kept speaking as he chewed. "Yer a little green yet. I shouldn't imagine it'll take ya long to learn the way of things." He grinned, showing bits of food in his teeth.

The heat did not disperse but flared from Philip's neck onto his face. The suggestion that he was inadequate for the job, that he refused to beat his slaves because he was too fainthearted, both humiliated and angered him. "I don't know what you've heard, but Mr. Braithwaite was completely out of line, sir. The woman—the *young* woman—he was flogging was injured, and—"

"Now, now, my lord, no need to get yer hackles raised. Like I said, yer soft yet, and 'twill take a bit of time before you come to realize how things are done." John motioned to a footman to clear his plate and pointed toward one of the children, clearing his throat and glaring.

The child had slowed in his task, but at the look, he widened his eyes and pumped the large fan more quickly.

"It's true, my lord," Clarissa said, as if they were simply discussing the weather. "Negroes need to be kept in line, or they become lazy and . . . well, where would we be then? A flogging isn't pleasant to watch—it can even be tedious at times—but we're their superiors, and we can't allow them to forget it." She nodded her head and picked up her knife and fork. "They aren't civilized like the servants in England. These are *Africans*." She looked at him directly, as if making sure he understood her point, and then proceeded to saw at the slice of pork on her plate.

John turned back to Philip. "Now tell me what happened today that's got ya worried."

Philip's stomach turned at the casual way the Stapletons spoke about beating their workers, as if it were more unpleasant for *them* than the slaves. He had never believed himself to be a proponent for the rights of servants. He'd hardly given the lower class a thought in England unless one was negligent in his duty, but the idea of using a weapon to inflict bodily harm on someone . . . He shook himself out of his contemplations. It would not do to criticize his hosts or delve into a debate about the treatment of slaves. Mustering a polite tone and casual smile, he continued. "Not so much worried, sir. I only seek your advice."

John nodded for him to continue.

"Mr. Norton and I discovered a woman on the beach."

"A woman?" Clarissa's eyes grew even wider.

"Yes, at first we assumed her to be . . . deceased." He did not want to describe in what state they had found her while Clarissa was present. Although from her earlier comments, he did not think his hostess possessed an overly sensitive disposition. "Dr. Bevan is attending to her even now, but she had not awoken at the time I left for supper. Mr. Norton speculates that she could have washed ashore from a shipwreck. Maybe the storm a few nights ago."

"It's possible, I suppose." John smoothed his mustache. "The current and all. Have you any idea how long she was in the water?"

"None, sir. I thought to alert the constable in Port Antonio. Perhaps send to Kingston and Black River to inquire about a shipwreck, or if anyone is searching for a woman named Anna."

"Anna?" Clarissa said.

"Yes, she wore a pendant with the name on a gold disc."

"Not a very pretty name, is it?" She wrinkled her small button nose. "Certainly not elegant."

Philip was taken aback. He quite liked the name Anna, and while it was not as flowery as Clarissa or Jacqueline, it brought to mind someone who was delicate and feminine but not spoiled and demanding. "I think Anna is a very suitable name for a lady," he said, unsure why he felt it necessary to defend the stranger in his guest chamber.

Clarissa's round eyes took on a hard look. "Is this *Anna* a lady then? What is her age? Is she attractive?" She clipped off each sentence and folded her arms across her chest.

"I'm afraid her condition was such that it was impossible for me to tell anything about her at all, Miss Stapleton." His tone barely concealed his irritation with her questions.

John motioned for a servant to serve the port. "Aye, the constable will look into the matter. She could have come from anywhere. Hispaniola or even one of the smaller islands."

Clarissa excused herself to the drawing room while the men remained with their drinks. Philip felt the tension leave the room with her.

"Lovely girl, isn't she, Lord Philip?" John said with an affectionate smile when they sat back in their chairs.

"Yes, you are a lucky man to have such a daughter."

"She's likely the most eligible woman on the island." John's gaze bore into his.

Philip swirled the dark liquid in his glass, trying to think of something to change the topic. It seemed that every time he'd done so this evening, he'd ended up on a more uncomfortable subject than the last.

John drank deeply and set his glass on the table, squinting his eyes as he studied Philip. "I imagine you'd be immensely suitable for my Clarissa—and a member of the aristocracy to boot. But, I'll not rush things." He leaned back, folding his hands across his ample waistline. "Best to let young people take their course, if you know what I mean."

Philip was at a loss for words. The heat returned to his neck. He'd never met a man as brazen when it came to sensitive subjects. If he wasn't careful, he'd find himself leg shackled before the evening was out.

His host chuckled. "Cat got yer tongue, I see. I take that as a good sign." He stroked his mustache. "There's a bit of business I'd thought to discuss with you if you don't mind."

"Of course." Philip's words spilled out in a rush. He had never been so relieved to transfer topics in his life.

"It's about your big man. Head of a gang, I think he is."

Philip knew precisely of whom John was speaking. He'd seen Malachi a number of times over the last few weeks and had been extremely impressed with the man's physical strength as well as his sure way of directing the people beneath him. Malachi had a calm, assured manner that Philip found himself rather envious of. "Is there a problem?"

"No, no problem. I've had my eye on that one for years. A Negro with his skill and strength, he's an asset to any operation."

Philip remained quiet, not sure what John was getting at.

"I have offered him a position here at Kensington Estate numerous times, but he's refused. I suspect Horace Braithwaite may have had something to do with his response, but now that he's no longer overseer . . ."

Philip's chest was tight, whether from anger or frustration he did not know. There was much he didn't understand about the way of things on the island, but he did know that his slaves were his property and any attempt to acquire them should be taken up with him or Mr. Norton. "And may I ask, sir, why you thought it acceptable to offer employment to my worker instead of speaking to my overseer or myself about his purchase?"

"His purchase?" John's face split into a grin. "Like I said, you've much to learn. I suggest you begin by determining which of yer workers are bondsmen and which are free."

"Malachi is a free black?"

"Aye, purchased his papers years ago. He's had many an offer for higher paying positions, but for some reason he's remained where he is as the mere head of a gang at Oakely Park."

Philip considered this information. Why would Malachi settle for lesser paying duties when he was free to choose his own situation? Was it truly because of Mr. Braithwaite? Philip had seen how cruel the overseer could be and had witnessed his demeaning treatment of Malachi. If he'd the opportunity to get away from a man who mistreated him, why didn't he?

"I plan to make him an offer again. Just thought I'd inform you—one gentleman to another."

"Then we shall see what Malachi chooses to do." Philip raised his glass and smiled, but the expression was forced. He knew precisely what John had seen in Malachi—the man was strong and capable. But he could not imagine that, given the choice, Malachi would be content to work for these people. He hoped the man would at least give him the opportunity to match John Stapleton's offer.

As Philip rode along the jungle road back to Oakely Park two hours later, he attempted to sort through the things he'd learned. He wondered again about Malachi and what had kept the man at his menial position. He didn't imagine Malachi could have feared Mr. Braithwaite physically. Had Mr. Braithwaite been holding something over him? Was he being blackmailed? What was the large man's reasoning?

He changed his train of thought to John Stapleton's obvious hints that he should consider marrying Clarissa, an alliance that would more than double his assets. He imagined what his father would think when Philip told him how he'd increased his earnings. The marquess would be immensely proud and Philip's brother immensely jealous. And the woman herself, Clarissa was . . . well, she was wealthy, and . . . he was certain she possessed other desirable attributes. He simply hadn't had the opportunity to discover them. He thought he could possibly endure her tiresome conversation, pouty mouth, and bouncing ringlets for a few minutes a day. How much time was a man obliged to spend with his wife anyway? The foliage on the side of the road rustled, and his horse skittered.

Philip lifted his pistol and spoke in a low tone to calm his mount. He peered into the dark jungle surrounding him, but the only light came from slight glow of the moon illuminating the path. He urged the horse forward at a quicker pace that matched the increased speed of his heartbeat.

The image of a woman floating through the dark sea arose in his mind. The very thought of the helplessness she had likely felt and the terror that must have coursed through her veins was the stuff of nightmares. What kind of a person possesses the strength of mind to push aside her panic and figure out a way to bind herself to an oar when every instinct within her should have set her to fits of hysteria that would have resulted in her drowning? He imagined that Jacqueline would have fainted dead away at the first instant or spent her dying breath determining who was at fault for her plight. Likely she would be most furious that her clothing was wet.

He wondered how Anna fared. Was she well? Had she awoken? Had she— His heart felt heavy at the other possibility. He did not know why the idea of this stranger's death made him sad. Perhaps because he still did not have many acquaintances in Jamaica, or perhaps because he had yet to solve the mystery of how she had turned up on his beach. *Anna*, he said under his breath. What a charming name.

Chapter 5

HER SKIN FELT HOT AND tight. Her eyelids were heavy, and her head ached. She heard hushed voices nearby but neither recognized them nor understood what they were saying. And she was so tired. She fought against the darkness that tried to creep back over her and, with a concerted effort, opened first one eye then the other.

It took a moment for her vision to focus. Her mind was hazy. Where was she? She took in the large four-poster mahogany bed, the thin curtains hanging from the canopy, the whitewashed walls with dark wood trim, and exposed ceiling beams. None of it looked familiar. She turned her head to the side, wincing at the pain, and wondered why her body felt so sluggish. Was she ill? Two people stood in front of the large, shuttered windows, although she couldn't make out any details through the gauzy fabric of the curtains around the bed.

She tried to speak, but the sound that escaped was little more than a raspy groan. She swallowed and tried again.

The people stopped their conversation and hurried to her, pulling back the curtains. Standing over her was a young man with light-orange hair, wearing round-rimmed glasses, and a dark-skinned woman with her hair bound in a scarf. Her heart pounded. She didn't recognize either of them. She tried to sit up, but a jolt of pain shot through her head and she groaned again.

"Just lay still, miss," the man said. "I'm Dr. Bevan." Up close, she saw that freckles covered his hands and face.

"Where am I?" she croaked. She moved to sit up again, feeling incredibly vulnerable lying prostrate with two strangers standing over her.

"You're at Oakely Park," Dr. Bevan said. "You suffered a trauma, but you're safe now." He motioned to his companion. "Betty is the housekeeper."

Betty lifted her chin and inclined her head in a gesture better suited to a queen than a housekeeper.

Oakely Park? She willed herself to think. The words did not sound in the least familiar. How did she get to this place? And what had happened? She gritted her teeth and pressed her arms into the mattress, trying to raise herself onto her elbows.

"Do not exert yourself." Dr. Bevan slipped a hand behind her back and lifted her slowly forward.

The pain in her head was nearly unbearable, and she closed her eyes when the room started spinning.

Betty placed pillows behind her, helping her to a nearly sitting positon, then poured a glass of water.

The drink felt cool on her dry throat. "Thank you." She touched her head and found it wrapped in a bandage. Her arms were slick, covered in some type of oil, and her nightclothes were unfamiliar.

Dr. Bevan sat in a chair next to the bed. "Do you think you've the stomach for some food? Perhaps a bit of broth?"

She nodded, and Betty left the room. "Please, can you tell me what happened?"

"Lord Philip found you on the beach three days ago."

None of the doctor's words made any sense. "Lord Philip? The beach? But how did I . . . ?"

"Your skin is burned, and you suffered from extreme dehydration—which could explain your confusion." He leaned forward to help her take another sip and then sat back in the chair. "Based on your condition, we believe you were exposed to the sun for quite some time, and though we cannot be sure, we theorized that you may have been washed ashore from a shipwreck."

Her mind reeled, but she couldn't uncover any memory of a shipwreck—or a ship. She breathed faster. Why couldn't she remember? "A shipwreck? I don't . . ." She'd been on a ship? From where? Panic swelled in her chest. She couldn't remember where she'd come from. She tried harder, trying to think of who might be searching for her.

She came up with nothing. Not one name, not one face. She pushed her mind, willing it to remember *something*, but found only emptiness.

"I don't remember," she said. "I don't remember anything." Her heart pounded so forcefully she could feel the banging in her aching head. She struggled to control a surge of terror. "Doctor, I— *Who am I*?" She pressed her eyes closed, searching through her mind, but where there should be memories, it was entirely blank. Her throat swelled, and she thought she would choke. Her arms and legs began to tremble.

"Miss, you must calm yourself. Like I said, dehydration can cause confusion."

Her trembles caused her teeth to rattle. She tried to compose herself, to breathe deeply and still her shaking. It was no use. "Doctor, it is not confusion. I can think; I can speak. I can recite a sonnet if you wish. But I do not remember anything about my life. How old am I? Do I have a husband? Children? Where am I from? What do I look like? I do not even know my own name." She brushed her fingers over the base of her neck, unsure of what comfort she sought there, but not finding it somehow increased her distress.

Dr. Bevan drew his brows together. He pinched his chin and tapped his finger against his lip for a moment. "Your name is Anna." His expression remained thoughtful as he watched her reaction.

She let it settle in her mind. *Anna.* She felt nothing. The name did not seem any more familiar to her than any other. "Anna?" She focused on the word, hoping it would unlock the chamber in her mind where she knew the rest of herself was hidden. "I do not recognize the name. How do you know it is mine?"

"A necklace you were wearing. The pendant was carved with the word *Anna*."

She touched the base of her neck again. A sob rose in her throat. "Why can I not remember, Doctor?" The shaking increased.

Dr. Bevan took her hand. "I have read about such a condition. *Amnesia*, it is called. I do not think it manifests the same in every instance, but I fear becoming upset will only impede the process of you memory returning. Do you understand? You must calm yourself."

Anna nodded. She concentrated on her breathing and willed her pounding heart to slow. He helped her to drink again, and she turned her mind to other questions that the doctor would have the answers to. "Where is Oakely Park, Doctor?" A small sob hitched her breath, but she focused on the man next to her.

"It is a plantation on the north shore of Jamaica, nearly fifteen miles west of Port Antonio."

Anna could see the map of Jamaica clearly in her mind and wondered how it was possible. "I know about Jamaica. This side of the island is quite sparsely populated, if I remember correctly." She continued speaking, hoping to keep from sinking back into panic. "A jagged shoreline makes landing a ship difficult, and the Blue Mountains lie between here and the larger cities of Spanish Town and Kingston."

Dr. Bevan's brows drew together again. "I wonder if you are from the island," he said. "Although your easily burned skin and accent indicate otherwise."

"I do not know," Anna said. Was she a colonist? Were people right now searching for her? People whom she could not— She shook her head as the fear began to rise again. "Lord Philip, I think you said. Is he the owner of Oakely Park?"

Dr. Bevan nodded and then raised his gaze as Betty entered. "Lord Philip has left for the evening to attend a dinner party at another plantation," he said to Anna.

Anna sipped at the chicken soup until the pain in her head became too strong and her eyelids too heavy. She kept her mind on the things she knew for sure.

Jamaica. She could remember various facts about the island and its history but was unable to conjure an image of anything besides the map.

Lord Philip. She wondered what type of man he was. She pictured a wealthy British plantation owner with his hundreds of dark-skinned slaves and found the image in her mind did not portray him in the most flattering light. *Lord Philip*, she thought to herself as she drifted into sleep. She wondered if the man was as unpleasant as she imagined.

Chapter 6

Philip sat at the dining room table waiting for his breakfast, as was unfortunately becoming his habit. He did not even spare a thought to the tardiness of the meal today but stared instead at Dr. Bevan. "What do you mean she has no memory? How is this possible?"

The doctor pinched his chin, looking thoughtful as he spoke. "The condition is unusual but not unheard of. I have read of similar cases, sometimes brought on by an injury to the head. Or when the patient has suffered a particular trauma. It seems Anna has endured both."

"Will her memory return?"

"I am afraid I do not know, my lord. I have no personal experience with a case like this. She seems to have some knowledge of the island. She could even be a resident. Perhaps something at Oakely Park will rekindle her memory."

Philip drummed his fingers on the table. He was not sure precisely what it was about the situation that frustrated him. Anna had not been an inconvenience; she'd not been a bother at all, but he'd counted on her waking fully recovered. He didn't realize how anxious he'd become to know the full story of her adventure, and now it seemed the situation wouldn't wrap up cleanly at all. "And how long will it take?"

"I cannot say. There is no way to know. She could recover her memories at any moment—or never." He knitted his fingers on the table before him, his expression softening as he leaned forward. "She is, as you can imagine, quite upset. I gave her a dose of laudanum last night to calm her."

"She has no memory whatsoever?" He knew he was repeating himself, but the entire situation seemed so implausible.

"Anna is very bright, my lord. She recalls facts and information about the world. But somehow she seems to have forgotten her own place within it. When she attempts to remember anything about her life, she finds nothing but darkness—a void."

Philip tried to imagine how she must feel. Not to remember one's family or any personal history would be extremely distressing. Anna must be terrified to find herself in such a condition. In his mind appeared the image of strings wrapped around an oar, and he reassured himself that she would bravely cope with her fear. That was the kind of woman Anna was.

He realized the path his thoughts had taken and shook his head, rolling his eyes to the heavens. His assumption that he understood this woman from a few bits of fabric wrapped around a piece of wood was ridiculous. It was obvious that he was in need of some sort of diversion to take his mind off inventing personality traits for people he'd never met. And besides, what if her injury had addled more than her memory?

He turned his attention back to Dr. Bevan, unnerved by the way the man watched him through his small, round spectacles. "And her . . . disposition? Is there cause for concern?"

"I believe Anna's character, her likes, and her overall temperament are very much unchanged. She is quite amiable actually."

"Is there anything she needs while she recovers?"

The doctor shrugged. "I shall keep a watch on her injury, and she should remain calm. I believe her mind would more readily heal if she did not have any more strain." He stood. "We should all do our best not to cause her any distress."

"Of course."

Philip spent the next hour writing letters to the Governor-General and the House of Assembly in Kingston, asking for word to be sent to representatives of the fourteen counties on the island about a missing woman named Anna. He sent a messenger with the letters to Port Antonio and then asked Betty to see to the purchase of some clothing for his houseguest.

Philip and Tom supervised the repair of an outer wall of the hospital. Bricks were brought in by donkey cart, and the workers carefully supported the ceiling with beams while the damaged wall was removed and a new one built. Lacking the patience to simply watch, Philip stripped off his jacket and waistcoat and heaved bricks and beams alongside the others.

His mind did not stray far from the topic of Anna and her strange loss of memory for the remainder of the day. How would it be to have no memory of his life? There were parts he wouldn't mind forgetting—such as the situation with his brother and Jacqueline—but to forget his home, his friends, his mother? The thought weighed heavily on his mind.

He wiped his brow and surveyed the brick wall with a swell of satisfaction.

A small girl approached from the direction of the slave village, carrying a bucket of water with two hands. A man stepped quickly to her and took the heavy bucket, squatting down to her height as he said something that Philip could not hear. He rubbed the top of her head with his palm. The girl laughed, swatting his hand away. The sight warmed Philip's heart. He'd seen men of his acquaintance act with similar teasing affection to their children. The man dipped a tin cup into the bucket, offering Phillip a drink of cold water.

They worked steadily until late afternoon, and Philip returned to the Great House that evening dirty and covered in sweat. He bathed and dressed for dinner, stepping out onto the veranda and enjoying the feel of the cooling air on his face. As Tom said, night came fast in the tropics, and sometimes it was even chilly in the evenings. He leaned his forearms against the wrought-iron railing and blew out a heavy breath.

A movement on the edge of his vision caught his eye, and he turned his head, expecting to see Betty or Ezekiel but stopped short.

A woman stood on the veranda near the far corner of the house, holding the railing with one hand—a *young* woman. As she twisted toward him, the setting sun behind her cast a golden halo around her head. She wore a long nightdress that didn't quite touch the floor. With one hand, she held a light blanket wrapped around her narrow shoulders. Her blonde hair was loose and damp, hanging in waves nearly to her waist.

He turned his gaze away from her bare feet, remembering that he was first and foremost a gentleman and he should behave as one and not scandalize this woman by staring at her ankles. When he looked closer, he noticed bruising on her forehead, and the damage to her skin was evident, as it peeled in thin sheets on her face and arms. In spite of it all, she was supremely beautiful.

She held his gaze with bright eyes and twisted her head slightly to the side. Philip realized his mouth was open, and he was staring like a fool.

"Are you Anna?" he asked. He could not believe that this lovely young woman was the same ghastly looking person he'd found on the beach. And he also could not believe the stupidity of his question. *Who else would she be?*

She nodded. Her light brows pulled together. "I am sorry, sir, you have the advantage of me. I do not know your name. Are you perhaps Mr. Norton?"

Philip pulled himself from his temporary stupor. He walked to her and gave a small bow. "Pardon me, I seem to have forgotten myself. Lord Philip Hamilton, at your service." It was highly improper for a gentleman to speak with a lady to whom he'd not been introduced, but under the circumstances, he supposed it was much less rude than tipping his hat and walking away. She was, after all, his houseguest, and they *had* ridden on his horse together.

"Lord Philip." She curtsied, maintaining her hold on the railing. "I was told that you brought me to Oakely Park. How is it that you do not recognize me?"

"You look very . . . different than when I found you. I am afraid I did not expect you to appear . . . as you do." He was blathering like a fool. When did he lose the ability to string words together?

"You look different than I expected as well, my lord." Her lips twitched the slightest bit, and if he wasn't mistaken, a bit of color rose to her cheeks. The effect was enchanting.

Philip raised his brows. "And why is that?"

The color spread. "I assumed you would be . . . older." She slid her gaze to the side.

Philip wished she would look back at him. He hadn't quite finished determining the exact hue of her brown eyes. "Well then, we are well met, miss."

She looked up at him and smiled although he saw a bit of a wince around her eyes. He wondered if her injury pained her.

"Indeed, my lord. And I owe you my thanks. Dr. Bevan told me if you had not rescued me, I would have surely died on the rocks. I am indeed grateful for your actions. And for your gracious hospitality."

"It is my pleasure, Miss, ah . . ." He lifted his hand, palm up. "What shall I call you? I can hardly call you by your Christian name."

Anna's countenance crumbled. Her hand tightened on the rail, and she lowered her gaze. "I do not know my surname, my lord."

He could have kicked himself for such an insensitive question. He remembered Dr. Bevan's warning about causing Anna more distress. Not that he needed the reminder; the sight of her dejected expression drove the point home better than anything the doctor could have said. He tried to think of something that might put her at ease.

"You have given me a rare opportunity, miss." Philip crossed one arm in front of his chest and tapped his other finger to his temple theatrically. "It is not often that a person is able to assign a name to a new friend."

Anna looked up, and her lips lifted in the slightest smile.

Philip was encouraged that he'd struck on the right strategy for cheering her. "Let me see. Shall I call you Miss Water-Nymph?"

She wrinkled her nose and shook her head.

"Very well then. Miss Black-Rock?"

"My lord, you are really quite awful at this."

"I shall hit upon the perfect name. Miss Sand-in-Her-Hair."

A small giggle escaped her lips. "And shall I repay the favor, my lord? Shall I give you a name as well?"

"And what name would you give me?"

Anna squinted her eyes as she studied him. The pink returned to her cheeks. "I shall have to wait until I know you better. As of now, all I know about you is your tendency to bring home objects you find at the beach." Her eyes twinkled, and he decided the golden-brown was nearly the exact color of toffee.

Philip laughed aloud, pleased that his plan to lift her mood had been successful.

"My lord?" Ezekiel stepped onto the balcony with a strip of fabric in his hand. He bowed low, sweeping his hand in front of him. "Shall I tie yo' cravat, my lord?"

"No, thank you, Ezekiel." Philip took the hopelessly wrinkled cloth. "Tell Betty I shall be down for supper in a moment."

"Right away, my lord." Ezekiel flashed his cheery grin and hurried back through Philip's bedchamber door.

Philip turned back toward Anna, who regarded him with her lips slightly pursed and a brow raised.

"Your valet?"

"Yes." Philip lifted the wrinkled cloth. "Although the situation does not bode well for the state of my wardrobe."

Anna smiled, but her eyes remained thoughtful. "You are indeed different than I imagined, my lord."

"I am not sure if I should take that as a compliment . . ." Philip's words trailed off when she lifted a hand to her forehead.

Anna's face paled, and her grip on the railing tightened. "I am sorry, my lord, but please excuse me." She released her grip, and Philip caught her arm.

"Are you all right?" He sucked a breath between his teeth at the sight of her ashen skin.

"Yes, just a bit dizzy. I need to rest."

"Come, you must lie down. I will send for Dr. Bevan." He led her carefully around the corner of the house toward her bedchamber door.

She leaned more heavily against him. "I am sorry."

Anna was slight, nearly frail, but not petite. The top of her head was approximately the height of his chin, Philip noticed. When he reached the doorway, he brushed aside the curtains and glanced into the guest chamber, fully aware of the impropriety of accompanying her inside. There was no maid or doctor, but he could not simply abandon her at the doorway in her condition. It only took one glance at the expression on his companion's face, and he did not hesitate. He led her to the sofa and helped her to sit.

"Forgive me, my lord," Anna murmured. Her eyes were squeezed shut, and she kept her hand against her forehead as she lay back against the headrest.

Philip placed a blanket over her lap. "I shall fetch Dr. Bevan right away," he said. His chest was tight with worry. Anna's face looked gray against the white sofa.

"Thank you," she whispered. Her head leaned to the side, and a strand of hair fell across her cheek.

Philip reached to brush it away but pulled back his hand. What had gotten into him? He hurried to the door, glancing back quickly before stepping into the hallway. Where was that blasted doctor?

Chapter 7

Three days later, Anna sat in the shade beneath a cluster of mahoe trees. Insects buzzed in the undergrowth, and a chorus of birds called in the canopy above. She tipped her head back to admire the different colors of leaves and hibiscus flowers. The flora surrounding the Great House at Oakely Park took her breath away. Was it familiar at all? Dr. Bevan had told her she could possibly be from the island, but if that were the case, wouldn't she remember something? It all felt new and strange. She concentrated, delving deeply into her mind for any memory of bright plants and their heady fragrance.

"Will dere be anyt'in' else, miss?" Ezekiel placed a tray on the table and stood with his hands behind his back.

Anna realized she'd been clenching her teeth as she'd searched, frustrated, through the blank spots of her memory. She glanced to Betty, who sat in another chair, waving a fan in front of her face and at the small table with a pitcher of juice and two glasses between them. Betty was as close to a friend as Anna had at Oakely Park, and she was grateful the woman had agreed to attend her this afternoon. "Thank you, Ezekiel. This is perfect."

Betty said something to him that Anna didn't understand. Ezekiel squeezed Betty's hand and then grinned and hurried away.

Anna studied his gait as she watched him walk unevenly back toward the Great House. One leg appeared to be shorter than the other, and his foot curled inward. She wondered if he had been born with the deformity or if he'd suffered a debilitating injury. And what was Betty's association to the boy? Were they related? She glanced at her companion, searching the woman's profile for any resemblance. "Thank you for sitting outside with me, Betty."

"Lord Philip an' de doctor tell me dat you should no' be left alone," Betty said. Her low voice and accent made her sentences sound as if she were singing or chanting.

It was not the most gracious reply, but Anna forged ahead. "And please tell your friend—I do not know his name . . . the large man?"

"Malachi." Betty still didn't turn toward Anna.

"Please give Malachi my thanks for bringing furniture outside so I could enjoy the sunshine."

Betty nodded stiffly; her gaze still followed Ezekiel as he climbed the main steps.

Anna didn't want to spend her entire afternoon sitting awkwardly next to a woman who responded only with stilted sentences. She determined to break through Betty's guarded exterior. Perhaps speaking about her family would soften her. "Is Ezekiel your son?" Anna asked.

Betty turned toward her, raising her chin and turning her head slightly to the side. The gesture was one Anna was coming to recognize as typical of the housekeeper. Betty's actions projected a stately quality that fascinated Anna. Her manners seemed so unlike a servant. "His mot'er was my dear friend," Betty said evenly.

Was? Anna looked closer at Betty's expression. Her self-assuredness was not quite so strong. "I am sorry. How long ago did she die?"

"When Ezekiel was very young. We—I did not know dis fo' a long time. She was far away, at a plantation near Whitehouse." She held Anna's gaze confidently, but Anna thought she saw a hint of nervousness. "I care fo' him now."

Anna studied Betty for a moment. The story was vastly incomplete. How did the two women know each other? And once Betty had learned of her friend's death, how did she arrange to bring Ezekiel to Oakely Park? Was it a common thing for slaves to keep in contact across long distances? To send for the children of their deceased friends? Betty's expression was closed, and Anna could tell that she didn't want to volunteer any more information about how Ezekiel came to be in her care.

Anna was immensely curious but changed her line of questioning, hoping that Betty would come to trust her enough to share more of the boy's story. "I believe Lord Philip quite likes Ezekiel."

Betty's expression did not change, but Anna was beginning to notice the slightest shift in her eyes, which spoke volumes. "We two—Ezekiel and me—take care a de Great House together fo' a long time but is different wit' de massa in residence."

"I imagine so," Anna said.

"De lord is not used to de island ways. He say he is gonna find a valet. I fear Ezekiel be sent to de fields—" Betty stopped speaking abruptly, her eyes widening as if she worried she had said too much.

Anna did not know the extent of the child's disability, but she couldn't imagine him performing heavy labor with his painful-looking limp. "I will help you if you like," Anna said. "We should be able to adjust the household routines to include Lord Philip." She winked. "Caring for an aristocrat should not be too difficult. It is simply a matter of knowing his needs before he does." For a moment Anna wondered about her own experience with domestic matters. What part did she play? Was she a married woman who commanded a household of servants? Is that why she was so comfortable addressing Betty's concerns? She strained to remember, but search as she might, she could not find any bit of knowledge of her life.

Betty's expression softened into a small smile, and Anna was surprised how young the housekeeper looked. Thick lashes surrounded her dark eyes, her lips were full, and dimples formed on her smooth cheeks. She was quite beautiful when she didn't hide behind her unapproachable exterior. She lowered her eyes, poured juice into a glass, and handed it to Anna. "Dr. Bevan say you mus' remember to drink."

Anna took the glass and sat back, happy that she'd perhaps thought of a way to help Betty and Ezekiel as well as to repay Lord Philip for his care. Thinking of the man and the gentle way he'd assisted her to her bedchamber a few evenings earlier warmed her cheeks.

She'd remained in her room and not seen him since that night, but as she regained her strength, she wondered more than once what occupied Lord Philip's time.

Hearing the sound of horse hooves, she turned. Her heartbeat sped up, and her cheeks warmed further when she saw Lord Philip riding toward her with another man. Her flush must be due to her head injury and the afternoon heat, she rationalized to herself.

Philip sat tall in the saddle, nodding as he listened to the other man speak. He lifted his hat when he saw her, and his light hair fell over his forehead above pale-blue eyes.

Betty stood to the side of her chair and curtsied.

"Miss Anna, how do you feel today?" He dismounted and handed the reins to his companion, walking toward her. He bent down in front of Anna and looked closely at her face. "Are you certain you're quite well enough to be outside? Dr. Bevan seemed to think you had overexerted yourself walking about on the veranda the other evening."

Anna found herself unable to look into Philip's blue eyes while they studied her so intently. She kept her gaze on her hands circling the glass in her lap. "I am much better, my lord. Between the sunshine and Betty's willow-bark tea, my bouts of dizziness are nearly gone.

"I am glad to hear it." He nodded once and stood, removing his riding gloves. "Please allow me to introduce Mr. Tom Norton, the plantation overseer."

"How do you do, Mr. Norton?" Anna raised her gaze to the other man. He was young, she thought, and also very handsome, though he lacked the air of confidence Lord Philip seemed to carry so easily. Tom's eyes were gray, and his hair was a light brown, tied at the base of his neck with a string.

Tom tipped his head forward, bowing a bit awkwardly from his position on his horse. "I am glad you are well, miss. Last I saw you, well, I'd not have imagined you to be looking so lovely a mere week later."

"Thank you, sir." Anna felt her blush return in full force and searched her mind for a neutral topic. "You have a beautiful horse, sir." As soon as she said it, she mentally chided herself for such a stupid statement.

"Do you ride?" Mr. Norton asked.

Anna blinked. Did she? "I . . . I am not certain whether I do or not."

"We shall have to find out, don't you think?" The overseer smiled, and his eyes twinkled. "I think a ride with such a lovely lady would be quite a pleasant way to spend the day."

Anna felt her own smile grow. She quite liked Tom Norton.

"Return the horses to the stables, if you please, Mr. Norton," Lord Philip said in a clipped tone. He tapped his riding crop against his leg. His jaw was tight, and Anna wondered if Mr. Norton had done something to displease him.

Tom tipped his hat to Anna and rode away, leading Lord Philip's horse.

Anna noticed that Philip's eyes had lost a bit of their brightness, and she thought that spending the day riding in the heat must have tired him.

Betty must have assumed the same. "A drink, my lord?" She poured a glass of juice and held it toward him.

"Thank you."

"If you stay wit' Miss Anna, my lord, I see to de afternoon tea." Betty curtsied again and departed.

"Of course." Philip moved into the seat next to Anna.

"I must thank you for the gowns," Anna said. "They are beautiful. It was very kind of you, though unnecessary to purchase so many."

Philip's gaze moved quickly over her dress and back to her face. "I am glad you like them, but I shall have to defer all credit to Betty. Apparently she has excellent taste." He raised his brow then took a long drink, stretching his legs out in front of him and crossing one ankle over the other. Anna noticed his jawline was sharp and his chin strong. The face of an aristocrat. "What a pleasant location for a picnic. Was it your idea or Betty's?"

Anna was grateful he'd changed the topic from her clothing. His appraisal had made her feel very exposed. "I admit I was tiring of staying in and asked if we might sit outside. But Betty was the one who arranged for Malachi to relocate the furniture."

Philip nodded.

Anna wondered what he thought of Malachi. She found the enormous man utterly terrifying. Was he dangerous? "Do you know who he is, my lord? A large man with . . ." She touched her fingers to her cheekbone and around her eye, indicating the placement of Malachi's scars.

"I do know him. Malachi is a fine worker, one of the few at Oakely Park born in Africa. Mr. Norton told me the marks identify which tribe he belonged to." He turned his gaze fully to Anna's face and must have seen her unease. "Does he frighten you?"

"A little," she said. That morning, Anna had walked into the main hall and come face-to-face with the dark man. His appearance and size along with the suddenness of the encounter had caused her to squeal. She'd hurried back into the drawing room to join Betty and had stayed inside, watching through the window until Malachi had finished carrying the furniture and she was certain he was gone. Just thinking of the incident made her heart beat faster. She winced as she thought of how the raised marks must have been formed. "The marks are curious, aren't they, my lord?"

"I suppose it seems that way to us, but to Malachi and his people it is the way of things. Only a very few slaves in Jamaica bear the marks. Since the abolition of the African slave trade, I'm told nearly all of the workers on the island were born in the West Indies."

"They do not know where they are from," Anna said. She could not help but lower her eyes as she placed her glass on the table, wishing she did not feel so despondent. Where was *she* from?

Philip clasped his hand over hers, and she raised her gaze. "Are you feeling well enough to take a short stroll before Betty delivers the tea? I promise we will walk slowly, Miss . . . ah, we never did settle upon a surname for you, did we? I shall have to keep thinking."

Anna rose to her feet and allowed a small smile at his obvious attempt to cheer her. She knew she should not permit herself to grow melancholy whenever she thought of her lost memories, but it was difficult to feel like a complete person when so much of her identity was missing.

Philip tucked her hand beneath his arm, settling it into the bend of his elbow. "You will tell me if you become too tired or if you feel any pain, won't you?"

"Yes." Anna lowered her face, grateful that her loose curls hid her expression. Lord Philip was clearly a much more thoughtful person than she'd imagined a wealthy plantation owner to be. He was concerned for her health as she imagined a good host would be for any guest at his home. There was no reason for her to become so flustered in his presence, but try as she might she could not prevent her fingers from tingling where they touched his arm.

He led her at a slow pace down the main path beneath the rows of palm trees.

Anna did her best to put aside her anxiety and decided she would steer the conversation away from herself. "Betty tells me you've not been at Oakely Park long, my lord."

"It is true. It was just over three weeks ago that I landed in Kingston for the first time."

"And how do you like Jamaica?"

He turned his head and seemed to be considering for a moment. He pressed his lips together then moved his gaze to hers. "It is beautiful."

Anna knitted her brows. His answer was perfectly acceptable for polite company. She supposed he intended to keep their discussion from any realms too personal. Anna felt a small sting of disappointment. She'd hoped to become better acquainted with Lord Philip, to possibly become friends, but apparently he did not feel the same. Very well then. She would restrict her conversation to neutral topics.

She glanced at Lord Philip. The corners of his mouth were pulled down, and his brow was wrinkled. He appeared to be contemplating, and she wondered whether she'd upset him. His gaze found hers and his lips lifted in a smile, but his blue eyes remained thoughtful.

"Where did you and Mr. Norton ride today?" she asked, hoping to return him to his former good humor.

"With the majority of the fall harvest complete, we visited the pastureland to look over the livestock." He lifted his chin toward the fields from which they'd ridden.

Anna glanced in the direction he indicated. "I didn't realize there was pastureland. I assumed a sugar plantation consisted entirely of sugarcane fields."

"Oakely Park is nearly five hundred acres divided between cane cultivation, woodland, pastureland, and provisions such as orchards and vegetable gardens." He spread his hand through the air in a grand gesture. "It takes more than sugarcane to keep the plantation running."

"Now that the harvest is finished, is the majority of your effort turned toward another of these endeavors?" Anna asked.

"We will finish processing sugar, treacle, and rum, and then prepare the products for shipment. Then we will tend to other parts of the property that are neglected during harvest season. However, cane is where a plantation makes its living, and we shall plant again as soon as possible."

Anna liked watching him speak about Oakely Park. Philip's eyes glowed with a combination of excitement and pride, something she wouldn't have expected of a nobleman. "Based on your knowledge, one would think you'd operated a sugarcane plantation much longer than merely a month, my lord."

"Thank you." He patted her hand that rested on his arm. "I suppose it is not in my nature to idly observe. My mother would tell you that I am impatient and at times hotheaded, but I like to think she intends it in the nicest way possible."

Anna laughed. "It sounds more like ambition to me."

"I am certain that's what she meant." Philip rolled his eyes as a teasing smile played over his lips. She was certain he'd charmed many debutantes in London with that smile. He stopped walking and inclined his head, turning them back toward the Great House.

A hundred questions fought their way to the tip of Anna's tongue. She wondered about Lord Philip's mother. Did he miss her? Why did his mother call him hotheaded? How had he learned so much about the plantation in such a short time? She wondered what had brought him to Jamaica alone. Surely a man with his connections should have a wife and family to accompany him across the sea. She remembered how Philip had avoided speaking personally and pressed her lips closed. She didn't want to cause him any discomfort.

She glanced up and saw that he was watching her with his tongue pressed into his cheek in a puzzled look. Anna thought quickly for something to explain away the frustrated expression on her face. "It is too bad you must wait months for sugar. Is there not another crop as profitable?"

Philip's confused expression grew, but he blinked it away, his manners obviously taking over. "Mr. Norton attempts at every opportunity to convince me that coffee will one day be as profitable as sugar. There is a spot in the mountains at the far end of the plantation where he is certain we will make our fortunes with a coffee farm."

"And what do you think?"

"I confess I am skeptical." He lifted his brows, and his lips twisted in a smile. "You see, I am not *always* impulsive. I should like to research the matter first. And I have not seen the site. Last time we traveled in that direction, we were distracted by a young woman on the beach. Miss Sopping-Gown, I think she is called."

Anna rolled her eyes to the heavens, causing him to laugh.

"I should like to see the location in the mountains. And all of Oakely Park. Will you take me?" She surprised herself with the boldness of her question, but his laughter had raised her confidence. Besides, she was growing increasingly bored in her bedchamber. Dr. Bevan had said that any small thing might trigger the return of her memory, and so far, sitting in the Great House had not done it.

They reached the shade of the mahoe trees once again. Betty had placed a tray with a tea set, fruit, and sliced bread on the small table under a piece of netting to protect it from insects. Philip took her hand from his arm, assisting her as she sat in her chair.

Anna had not realized how tired she was, and her dizziness was returning, but the fact that Lord Philip had not answered her request was worse than either ailment. Her stomach grew heavy. She touched her fingers to her forehead and closed her eyes.

"Miss Anna," Philip said after he'd remained silent far too long, "I should like nothing more than for you to accompany me on a tour of the plantation."

She lifted her gaze and found that he had crouched down in front of her.

He took her hands. "But I must be certain that you are well. Dr. Bevan fears that overexertion could impede your recovery."

She wondered if Lord Philip worried that if she didn't regain her memory, he would be trapped with a houseguest forever. But the thought melted away as quickly as it formed when he lifted one corner of his mouth in an expression that she was certain must have set the hearts of London's ladies fluttering. Her own heart was not immune to the effect, and she wondered again how it was possible that this man was unattached. "I am recovering quickly, my lord."

He stood and clasped his hands behind his back. "Tomorrow I will be in Port Antonio, but the day after I planned to ride to the stills. Early, while it is still cool." He moved to the table and placed a slice of cassava bread on a small plate and offered it to her. "If you feel well, would you accompany me? It is not far."

"I should like that very much, my lord."

Philip served himself a piece of bread and sat. The half smile returned. "Not many ladies would—it is not exactly a carriage ride around Hyde Park or an evening at the theater."

"But I shall enjoy it just the same," Anna said. She was delighted to have something to look forward to after convalescing for a week. She was curious about the workings of the plantation, and truthfully, she was curious about Lord Philip. What sort of man was he? Everything she had seen indicated that he was kind and thoughtful and intelligent. But he was also an unmarried member of the aristocracy who lived alone in a colony four thousand miles away from England. What had brought him to this place when most men in his position allowed others to manage their holdings on their behalf?

Anna was still contemplating the mystery of her host while she prepared for bed that evening. She stepped onto the veranda, leaning against the railing to breathe in the fragrance of the plumeria blossoms beneath her.

Murmured voices drew her attention, and she stepped around the corner to the back of the house, squinting as her eyes became accustomed to the darkness. Although she could only make out shadows, there was no mistaking the forms of Malachi and Betty. They stood close, speaking in low voices. The couple embraced, and Anna hurried away, realizing she'd intruded on a private moment.

As she slipped between the gauzy curtains into her bedchamber, Anna had the thought that perhaps the mystery of her own identity was just one of many secrets at Oakely Park.

Chapter 8

PHILIP GLANCED OUT THE WINDOW at the lightening sky as he finished shaving. He felt anxious to get riding before the sun became too hot. He'd returned from Port Antonio late the night before, disappointed that there was still no word from the Governor-General, and hadn't seen Anna upon his return. How had she spent her day? Was she still planning to join him this morning? He was surprised by how much he anticipated their outing, obviously a testament to the isolation of Oakely Park. He was in desperate need of society when a ride to the stills was the high point of his month.

He stepped into his dressing room, where he knew Ezekiel would be waiting, bracing himself for another disappointment at the state of his wardrobe. He found that he was becoming accustomed to and even looked forward to a morning greeting from the boy. His practical side told him he really should hire a valet. His clothing was in a dreadful state. As far as cheerful and helpful went, he'd never replace Ezekiel, but as a personal attendant, the poor child was sadly lacking.

"Good mornin', my lord." Ezekiel bowed in his customary manner, but instead of offering a pile of rumpled clothing, the boy opened the wardrobe door, displaying a row of clean shirts hanging in an orderly line. "And which trousers you prefer today, my lord?"

Philip blinked slowly, raising his brows as Ezekiel spread his hand to indicate the equally cleaned and ironed breeches hanging next to the shirts.

"The gray buckskins, please," Philip stammered, purely out of habit. He wondered if he might have been out in the sun too long the day before. Had he awakened in the wrong house?

Ezekiel's smile widened as he fetched the clothing and assisted Philip in dressing. The child produced a starched collar, and not knowing what else to do, Philip leaned forward as the boy fastened it and finished it off with a cravat.

Philip blinked again and stared dumbfounded in the mirror, studying the knot, which, to his astonishment, was entirely satisfactory. Surely much better than the pitiful efforts he'd made himself over the past month. "Ezekiel, where did you . . . ?" He waved his hand toward the wardrobe and then to his cravat. "How did you . . . ?"

Ezekiel picked up Philip's nightclothes, shaking them out and hanging them on a hook in the wardrobe before carefully closing the door. "I been practicing, my lord." He smiled and held his head high. "And you be wearing yo' top boots today, my lord?"

Philip nodded and gaped at the freshly blackened and shined boots. He selected a waistcoat and jacket and found both cleaned and brushed. The small tear in the shoulder of his jacket had been repaired. He stared at Ezekiel, shocked and overcome with gratitude for something he'd taken for granted his entire life. He couldn't imagine how the boy had learned all of this in one day. And the work it must have taken to wash, repair, and iron all of his clothing . . . "This . . . it all . . ." He patted the boy on the shoulder. "Excellent work, Ezekiel."

Ezekiel's grin grew impossibly large. "Will dere be anyt'in' else dis mornin', my lord?"

"No. That will be all." Philip couldn't help but grin himself at the boy's high spirits. He picked up two parcels as he left his bedchamber and started down the stairs. But he paused with his hand on the rail as the smell of food reached him. He'd certainly never been assaulted by smells of a warm breakfast at Oakely Park. A moment later, he stepped into the dining room and stopped short.

Anna and Betty stood at the sideboard and turned toward him when he entered.

Betsy curtsied, placed a pitcher of juice on the table, then hurried out of the room toward the kitchen building.

"Good morning, Lord Philip," Anna said, dipping in a small curtsy. Her hair fell in waves over her shoulders. He imagined it would be painful to pin it up, and he had to admit he liked it loose. She wore a gown that would have set the ladies of London green with envy. The cut was obviously French and it was made of a beautiful pale-blue silk, both things the war had deprived the British of. He didn't think the style would appear as lovely on many women, but Anna's slender figure carried it perfectly. No matter Betty's shortcomings, she knew how to select dresses.

His attention was so captured by his houseguest—her hairstyle and her apparel—that he didn't notice the plate she held toward him until she took a step closer. He pulled his mind back to the moment at hand but found that the situation in his house was not any more comprehensible. He was still at a loss to explain the changes. Breakfast was served on time. Ezekiel had transformed overnight into a competent valet. Perhaps he was still abed and dreaming, or perhaps his hallucinations were a symptom of the onset of malaria.

Anna still held the plate toward him. She cleared her throat, and he realized he was standing in the doorway with his mouth open.

He looked at the young woman before him, and the strange happenings made a bit more sense. He deposited his parcels on a chair and moved to take the plate. "Thank you, miss."

Anna's brows drew together and then smoothed pleasantly. "I hope you slept well."

Philip scooped fried plantains onto his plate and then added some breadfruit and salted fish. "Quite well. Actually I have doubts as to whether I have fully awakened."

"And why is that, my lord?" Anna sat at the table.

He joined her. "I rose to a very different household than that of yesterday." Philip reached for the pitcher, only to have Ezekiel hurry from his station to fill their glasses. Apparently, the boy had become a capable footman as well. "It seems that someone has organized Oakely Park's domestic schedule and trained the staff in their duties."

Anna pursed her lips as if she were pondering as well, then she took a bite of cassava bread. But a smile pulled at her mouth while she chewed. She darted a glance at him and then back to her plate.

"You do not have any idea what might have brought about this transformation, do you?"

Anna shrugged and lifted her gaze to his. "You have very capable servants." Her toffee-colored eyes were wide with feigned innocence. "I do not think it would have required much training—if indeed someone did train them."

Philip tapped his chin. "Whoever this person is, I find myself immensely in her debt. She is much more capable than I when it comes to household management."

"Perhaps she was simply grateful for the kindness you've shown her."

Philip glanced at Anna's hands while she cut a piece of breadfruit and noticed that they were red and chapped. She must have done much more than merely instruct the servants. The amount of laundry alone would have taken one boy all day, and he felt a warmth in his chest accompanied by a tingle of guilt when he realized that Anna must have worked alongside Ezekiel.

When Anna saw him gaze at her hands, she hid them beneath the table. "I do hope your plans have not changed today."

"Not at all. In fact, I acquired a suitable mount and sidesaddle in Port Antonio yesterday so you would have an easier time of it."

Anna pressed her fingers to her lips. "Oh, my lord, you did not need to—"

Philip held up a hand to stop her. He shook his head, remembering that in spite of the secretive happenings at Oakely Park, he was still the master of the house. "Let us agree there will be no more 'You shouldn't have' or 'I am in your debt' between the two of us." He leaned closer and allowed a smile to lift his lips. "After all, we are friends, are we not?"

Anna's cheeks reddened at his words. "I hope we are friends, Lord Philip," she said, touching her finger to the base of her neck.

He noticed again how fetching she looked in the dress, and the thought sprung into his mind that he was glad Mr. Norton wasn't here to admire her. He had shocked himself with the surge of anger he'd felt toward his overseer when he'd flirted with Anna. But he couldn't say why it had bothered him to the point that he'd snapped at Tom and dismissed him. Perhaps the heat had gotten to him. Come to think of it, Dr. Bevan had also shown a particular interest in Anna. He would need to keep a closer watch on the men—and on Anna, as there were few women on the island and far fewer who were lovely and delicate and . . . He ground his wayward thoughts to a halt. "Very well then, if you are finished with your meal, Miss Secretly-Launders-Waistcoats . . ."

Anna cringed, wrinkling her nose, but a small giggle burst from her mouth. "My lord, that is the worst name so far."

"Yes, it did not quite roll off the tongue the way I'd hoped." He pushed his chair back and stood, shrugging as he dropped his napkin onto the table. "I shall have to keep trying." He fetched the parcels. "I failed to find a riding habit in the thriving shopping district of Port Antonio, but I did acquire a cape that I think will do the job nicely, and silk is much cooler than wool." He tore off the paper and unfolded a buff-colored cloak.

"Oh, it is beautiful." Anna rubbed the cloth between her fingers. "My lord . . ."

Philip waggled his finger back and forth like a pendulum. "Remember, friends."

Anna opened her mouth then closed it. She smiled. "Thank you."

"You are very welcome." He opened the other parcel and laid a parasol and a pair of kid gloves on the table. "I did not think you would be comfortable wearing a hat with your injury. And truth be told, the selection was rather sparse."

"This is all perfect." Anna slipped her hand into the gloves and tied the cloak around her shoulders.

Ezekiel delivered Philip's hat and gloves and then hurried out the door to the stables. Philip and Anna followed and waited only a few moments before the boy returned with two saddled horses. He led the animals to a stone mounting block at the side of the front steps.

Philip watched Anna, wondering what was happening in her mind. Was she frightened? She didn't appear to be. Did she know how to ride? Perhaps something as simple as mounting a horse would bring back her lost memory.

Anna shook back her hair as she neared the horse. "What is her name?" she asked, nodding toward the gray speckled mare.

"She has none that I know of." Philip patted the horse's neck. "Perhaps I should give her one."

"I think that is a terrible idea, my lord. Unless you are better at naming horseflesh than houseguests." She pursed her lips and quirked a brow, her eyes sparkling.

Philip had seen that precise expression on ladies of the *ton* as they'd flirted and teased—even Jacqueline had used it often—but on Anna the look made his knees feel like jelly. And she did not even seem to know she was doing it. He couldn't imagine the power this woman would have if she were to employ her flirting energy to its fullest potential.

"Smokey," he blurted.

"The horse's name?" Seeing his nod, she smiled. "It seems I was wrong, my lord. Smokey is just the name for this lady." She turned to the mare. "What do you think, Smokey?" Anna ran her hand down the horse's neck and stepped up onto the mounting block. She lifted her foot, placed it in the stirrup, and pulled herself into the saddle in one swift motion, arranging her cloak over her legs. "Apparently I do know how to ride," she said, looking surprised and rather pleased. She took the riding crop and the parasol Ezekiel held up to her. "Thank you, Ezekiel."

Philip noticed the conspiratorial smile that passed between the two of them, and he thought he even saw Anna wink at the boy. The warm feeling in his chest returned, and he pushed it down, quickly mounting his horse and starting up the path ahead of Anna. He needed a moment to get his emotions under control.

He'd spent the last few months constructing and fortifying a wall around his heart. This woman and boy had managed to crumble part of it away in merely a few weeks. Philip felt intensely vulnerable when it came to the two, and it frightened him. He worried that he had come to care too much for them. The fear of being hurt again was all it took to shore up the battlements and ensure that he was strong enough to withstand the assault.

Anna joined him on the road, looking as comfortable in a saddle as anyone he knew. When they reached the top of the hill, she reined in next to him. "It is magnificent," she said in a breathless voice. The wind lifted her hair, and she shook it out of her face.

Philip followed her gaze over the leafy jungle up the jagged purple mountains covered with wisps of volcanic steam and down to the deep blue of the sea, where pelicans soared and swooped into the water. He pointed out the various areas of the plantation and watched Anna's eyes narrow thoughtfully and her face fill with excitement and interest—precisely how he'd felt when he'd sat in this spot for the first time.

"Shall we see the stills then?" she asked.

They rode toward the cylindrical stone buildings, and once they arrived, she leaned over to hand him the parasol while she dismounted.

As they walked through the buildings, Philip explained how the rich, dark treacle was the wastage from the sugar process and in the stills it was converted to rum.

Anna watched the entire process, paying attention to every step. She studied the liquid bubbling in copper pots and the pipes siphoning between them as the fermented juice was distilled into alcohol. She watched as workers filled large barrels with the finished product. The sweet and pungent aroma was strong enough to cause Philip's eyes to water, but Anna didn't seem bothered by it.

They stepped outside. "And what is this?" Anna pointed to the shallow pots on the ground.

"Adding treacle that has caramelized in the sun improves the rum's flavor," he explained. He smiled at her curiosity and was surprised by the questions she asked. She was not merely going along with him to pass the time and nodding disinterestedly as would most ladies he knew. She was truly fascinated by Oakely Park, and it gave Philip an immeasurable amount of pride to show it to her.

They watched as hogshead barrels with the Oakely Park symbol were filled with treacle, rum, and sugar crystals and transported to a shed.

"Tomorrow, the first shipment of our crop will travel to Port Antonio," Philip told her. "Malachi and his gang will leave with the mules and carts at first light."

"You must be so proud, my lord. To see all the hours of labor packed tidily away and turned into profit." She patted a hogshead barrel. "It must be immensely rewarding."

She had expressed his feelings completely. High marks at the university, a successful day hunting, even winning a considerable wager at cards—*nothing* in his life had ever compared to the satisfaction of laboring with his workers and seeing the end result. He didn't think any of his friends in London would understand if he tried to describe the sensation. They would all think he'd gone mad, laboring in the fields with slaves. He blew out a breath. Perhaps he had. But he was managing the plantation according to his own system. Not his father's and not Horace Braithwaite's. And it was prospering.

He looked to where Anna leaned back, resting against a barrel and realized that he'd kept her much longer than he'd intended. She must be exhausted and hungry. Dr. Bevan had warned against too much exertion.

When she saw him walking toward her, she straightened and smiled brightly although she blinked a few too many times.

"Miss Hogshead, I fear I am going to incur the wrath of Dr. Bevan if you do not rest."

Anna did not argue or object to the surname, which in itself indicated how tired she must be. She took his arm, and as there was no mounting block, he brought Smokey to a low, moss-covered wall where she could step up.

They rode back toward the Great House at a slower pace. Philip told himself that it was because he was worried for Anna's health, but truly, he'd enjoyed the day and was reluctant for it to end. He glanced at her, noticing again how tired she looked. "I hope you will feel free to take Smokey for a ride whenever you like."

"Thank you. I would enjoy that."

"As long as you are careful to stay within the boundaries of Oakely Park, you will be safe."

Anna nodded.

He glanced at her and cleared his throat. "Miss, I'd like to ask you a question if you don't mind."

She turned her gaze to him. "Of course, my lord."

"The other day when we talked, you asked how I liked Jamaica, and I'm afraid I disappointed you with my response."

Anna looked at the road ahead and remained silent for so long he feared she would not answer. The plodding of the horses' hooves sounded loud to his ears, and he nearly spoke to fill the silence.

But finally she turned to him. "I *was* disappointed, sir. Your answer seemed . . . I suppose I'd asked the question in hopes to learn more about you." Even in the shade of her parasol, he saw her face redden.

He was surprised by her honesty and knew he could not respond with anything less. "My answer was . . . trite . . . because my feelings about Jamaica and Oakely Park are complicated. I do not know if even I understand them."

Anna watched him. She nodded slightly, encouraging him to continue.

"I love it and hate it. It is hot and full of mosquitoes and wind and violent storms. I miss London desperately. The society that was my life—my family, friends. But at the same time, I feel a fierce attachment to this land that I cannot explain. I have never worked harder or felt more pride in anything. I do not know how to even begin to describe the feelings I have, and when you inquired I found it was simpler not to try."

They drew near to the house, and Ezekiel hurried from the stables to meet them.

Anna reached to touch Philip's arm. "You do not need to explain, my lord. It is difficult to describe emotions for something one is passionate about." She spoke in a soft voice.

Philip met her gaze for a moment before he dismounted. He held onto Anna's waist as she climbed down, then he offered his arm.

Anna pushed her hair back over her shoulder and slipped her hand beneath his elbow. "You were very brave to come to Jamaica alone, Lord Philip, whatever your feelings."

"No more than you, surviving a shipwreck," he said as they walked up the steps to the house.

"I do not know if I was brave or not." Anna glanced at him then away.

"Mr. Norton and I found an oar with strings from your gown wrapped around it. I could never hope to be as brave as a woman who bound herself to a floating piece of wood in the middle of an ocean."

Anna squeezed her eyes shut. After a moment she blew out a heavy breath. "I wish I remembered. I look in the mirror and see a stranger. My own name does not sound familiar to me. I do not know whether I have a family or . . ." She raised her gaze, and he saw tears in her eyes.

"Anna, I know you do. And I know they miss you. Somewhere, people who love you are searching frantically, worried out of their minds. How could they not be?"

She blinked, and the tears spilled over. "I do not know. Maybe there is no one."

"Impossible," he murmured. He offered her a handkerchief.

Anna took it and dabbed her eyes. "I am sorry, my lord. I do not mean to ruin such a lovely day with my self-pitying."

Ezekiel hurried through the door and took Philip's hat, Anna's parasol and cloak, and both of their gloves.

Philip lifted Anna's hand and turned it over, placing the necklace into it. "I'd meant to give you this earlier. I took the liberty of having the clasp repaired while I was in town."

She studied the gold disc, brushing her finger over the inscription. "I wore this necklace?" She raised her eyes and, seeing his nod, looked back down at it. "Why don't I recognize it? Not even a bit?"

"I am sorry." He had hoped that the sight of her necklace would bring her memories tumbling back. He gritted his teeth, feeling helpless to do anything for her.

"I think I'll lie down," Anna said. Her shoulders slumped. "Thank you for today, Lord Philip. I enjoyed it immensely."

He didn't know what to say. Everything that came to his mind sounded pathetically inadequate. Standing in the main hall, Philip watched Anna ascend the stairs, wishing he knew how to help her or at least comfort her.

Philip was met in the drawing room by Ezekiel, who offered a glass of brandy which Philip readily accepted. He sat heavily in a chair in the bow of the window, watching the colorful birds flitting through the trees as his mind turned over the events of the day.

He knew what he had told Anna was true—a woman as intelligent and beautiful as she would be missed. His stomach grew heavy as he considered who might be missing her. Anna was undoubtedly adored by someone. A husband, a fiancé . . . He realized he was clutching the arm of the chair and forced his fingers to relax.

What he truly feared was not that Anna would never remember but that she would regain her memory and leave. He hated himself for the thought and chased it away, recalling the promise he had made to himself as he'd left London with his heart and pride torn in two. He had vowed to marry a wealthy woman who would increase his holdings. And he would not fall in love. He wouldn't risk allowing himself to care for someone. That path only led to pain.

He curled his lip as he thought of Clarissa Stapleton. He really should reciprocate the dinner invitation, and perhaps Clarissa would improve as he knew her better. He hoped to at minimum be able to tolerate her. He did not worry that she would break his heart. At least in that he was safe.

And as for Anna, he would treat her as a friend, a houseguest, and behave as her guardian. Once her memory returned, he would see that she was reunited with those who loved her. He would keep a closer watch on his heart's ramparts lest the woman and her charms found a way inside. His heart had been battered enough, and he feared Anna was one who could wound it beyond repair.

Chapter 9

ANNA WAS HEARTILY ASHAMED OF herself for the way she'd behaved to Lord Philip the day before. The outing had been perfect. She'd been fascinated with the stills and everything else about the plantation. She worried that she'd been annoying, asking so many questions. She'd wanted to see it all, to understand the workings of a place so extraordinary. But her frustration and despair over her lost memory had cast a pall over the day. After Lord Philip had been so attentive and had even purchased a horse for her to ride.

She clenched her fists on the dressing table, looking into the mirror. If only she could remember. She touched the pendant at her throat. "Who are you, Anna?" she said aloud to the reflection.

She sighed, arranging the hairbrush and other implements on the table before her. A flash of something familiar fluttered through her mind, so thin she couldn't grasp it. She chased it, searching the deep corners where she should find memory, but it was gone. Anna looked at the dressing table again. The positions of the various items had sparked something. She must have a dressing table of her own. Somewhere. But where? She clenched her eyes shut and pushed again, probing through her mind, but found nothing.

She felt as if something heavy had been put onto her shoulders; she shrugged to shake it off. It would not do to be melancholy. She'd already ruined her lovely day with Lord Philip by feeling sorry for herself. The wisp of memory had come when she wasn't trying, and if that was the case, she would simply not think about it and perhaps another would appear.

Anna combed through her hair gently, but her injuries were still too painful to pin it onto her head, so she left it loose. She dressed and made her way to breakfast, hoping for an opportunity to apologize to Lord Philip and thank him again for the previous day's outing.

A wave of disappointment washed over her when she arrived in the dining room and Ezekiel told her Lord Philp had ridden to the pastures for the day. She felt her shoulders slump but found it impossible to remain discouraged in the boy's presence.

She thanked him when he filled her glass. "It appeared yesterday that Lord Philip was very pleased with his valet," she said, winking.

"I did it all, everyt'in', just de way you tol' me, Miss Anna. Even de special knot."

"His lordship's cravat looked very fine, indeed." Anna loved saying anything that produced the boy's white-toothed grin. His entire face shone when he smiled. She could not imagine even the wickedest person to be immune to Ezekiel's charm.

"Lord Philip say you may wish to ride de horse today?"

Anna experienced a brief skip of her pulse at the idea that he had left instructions concerning her, but she shook her head to clear away the thought. It was typical for a host to see to the welfare of his guests when he was absent. She needed to rein in her emotions. "I would like that," she said.

Once Anna had finished her meal, she followed Ezekiel toward the stables. She was tempted to ask about his limp but did not want to hurt his feelings if he was sensitive about the topic.

As they rounded the side of the house, a large lizard with a long tail scurried toward them from the trees. The reptile was at least five feet long with a row of spines down its back. Anna's muscles clenched, and her heart hit the inside of her ribs. She clung to Ezekiel's arm and screamed.

The lizard darted toward a tree and ran up the trunk, disappearing into the canopy. Anna thought she might collapse. "An iguana lizard?" she asked between gasping breaths. Realizing she was still holding the boy's arm in an iron grip, she released her fingers.

"Dey will no' hurt you, Miss Anna." Ezekiel laughed. "You scare him worse dan he scare you."

Anna managed a weak smile. "I'm glad you are with me, Ezekiel, or I might have fainted dead away." She clenched her hands against the trembling. She needed to develop a stronger countenance if she was going to prevent herself from appearing ridiculous.

The boy continued to laugh as they entered the stables. He slipped a bridle over the mare's head, led Smokey out of the pen, and then quickly strapped the lady's saddle on the horse.

Anna looked around the well-maintained building. Two carriage horses stood in pens on the far side, and she assumed the empty stall belonged to Lord Philip's mount. She wondered how long it took the boy to feed and clean up after the horses in addition to his duties inside the house. "Do you care for the stables all on your own?" Anna said as she rubbed Smokey's nose.

"No, he come—" Ezekiel clamped his mouth shut. His eyes slid to the side, and he turned away, leading the horse through the stable door into the sunlight.

Anna wondered at his strange behavior. Did he think he would be punished for having assistance in the stables? Was the boy truly expected to manage the stables and serve as the footman and valet? She knew she had made him ill at ease and did not ask any other questions, thanking him once she'd mounted Smokey.

She paused, contemplating which direction to take. She didn't want to ride toward the pastureland and bother Lord Philip—not after she'd left him yesterday in tears. She pulled on the reins and turned the horse in the opposite direction, down the lane past the hospital and offices and blacksmith's forge. A plantation was truly a small city unto itself. She was curious about each place and hoped Lord Philip would give her a tour of the other plantation buildings.

Ahead she saw the cluster of cabins that Lord Philip had told her made up the slave quarters. She rode closer, studying the small structures. Each cabin was built with masonry walls on the lower half and finished with woven wattle covered in mud and hardened in the sun. The roofs were thatched palms held up by wooden poles at the corners.

The structures were surrounded by colorful gardens. She recognized the plants from the time she'd spent helping Betty in the kitchen. Yam vines climbed up sticks. The purple leaves of the sweet potato plant flowed over hillocks. It all appeared neat and well maintained, which Anna admitted she had not expected.

Elderly men and women as well as small children peered at her from doorways and yards. Some held infants; others tended gardens or ground cassava roots into flour. Anna realized the village was nearly deserted because the majority of workers were in the fields. The older slaves must be responsible to care for those still too young to labor. The children waved and grinned as she passed.

She wondered which house belonged to Betty. Did Ezekiel live with her?

She continued down the lane, considering the lives of the people at Oakely Park. They all had a place. The gang leaders supervised workers, the elderly cared for the children, the bookkeepers managed ledgers. Everyone had a purpose. Everyone *belonged*. But where did Anna belong? What role did she play in life? Right now, she felt as though she were floating, not able to find the niche where she fit. Would she ever remember?

She reached a wide-open plain and prodded Smokey into a gallop. They rode through fields separated by low prickly hedges, nearing a forested area. Sprinting on horseback was familiar to her, and she wondered where she had done it before. In England? Elsewhere on Jamaica? Her heart was light as she flew over the ground.

Without warning, a torrential rain began to fall, and in an instant, Anna was drenched. She looked around for shelter but saw none through the downpour. She did not want to go close to the trees for fear of an iguana lizard falling on her. Recalling how quickly the large animal had moved, she decided to avoid the trees altogether.

A bolt of lightning lit the sky, and the wind lashed her hair against her face. Something hovered just outside her consciousness, and for an instant, a memory of a similar storm flashed into her mind. But Anna didn't stop to dwell on it. It hadn't ever worked when she'd tried to force a memory. She turned the horse toward the edge of the property, hoping the high wall marking the inland boundaries of Oakely Park would provide a bit of protection. Once she reached the property line, she rode Smokey as close to the stone wall as she could.

The rain stopped as quickly as it had started, leaving the land sparkling and clean. Steam rose from Anna's clothes as the clouds moved away and the sun heated the air. She shook her wet curls over her shoulder, and they slapped against her back.

By the time she had followed the wall all the way to the main entrance, she was nearly dry—a benefit of wearing silk—although her gown was wrinkled and clung to her. Near the wrought-iron gates that led to the road, she saw a dark form on the ground and squinted to identify it. Had something fallen from a cart? As she drew closer, the shape moved, and a jolt of terror shot through her as her first thought was of a reptile. She clutched the reins and started to turn Smokey back toward the Great House, but the figure shifted again, and she saw that it was a man.

"Hello?" she called but didn't receive an answer.

Anna's heart thumped as she debated whether to approach the person. She edged the horse closer, wondering whether he was injured or drunk. Was it a highwayman merely pretending to need assistance? Would he jump up and carry her off as soon as she approached?

She prodded the horse around until she could see the person's face. *Malachi!* Why was he here? She'd thought his gang was driving the barrels to Port Antonio for sale. What had happened? Had he met with misfortune? Did he drink too much rum?

Anna reined in the horse. Malachi lay slumped with his shoulders resting against the gate. His head leaned to one side. The whites of his eyes contrasted starkly against his nearly black skin. He did not move though he was watching her.

Her gaze moved over him, and she saw his coarse tan shirt was streaked with blood. She could see the raw pink skin of a wound on his shoulder and another on his arm. If he didn't get help, she feared he would bleed to death.

She looked down the road that led to the Great House. She could ride for help, but would they make it back in time?

He continued to watch her. His marks looked like an evil mask around his eyes, and Anna's insides felt as though they were being squeezed. She could not imagine a more terrifying person, and she was alone with him. How could she . . . The image of Betty's face rose in her mind, and Anna remembered the embrace she had witnessed. Her throat thickened. She set her jaw and felt her temperature rise as she pushed aside her fear.

Anna climbed down from Smokey's back, dropping to the ground. She wrapped the reins around a bar of the gate and took a step toward Malachi. And then another. Her heart pummeled in her chest. "Sir? Malachi?"

His only response was a slow blink.

Anna knew she was wasting precious time and forced herself to move closer. She knelt in the mud next to him and looked at his shoulder. The wound was round. A musket ball? "You need help. Can you get onto my horse?"

Malachi blinked again. His muscles strained as he pressed his hands against the ground, but the movement caused the blood to flow faster.

"Stop." Anna pressed her hand against his chest. "We must bind your wounds first." She slipped off her glove and then removed her cloak, wincing as she tore the beautiful silk. "I do not think I have ever done this before," she muttered, more to herself than to him. She wound the strips around his arm, tying it off, and then turned to his shoulder, unsure of precisely how to proceed. "The main thing is to stop the bleeding," she said, unsure why she felt the need to keep up a dialogue.

When she placed a folded piece of cloth against his wound, Malachi drew in a heavy breath through his nose, but he didn't move.

"It is hurting you. I am sorry." Anna tried to be gentle as she wrapped the strips beneath his arm and around his chest to hold the cloth in place. The light silk was quickly saturated with blood, but she hoped it at least reduced the flow.

She moved Smokey as close as she could without trampling Malachi. "If you use the bars to pull yourself up, and perhaps lean on me . . ." She helped him bend forward and grab with one hand onto the metal gate. He did not move his injured shoulder. She crouched beneath his arm and pushed against his chest as he rose shakily to his feet. Once he was standing, he released the bar and rested his weight against Anna for an instant before grabbing the saddle.

Anna's knees buckled, and she pressed her side against Smokey to keep herself upright.

Malachi did not make a sound, though his face was twisted in pain as he pulled himself with one hand up onto Smokey's back. He sagged crosswise over the horse, his legs hanging on one side and his arms on the other.

Anna moved around to pull him astride, but Malachi's eyes were closed. He didn't answer when she spoke to him, and she realized he had fallen unconscious. After ensuring that he was still breathing and his shoulder was bound tightly, she led the horse slowly down the lane. She checked every few minutes to make sure he did not slide off one side or the other. She was grateful he was unaware. The movement of the horse would have been agony on his shoulder. Instead of proceeding to the Great House, she veered from the path through the trees toward the hospital.

Anna spotted a young girl and called to her, telling her to fetch Dr. Bevan and then Betty.

Anna hadn't realized how tense her shoulders were until she saw the doctor running toward her. She nearly wilted with relief.

"Miss Anna! Are you injured?"

Anna glanced down at her blood- and mud-spattered clothing. She shook her head. "No."

"What on earth happened?" Dr. Bevan crouched down to look at Malachi's face and pinched his dangling wrist between his fingers.

"I do not know. I found him at the main gate."

"And you brought him here yourself?" Dr. Bevan stared at her for a moment and then instructed two men to bring Malachi into the hospital.

Anna nodded and followed the doctor inside, too exhausted to say anything more.

Chapter 10

PHILIP LEAPED OFF HIS HORSE and ran into the hospital. Tom was right behind him. The messenger who had found them in the pastureland hadn't told them any details, only that Malachi had been found, nearly dead from blood loss. Where were the other members of his gang? What had happened to the shipment? His mind had churned over various scenarios in the past half hour, none of them good.

He hurried through the door but stopped short when his gaze landed on Anna slumped in a chair, her eyes closed. Her hair was matted and her gown filthy and covered in blood. A sudden cold spread from his core, and his heart plummeted. "Anna!" He knelt and clutched her shoulders as a jolt of fear shot through him. "Anna, are you hurt?"

Anna blinked slowly and looked up at him with bleary eyes. "No, my lord. Malachi is hurt," she said in a drowsy voice. "I was just tired."

Relief washed over him, and he stood quickly, resisting the impulse to pull her into his arms. He let out a breath.

She rubbed her eyes and stood.

Philip couldn't help noticing that despite her disarray, she looked extremely charming as she awoke, blinking and yawning. He glanced at Tom, who, judging by his expression, had noticed the same thing.

Before Philip could think of a reason to send Tom away from the hospital, Dr. Bevan entered from the back room, followed by Betty.

"What happened?" Philip lifted his chin toward the back room. "Malachi is injured?"

Dr. Bevan nodded his head. "A bullet wound to the shoulder and a deep slash, probably inflicted by a knife or a sword, to his upper arm."

Tom let out a low curse.

"He lost an excessive amount of blood and would have died for certain if Anna had not discovered him and brought him here."

Philip's gaze darted to Anna. *She had saved Malachi?*

She met his eyes briefly, and her cheeks turned pink.

He turned back to the doctor. "Did he speak? Where are the others in his gang? What happened to the shipment?" Philip balled his hands into fists, pressing them against his legs to keep himself from shouting.

"He spoke to Betty briefly, but his pain was such that I gave him a dose of laudanum to allow him some relief," Dr. Bevan said.

Betty wrung her hands, somehow looking pale beneath her dark skin.

Anna stepped across the room and put an arm around her shoulders.

"Did he tell you anything, Betty?" Philip could see that Betty was upset and tried to keep his voice even, but he was so agitated it was all he could do to remain standing in one spot.

"Malachi tol' me de highwaymen took de shipment. He does not know if any of de gang survive. And . . ." Betty's eyes widened. She leaned toward Philip, her eyes darting to each side. "De leader, he is de old *busha*." Her voice trembled, and she clamped her hand over her mouth as soon as she spoke.

Philip glanced to his overseer.

Tom's brows were drawn together. "Are you certain, Betty?" he asked.

Betty nodded.

Philip looked back at Tom. "Who is the old *busha*?"

Tom furrowed his fingers through his hair. "Horace Braithwaite."

Hot fury burned in his gut as Philip processed what Tom told him. *Horace.* That disgusting, vindictive man had killed his workers and stolen thousands of pounds worth of sugar, treacle, and rum. His insides writhed. He clenched and unclenched his fists.

"Come, Tom. We will deal with this at once. He will not get away with it." Philip strode through the hospital door, cramming his hat onto his head.

"Lord Philip," Anna said.

He turned as she rushed toward him.

"Where are you going?" she asked when she reached him. "Please say you are not going to challenge the criminals."

"I cannot allow this to go unpunished."

"Please. It is too dangerous."

He clasped Anna's hand, not caring that she could likely feel his shaking.

"I have heard you can be hotheaded and impulsive." She attempted to smile but couldn't quite make it. Her brows pulled together. "Do not allow anger to cloud your judgment."

Philip gritted his teeth and glanced down the dusty path toward the main road. He would never find Horace and his posse in the thick jungles. Although his impulse was to search the island with his weapon drawn until he found the foul-mouthed wretch, he knew the matter was best left to the authorities. The idea that Horace Braithwaite and his group could get clean away with Philip's hard-earned goods clamped his chest like a vice. "Anna, other survivors could be on the road. I must alert the authorities in Port Antonio. I cannot send another when it is my duty."

Anna bit her lip and touched her pendant. "The highwaymen could be waiting for you."

"Not likely," Tom said, leading the horses to join them. "They've fifty hogshead barrels to transport and hide. I imagine that will keep them busy for some time. Oakely Park's symbol is recognized in Port Antonio, and they'll never make it through the mountains without the Brethren appropriating some, if not all, of it." He brushed his fingers through his hair again. "Horace is smart. He'll have a plan. I'd not be surprised if he's got a boat ready to transport the barrels from some hidden bay."

Anna squeezed Philip's fingers, and he thought what a comforting sensation it was to hold her hand. "You will be careful, my lord?"

He wanted to smooth the worry lines between her brows. "I will be careful, Miss Rescues-Wounded-Men." The simple act of holding her hand had calmed him immensely. He was reluctant to release it, especially when she still looked so concerned.

"Are you ready, my lord?" Tom said.

Philip looked up to see that the overseer had already mounted his horse. He pulled his hand from Anna's and hurried into the saddle, unlatching the strap he'd fastened over the horse pistol. The weapon—even as awkward and heavy as it was—made him feel less vulnerable.

He glanced to Anna. She stood with her arm linked through Betty's, and the women watched the men ride toward the main gates. He couldn't help the warmth that spread through his chest at Anna's concerned expression, and he wondered again, *Who is she?*

***

Philip and Tom kept up a good pace, not only because they were nervous about whom they might encounter on the road, but they needed to reach any possible survivors and get to Port Antonio and back before dark. Tom had left orders for a cart to follow them as soon as the animals could be harnessed in order to return with any wounded or deceased workers they might encounter.

There was no question as to where the shipment had been attacked. Not three miles from Oakely Park, the road curved, and a thick copse of trees provided limited visibility. Evidence of the strike was all around them—broken tree branches, a cart that had smashed a wheel, a dead mule. But it was the sight of the lifeless bodies that turned Philip's stomach. The workers, riding or walking next to the carts, had obviously been taken completely by surprise.

He and Tom dismounted and began the gruesome task of retrieving the remains of his workers. Most were young, some only children. None had survived. Philip retched into the undergrowth. He recognized the man who had offered him a drink after they'd repaired the hospital wall. This man had a daughter. Philip's eyes stung.

They lifted and moved the bodies to the road, arranging them as respectfully as they could, and waited for the cart to arrive. As Philip looked at the row of workers his throat constricted, and he brushed his sleeve across his eyes.

"Don't worry." Tom leaned his back against the broken cart and crossed his arms. "It is only one shipment. We'll make up the damages by expanding our planting field next season."

Philip stared at the man. "Do you honestly think I am worried about the blasted sugar when my workers have been *murdered*?"

Tom shrugged. "Not a problem, my lord. The slaves will be even cheaper to replace than the lost barrels." He shook his head. "The mules are the biggest loss, but we can find more."

A rush of anger made Philip want to plant his fist in the overseer's face. "Mr. Norton, there are twenty-four people dead." He bit off each word. "Twenty-four people under our care. Twenty-four people massacred defending another man's—MY—property." Philip breathed deeply in hopes of calming himself and sparing Tom from becoming the recipient of the rush of anger that shot through his veins. "How can you be so cavalier about barbarity?"

"But, my lord," Tom spoke slowly as if he were speaking to a child, "they are only Negroes."

Spots of red burst in front of Philip's eyes. He thought of the smiling girl whose father would never return. He seized Tom's collar and shoved him forcefully against the cart.

"My lord . . ." Tom raised his hands, palms out, and looked at Philip as if he had gone completely mad.

Philip shoved him again and stormed toward his horse, mounting in one swift move. "Remain here until the cart arrives and help load the remains. When you arrive at Oakely Park, you are to relieve the workers from their duties today to bury and mourn the dead."

"But, my lord, it is early yet. We'll lose a half day of labor . . ." Tom's voice trailed off as he raised his gaze to Philip's.

"I will continue to Port Antonio alone."

"Are you certain, my lord?" Tom said in an unconvincingly concerned voice.

Philip turned his horse and urged it to a gallop. The pounding of the animal's hooves mirrored the turmoil inside him. This situation, this tragedy, his people, his sugar, his overseer. He had never been so completely furious as he was now at Horace Braithwaite. Even his brother and Jacqueline's deception paled in comparison. Philip felt violated. His property had been stolen, his people killed. And all because he had injured a loathsome man's pride.

Philip knew Anna would be disappointed, but he would not rest until he saw Horace Braithwaite hanging from the gallows, or even better, impaled by Philip's own sword. He never thought of himself as a man who would be driven by revenge, but today, the game had changed.

Chapter 11

Anna sat next to Betty in the hospital, not wanting to leave her friend and hoping she was providing some sort of comfort.

The day had given Anna much to ponder. She'd learned from Betty that Horace Braithwaite was the former overseer at Oakely Park whom Philip had dismissed the day he arrived when Horace lashed a slave girl. Anna listened to the horrible story, her stomach clenching in repulsion for Horace Braithwaite and her heart growing light as she heard of Philip's heroism. She had suspected he was a kind master, and Betty's tale confirmed it. Betty told Anna that the rations and the working conditions had improved immensely since Philip had arrived. Although the law allowed it, he firmly forbade corporal punishment of any kind. The workers were loyal to him, Betty had told her.

While they sat in the hospital, Ezekiel had burst through the door, his face wet with tears. Betty had spoken to him in the pidgin language Anna could not understand and took him to the back room to see Malachi, even though the man still slept.

When they returned a few moments later, Anna did not ask Betty or Ezekiel about his reaction. She knew the boy to be sensitive and kind. Perhaps he became upset anytime someone was injured, but her instincts told her there was more. She studied the pair as they sat, unspeaking. Betty nervously wrung her hands. Anna was saddened to see her friend so worried. She wished she could think of comforting things to say but decided to allow Betty to speak first if it was what she needed. Until then, Anna hoped her presence offered some support.

Suddenly Ezekiel's head jerked up, and he stood, moving to the open door. He motioned for them to join him.

When Anna peered outside, she saw that Mr. Norton rode ahead of a slow-moving cart and stopped in the road in front of the slave's cabins. People hurried from the houses. She followed Betty and Ezekiel down the road toward him.

By the time she reached him, he had dismounted and was speaking with Betty. From what Anna overheard, Philip had ordered a reprieve from the worker's duties in order for them to care for their dead. She moved to follow Ezekiel toward the cart, but Mr. Norton hooked his hand into her elbow, stopping her, and then moved to block her view. She'd only caught a glimpse of dark limbs piled on top of each other.

"You don't need to see that, Miss Anna," Thomas said. He turned her by the shoulders, leading her away from the cart and the slave village, toward the Great House.

Anna glanced back once and shuddered at the sight of a limp form being lifted off the cart. She took the overseer's arm and continued up the lane.

Questions tumbled through her mind. What had happened? How many people were dead? Where was Lord Philip?

Mr. Norton cleared his throat, and Anna realized he'd spoken while she was contemplating. "I'm sorry, sir. What did you say?"

He placed his hand over where hers rested on his arm. "I wondered if you might take tea with me. It feels like the entire plantation is deserted, and I wouldn't want you to be afraid, alone in the Great House."

The emotional day had left Anna feeling drained, and she wanted nothing more than to take a nap. "I shall not be afraid, sir. And Lord Philip will return soon, will he not?"

Tom's eyes narrowed the slightest bit, and Anna wondered if she had only imagined it. "Lord Philip is likely still in Port Antonio speaking with the constable. I do not think he will return for quite a while."

This time she was certain she saw displeasure in the man's eyes and wondered if something had happened. "I am very tired, Mr. Norton. It has been a long day for both of us. I do thank you for your invitation. Perhaps another time would better suit?"

"As you like, Miss Anna." Tom nodded curtly and left Anna at the Great House entrance. She had plenty to think about as she made her way up the stairs and changed out of her filthy gown. It was merely hours earlier that Anna had thought the iguana lizard to be the worst thing she would ever encounter, but she had been proven wrong. Twice. The moment her head touched the pillow, the physical and emotional strains of the day overcame even her most valiant efforts to contemplate the extraordinary happenings, and Anna slept.

***

Anna awoke in the dark. She felt for a moment that she was aboard a ship and even thought she could feel the rocking of the waves beneath her. She tried to see more of the memory, for she knew that's what it was, but it was simply a dark, swaying room. Anna assumed it would flutter away as the others had done, but it remained in her mind. And even though it was hardly anything, her hopes rose. The knowledge that there *was* something before, that she was from somewhere, that she had truly lived a life lit a small spark in the recesses of her mind, and she touched on the memory again, delighted that she could do so at will.

The events of the day moved to the forefront of her mind. Had Lord Philip returned? What had he discovered? Was he safe? She hurried from the bed and lit the candles in her room, lifting the candelabra and shining its orb of light into the dark hallway. She passed Lord Philip's bedchamber and saw that his door was open and he was not inside.

She stepped down the stairs, lighting the sconces on the wall as she went so the house wouldn't be dark when he returned. While she stood in the entryway contemplating whether she should go outside to the kitchen building to find something to eat or wait until the morning, she heard a thump from the drawing room. Perhaps Lord Philip was already home.

Anna walked down the hallway, anxious to tell him about the sliver of memory and to hear what had happened in Port Antonio. She stepped into the drawing room and found the source of the noise. Lord Philip sprawled in an armchair fast asleep. A glass tumbler lay on the heavy carpet where he must have dropped it.

Anna set the candelabra on a table and picked up the glass, tapping the carpet with her fingers to make sure nothing had spilled.

In the flickering light, she studied Lord Philip's sleeping face. The lines she'd seen around his eyes at the hospital and the tightness of his mouth were gone. He appeared unconcerned and carefree, almost childlike. She wondered if this is how he must have looked before taking on the responsibility of the plantation. What drives a man to leave a life of ease for one of hard work and worry?

She thought for a moment about waking him, but he looked so peaceful. She hurried up the stairs, took a blanket from his bedchamber, and returned, placing it over him. She moved an ottoman close for his legs then grasped a boot with both hands, tugging until she pulled it free, nearly toppling backward. She repeated the procedure with the other boot.

Anna studied him again, remembering what Betty had told her about how he treated his slaves and thinking how he'd stopped work at Oakely Park to give the laborers time to mourn their dead. She knew the way he managed the plantation was singular for a slave owner, and her chest warmed with an immense feeling of pride and gratitude. Lord Philip was a good man.

Once Anna had done all she could think of to make Lord Philip comfortable, she lifted the candelabra and turned to leave the room. She paused and reached a tentative hand to brush a lock of hair from his forehead. "Good night, my lord," she whispered.

His hand darted up and caught hers.

She gasped. "Lord Philip. I thought . . . Were you awake this entire time?" Heat flooded her face, and she jerked her hand away.

One corner of his mouth lifted in a smile. "I had the most enchanting dream."

Anna whirled and stomped out of the door. Her flush spread over her entire body in a burning layer of humiliation.

Lord Philip caught her on the stairs, darting past and turning to block her way. "Anna, please stop." He sat on the steps in front of her, so that they faced each other.

"It seems I've no choice, my lord." She pressed her balled fists on her hips and looked in every direction but at him.

"Please, Anna, do not be angry. I dozed in my chair and awoke to find you tugging off my boots. If I'd have let you know I was no longer sleeping, I fear I'd have missed out on the most pleasant thing that's happened to me in weeks."

Anna scowled dramatically. "I should have grabbed your shoulders and shaken you as you did to me in the hospital." She cocked a brow. "I, however, know how unpleasant it is to be awakened in such a manner and chose to be compassionate."

He smiled. "Leaving me in that chair all night after hours in the saddle would have been the farthest thing from compassion." He pressed his palms into the small of his back, stretching to the side. "My back already hurts like the dickens."

At the reminder of his hard day, Anna's anger softened. She sat on the stair next to him. "I'm afraid I have a policy to assist only one unconscious man to a bed per day, and as you know, my quota was filled this morning."

Philip laughed, but the lines returned around his mouth, and his eyes lost a bit of their sparkle. "We both had a trying day, I'm afraid, Miss Boot-Removal-Service."

Anna felt a rush of heat at the tenderness in his voice. Even when horrible things were happening, he tried to lift her spirits. She shifted on the stair so that her knees faced him. "Did you speak to the constable?"

Philip's eyes tightened. "I did."

"And will he . . . ?"

"He will not help us. I also spoke to the colonel in charge of the fort. With the Spanish invading Hispaniola, the soldiers are to remain on alert and are unavailable for local law enforcement." He rubbed a hand over his cheek. "Especially when the only witness is one black man."

"But all those people . . ." Anna's eyes burned at the injustice of it all.

"I know, Anna." He blew out a breath. "The constable was much more interested in the number of mules and the quantity and contents of the barrels than the people who were killed." He brushed a tear from her cheek that she had not even noticed. "We will figure something out. Perhaps I can appeal to the Governor-General of the colony."

Anna nodded. She didn't know what to say. How could the senseless murders of so many people be ignored?

He pushed his fingers through his hair. She could see that the deaths and the refusal of the constable to assist him weighed heavily on him. He had not even mentioned the loss of his sugar, which would impact him financially as well.

Philip scrubbed his hands over his face, and his eyes widened as if he suddenly remembered something. "Tomorrow"—he reached into his waistcoat and checked his pocket watch—"oh, it *is* tomorrow. I did not realize it was so late." He put away the watch. "I have invited our neighbor John Stapleton and his daughter, Clarissa, for dinner tonight. I am sorry I did not have an opportunity to tell you earlier, but I would be very happy if you would join us."

Anna looked at her hands resting in her lap. She'd come to love the isolation of Oakely Park. The idea of being introduced to strangers, having to explain her memory loss . . . She pushed aside her worry. Lord Philip had been the perfect host, and if she could repay him in some small manner by joining him for dinner, it would not matter if she were uncomfortable for a few hours. "Of course, my lord."

"The Stapletons know of your . . . memory impairment." The side of his mouth lifted again, and she knew he was teasing. "Do not be worried. And the day after our dinner party, Tom and I are riding to the coffee farm location in the mountains. Will you join us?"

Anna smiled, and her spirits lifted. "I would love to."

He leaned back and stretched his arm across a stair. "I knew you would."

"I remembered something tonight," she said in a quiet voice.

Philip's eyebrows lifted. "That is the first bit of good news I have heard all day. Do you want . . . is it something you wish to share?"

"It is not much. I remember lying in the darkness, and I know I am at sea. The boat rocks back and forth—and that's all. Not a very interesting memory, but I am certain it's real."

He studied her for a moment, perhaps waiting for her to say more. She could not read his expression. "Maybe your memory will return in small pieces. I do not know. But perhaps this means it is not lost for good."

Anna nodded. "That is exactly what I thought. I hope this is just the beginning."

Philip's expression was strange. He had seemed happy for her, but the smile on his face was strained somehow. She looked at him again and saw his brow furrow, just for a moment, and wondered if she had imagined it. Anna decided the day had been extremely difficult, and she could hardly expect him to be overjoyed with a strange bit of someone else's memory.

Chapter 12

ANNA GAZED AT HER REFLECTION as Betty carefully pinned up her curls. Her hair pulled on her tender scalp, and she winced.

"I be mo' gentle, miss," Betty said, loosening the pins. She stepped back, and Anna turned on the dressing table chair.

"Thank you, Betty." Anna slipped on her evening gloves, pulling them past her elbows, and stood to study herself in the mirror. Aside from a bit of redness on her cheeks from her sunburn, she looked fully recovered. When she'd seen the new gown, it had taken her breath away. The embroidery on the bodice and the lovely salmon-colored silk that hung in gentle folds to the floor . . . It was magnificent, and Anna felt like a princess.

"You are very beautiful tonight."

She smiled at Betty. "Thank you for your help. I know you must hurry to finish supper on time. Thank you for performing lady's maid duties in addition to everything else."

Betty took her hands. "You and Lord Philip are de good people. Don' forget it when you wit' de others."

Anna squinted her eyes and opened her mouth to ask what Betty meant, but the housekeeper shook her head and hurried out of the room. Anna did not want to dwell. It was obvious that Betty didn't care for the Stapletons, but it was just one evening, and Anna could endure a few hours with unpleasant people if it was what Lord Philip wanted. The new dress didn't hurt her confidence either.

She stepped down the stairs and into the entryway, turning when she heard someone clear his throat.

Lord Philip stood with his arms folded across his chest, one shoulder leaning on a door frame. "'Pon my word, Miss Anna. If you're not the loveliest sight I've seen in months." The side of his mouth pulled in a smile. He stood straight, walking toward her. He lifted her hand and bowed over it. Though they both wore gloves, the warmth from his touch sent a wave of heat up her arm, straight to her cheeks.

Anna dipped in a curtsy. "Thank you, my lord."

Lord Philip did not release her hand but continued to study her.

Anna wished her hair was loose and she could duck her face behind her curls. His scrutiny heated her cheeks further. She pulled her hand gently from his grasp.

Lord Philip seemed to come to himself and took a step back. "Shall we wait for our guests in the drawing room?"

Anna's heart tripped at his wording. *Our* guests. She worried that she was becoming too attached to Oakely Park and even more to its owner. She knew the illusion was temporary, but it was so easy to imagine herself a permanent resident here. Her heart beat faster, and she glanced at the man next to her as she realized the implications of her thoughts, grateful he couldn't see into her mind.

Was there another man somewhere that she loved? Another who sent heat to her cheeks with his smile? She would feel differently, she was certain, once she remembered her own life, but for now, Anna found herself very much content with the made-up version.

"They should arrive in ten minutes." Lord Philip snapped his pocket watch shut. He led Anna to sofa and sat in an armchair across from her. One side of his mouth rose in the slow smile that made her pulse speed up. "So, until then, what shall we talk about?"

***

An hour and a half later, Anna stood next to Lord Philip in the main hall as he welcomed his guests. Being a generous host, he gave no indication that he was annoyed with their tardiness. She curtsied when she was introduced to John Stapleton and again when she made the acquaintance of his daughter, Clarissa.

Anna didn't think Clarissa could have looked less pleased at the introduction if she had tried. Her eyes narrowed as her gaze moved slowly from the tip of Anna's head to her toes and then back. She closed her eyes and curled her lip as if she could no longer bear the sight and turned her head toward Lord Philip. Anna felt like she'd been deemed supremely inadequate.

When Betty announced dinner, Lord Philip turned to the group, opened his mouth, and then paused.

Anna understood his dilemma right away. Since he did not know Anna's parentage, he was unsure whether she outranked Clarissa. Who should accompany his lordship to dinner? She saw the indecision on his face as his eyes moved between the two ladies for an uncomfortable moment. Anna solved the quandary by stepping back and motioning with her head toward Clarissa.

Lord Philip shot her a grateful look that she did not think anyone else noticed. He offered his arm to lead Clarissa into dinner.

Clarissa snatched it and nodded once to the others, apparently quite proud of herself.

Anna and Mr. Stapleton followed.

In the dining room, Lord Philip sat at the head of the table. Anna sat on his left side and Mr. Stapleton on his right. Clarissa was seated next to her father, and she didn't bother to hide the fact that the arrangement did not suit her. She folded her arms and pouted with a huff, sending her ringlets into a frenzy of bouncing around her doll-like face.

Anna glanced at Philip, wondering what he thought about Clarissa's behavior, but he politely pretended not to notice and commented instead on the sudden rain the day before.

Betty and Ezekiel served the first course. Anna couldn't help but be irritated. Betty had worked all day and then had to reheat the meal because the Stapletons were so inconsiderate and couldn't be bothered with punctuality. She nodded her thanks to Ezekiel and had just brought a spoonful of sea-turtle soup to her lips when Clarissa set down her spoon with a clatter.

"Lord Philip told us that you have no memory, Miss Anna," Clarissa said.

"Yes, Dr. Bevan believes the phenomenon to have been caused by an injury to the head."

Clarissa raised her gaze to Anna's hair and then lowered her eyelids, tipping her head in an expression that left no doubt that she did not care in the least.

"The doctor thinks the condition is temporary, Miss Stapleton," Philip said. "He believes that eventually Anna should regain her lost memories."

Clarissa shot another glance at Anna and turned her body to face Lord Philip. "My lord, if I might be so bold—how can you be certain that she is who she claims to be?"

Anna pulled back in her chair. She couldn't believe anyone would speak so rudely about her while she sat in the same room.

Philip leveled a gaze at Clarissa. "Well, she has not claimed to be anyone—the exact opposite in fact."

"What if she is a charlatan? Or a . . . spy?" She whispered the last word and glanced quickly at Anna. "What if she is loyal to the *French*?"

Philip stared at Clarissa for a long moment. His expression seemed to waver between anger and amusement. "A spy at Oakely Park? If it is the case, she went to incredible lengths: exposing herself to the sun for days, wounding her head to the point that she nearly died of blood loss and dehydration in the hopes that someone would happen upon her and get her to a doctor in time to save her life."

Clarissa glared at Anna. "How can you trust someone without knowing her background? I would never allow a person in my home who conceals so much about herself."

Anna could not believe that the woman had not yet tired of her accusations. She tried to tell herself that Clarissa did not understand the true nature of her condition. Perhaps she was merely looking out for her neighbor. But the manner in which she spoke was uncouth to say the least. She wondered if she should excuse herself. Surely this contention was making Lord Philip uncomfortable.

Philip's brows pursed, and he wiped his napkin across his mouth, setting it on the table. "Now that you mention it, Miss Stapleton, she has been excessively interested in treacle. I wonder what the French would do with that information?"

Beneath the table, Anna felt Philip's leg bump into hers. She glanced at him, but he seemed suddenly interested in the pattern on the rim of his plate. The edge of his mouth pulled. Anna was relieved that he did not take Clarissa's words seriously.

Clarissa settled herself in her chair, folding her arms and turning up her nose at the soup when Ezekiel removed the bowl and replaced it with fruit. The bouncing of her ringlets reminded Anna of Medusa's head full of serpents.

Philip glanced between the two women and turned to Mr. Stapleton. "John, you must have heard about the attack on my shipment yesterday."

John swatted away Ezekiel's hand when the boy offered to take his soup. "I've heard reports of at least two other shipments stolen as well from other plantations. You lost fifty hogsheads and a few mules, I understand."

"I also lost twenty-four workers." Lord Philip's expression remained pleasant, but Anna knew if the Stapletons were better acquainted with him, they would have been wary when they noticed his eyes tighten.

Anna tapped her foot against his leg to let him know that he was not alone among these ridiculous people. She understood that he mourned the loss of his people even if the Stapletons did not.

"I do not think the others lost slaves." He looked thoughtful as he stroked his mustache. "But no matter. 'Tis only a few hundred quid to replace the Negroes. The sugar and rum—that there's the real loss."

Anna saw Philip's jaw clench. She thought quickly for something to say to change the direction of the conversation before he lost his temper. "Miss Stapleton, your gown is very lovely. I think the color is the perfect complement for your . . . ah . . . hairstyle."

Philip's leg bumped hers again, and he coughed into his napkin.

Clarissa waved her fingers over her plate, indicating for Ezekiel to remove it. "An *English* gown made by an honest English dressmaker. Another reason to mistrust you, if I may speak plainly, Miss Anna. I would not be buried in a French dress like yours. We are at war, you know." She sniffed. "Apparently you are not averse to purchasing plundered clothing from peddlers who acquire their wares from pirates. Some of us have standards."

Anna didn't bother to be offended. Clarissa's words had piqued her interest. Her clothing was French? And purchased from pirates? She hadn't even wondered when Philip said he had a difficult time finding clothing in Port Antonio, and yet Betty had produced an entire closet full of gowns.

Anna looked across the table. Mr. Stapleton was studying her intently. She tried not to squirm under his scrutiny. She hoped he was merely curious about her gown.

Philip cleared his throat. "I wonder, John, if you think I should try to plead my case to the Governor-General in Kingston."

Mr. Stapleton pulled his gaze from Anna. "Yer case? Oh, aye. The fifty hogshead . . ."

Anna did not focus on the men's conversation or Clarissa's glares in her direction but allowed her mind to wander. She touched on the memory of lying in a dark ship and wondered more about it. Had she been traveling to Jamaica? From where? Was she with her family? Did they survive the shipwreck? Or was the small wisp of memory something different altogether?

An image flashed in her mind. *A handsome man in a dimly lit room hands her a book. He smiles.* Anna tried, but she could not push the memory further. Who was the man? She knew she recognized him, but she could not think of his name or their relationship. Was he her friend? Brother? Anna breathed deeply. Was the man her *husband*? She pushed harder, trying to attach an emotion to the image.

"Miss Anna?" Ezekiel's whisper dragged her mind back into the dining room. He stood behind her chair, poised to pull it back.

She looked up and noticed that the others stood and the meal had ended. They were waiting for the ladies to adjourn to the drawing room while the men drank their port.

Anna stood quickly. She glanced at Philip.

His eyes squinted, and he turned his head to the side slightly, asking a silent question. He was concerned.

She nodded just a bit, smiling to assure him that she was well, and followed Clarissa down the hall, bracing herself for the time she would have to spend alone with the woman.

Clarissa sniffed as she looked at the furnishings in Lord Philip's drawing room. "Poor man. Oakely Park could certainly use a woman's touch." She sat in Philip's chair, resting her wrists on the chair arms like a queen.

Anna smiled as she imagined that Lord Philip would certainly have bumped her knee with his if he'd heard such a brash sentiment. Anna sat on the sofa across from Clarissa, and she thanked Ezekiel when he set a tea tray on the table between them.

"You do know that my father owns more land than anyone on this side of the island. Kensington Estate is very extensive." Clarissa let out a breath as if her extreme wealth was at times too much of a burden. "He is taking me to the governor's house party next week." She allowed her half-lidded eyes to travel around the room again. "Oakely Park is nice to be sure, but the decor is quaint and the food plain. It is hardly suitable for a fine lady of my tastes."

Anna pressed her lips together as a rush of irritation sped up her pulse. "I think Oakely Park is absolutely lovely just as it is," she said.

Ezekiel poured the tea.

"It will be soon enough if you take my meaning." Clarissa puffed out her lips and turned her gaze full force on Anna. "I think Lord Philip is quite taken with me." She batted her eyelashes. "And he'll need a strong wife, experienced with the ways of plantation life, if he's to survive here in Jamaica. Poor man is hopelessly out of his element."

Anna thought she would be sick. The very idea of Lord Philip with this woman made her stomach burn. "I am sure his lordship is aware of your charms and all you have to recommend you." She thought her reply seemed safe. There was no way he could not notice Clarissa, but Lord Philip would never consider an attachment to her.

"Of course he is. He would be a fool otherwise. And then all of this—" Clarissa swung her hand through the air, colliding with Ezekiel as he reached to offer her a cup of tea. Liquid splashed over Clarissa's glove and gown. The teacup flew, shattering with a crash against the wall.

"You clumsy fool!" Clarissa shrieked. She struck Ezekiel across the face. The boy hit the wall and collapsed, holding his hands in front of his face as she lifted her hand to strike again.

Anna darted toward her, seizing her around the waist and pushing her back into the chair. Then she sank down on the floor next to Ezekiel. She tugged on his arm and found an ugly gash bleeding on the side of his head. "How dare you strike this boy!" Anna cried. She looked around for something to stop his bleeding, and when she saw nothing nearby, she pulled off a glove, folded it, and pressed it against his wound.

Clarissa stood, her face red and her ringlets sticking out at odd angles. "When I am mistress of Oakely Park, I will not tolerate this vulgar treatment. Useless crippled Negroes and swindlers that masquerade as ladies will be thrown out into the jungle to fend for themselves." Spittle flew from her mouth as she yelled.

Ezekiel shrunk back, and Anna wrapped her arms around the boy, holding him tightly.

Clarissa jerked her head around as footsteps sounded in the hall. The men rushed into the room followed by Betty.

Clarissa's expression transformed in an instant. She pouted her lip and whimpered, "Daddy, the cruel Negro tried to hurt me." Covering her face with her hand, she howled and shook.

Philip just stared at the preposterous performance.

"That is not true in the least," Anna said, even though she was sure no one could hear her words over Clarissa's wails.

Betty knelt on the other side of Ezekiel and peeked beneath the bloody glove.

John took his daughter in his arms, patting her on the head like he would a small child. "What do you have to say for yourself, my lord?" He glared at Philip.

"Ezekiel would never harm Miss Stapleton," Lord Philip said. "There must be a misunder—"

Clarissa's wails grew louder, and her father led her into the hall.

Philip stood in the doorway, his expression wavering between anger and confusion as he looked at the women, injured boy, and then into the hall at his guests. His gaze met Anna's, and she lifted her chin toward the noise in the hall. He should deal with his guests.

Betty watched him go and then turned to Anna. "I take Ezekiel to de doctor," she said in a low voice. She laid her hand on Anna's cheek. "I knew you was one of de good people."

Anger bubbled up inside her accompanied by a constricting throat as she thought about the terror she'd seen in Ezekiel's face. No child should have to fear such harm. But Betty's simple words and gesture touched her heart so deeply that she could not find the words to respond. Tears prickled behind her eyes. She nodded, hoping Betty understood.

They helped the boy to his feet, and Betty took him from the room.

Anna peeked through the front door. Outside, Clarissa continued to cry while her father bellowed about nobody fetching their carriage or his hat quickly enough.

"Sir, if your daughter had not injured my manservant, he would have indeed retrieved your coach by now," Philip said. Anna could hear the frustration and anger in his clipped tone. He turned toward the house and caught her gaze for an instant, shaking his head before he started toward the stable.

Anna moved away from the door. She pulled the pins from her hair as she climbed the stairs. The easing of the pressure on her sore scalp was a relief. Once she reached her bedchamber, she threw herself on the bed, not caring that she still wore an embroidered French silk dress.

A torrent of emotions washed over her. She didn't know whether she wanted to pound her fists on the pillows or to pull them over her face and sob. She wouldn't do either while that wretched woman still shrieked outside her window. Eventually the noise quieted, and the sound of horse hooves and carriage wheels told her that their repulsive dinner guests had departed. She lay on the bed long after the noise faded, imagining the Stapletons getting farther and farther away—and perhaps dropping off a cliff into the sea.

Anna sat up and pulled off her other glove. She was making a habit of ruining beautiful clothing, she thought with a grimace. Now that there was no chance of encountering the Stapletons, she decided she would go to the hospital to check on Ezekiel. She stepped into the hallway and nearly collided Lord Philip as he raised his hand to knock on her bedchamber door.

"I thought you would not wait in your room," he said. "Might I assume you are walking to the hospital?"

Anna nodded her head.

"I hope you don't mind a companion. I myself am quite concerned about my valet."

Chapter 13

Philip was grateful that Anna had agreed to join him as he walked to the hospital. He'd worried that she might be angry with him or too upset by the horrendous evening to wish for company. He couldn't imagine any scenario where the evening could have gone worse. He lifted the lantern he'd found in the stable and glanced at her as they stepped through the front doors.

Anna raised her face to the sky, and he followed suit, watching the shadowy bats swooping to catch insects. He'd only occasionally seen a bat before he came to Jamaica, but on the island they filled the sky every night. He followed her down the steps.

Anna breathed in. "I love that aroma," she said. "I can smell it from my window."

Philip gestured to the small bushes next to the stairs. "Plumeria. It is more fragrant at night." He offered his arm, and they started down the road.

She glanced at the shrub's white flowers as they passed.

Philip wasn't sure exactly how to broach the uncomfortable subject of what had transpired that evening. Best just to jump in with both feet. He laid his hand over hers. "I wanted to make sure you were not distressed after the . . . events with the Stapletons."

Anna frowned and glanced at him. "By 'events,' are you referring to the insults to me, my clothing, your management of the plantation, and your choice of servants? Or perhaps the completely uncalled-for violence against a child I care for?" She pulled her hand from his and crossed her arms in front of her. Her strolling turned into a quick march, and Philip had to hurry to keep up. "I do not remember a time when I have felt *more* distressed—although I have only the past weeks to use as reference." The lantern light flickered over her face, which remained unnaturally devoid of emotion.

Philip almost wished she would scream, or cry, or *something*. "I don't suppose an apology would make a difference?"

"Are *you* apologizing to *me*?" Anna stopped walking. She took a step backward and turned to face him, her nostrils flared. "My lord, *you* are not the one who should be sorry, unless it is for living on a plantation near those horrid people. And it is Ezekiel who deserves an apology from that"—she clenched her teeth together—"that *woman*."

"I should not have allowed—" Philip began.

Anna held up her hand. "You did not allow anything. I will not permit you to shoulder the blame."

"Nevertheless, it is my home and my responsibility." Philip could see her anger simmering in her eyes. "I am glad you were there to protect Ezekiel." He took her hand again, slipping it back into the crook of his elbow, and they continued walking.

Anna pursed her lips and remained silent. Her hand was tight on his arm.

He glanced at her, unable to read her expression. "I did hope to remain in the good graces of *one* dinner guest," he said. "Will you be all right, then?"

"If Ezekiel is kept completely away from Clarissa Stapleton forever, I shall be," Anna said.

After Anna had endured an entire evening of insults, Philip could not believe that she thought only of the harm done to Ezekiel. He patted her hand on his arm. "It is not much farther," he told her for lack of something better to say. The lantern's flame cast strange shadows around them, and he was glad that in his pocket was a small blunderbuss pistol he'd purchased the day before in Port Antonio.

Anna shivered.

"Are you cold?" he asked. "We should have brought a wrap." She was still wearing her light evening gown. Her hair was down over her shoulders, and with her flashing eyes and heightened color, he thought she could not have looked more fetching if she tried.

"I am not cold, my lord. Just remembering."

"That is something I do not hear from you often." He smiled and bumped her with his shoulder to show that he was teasing.

"It is not from my mysterious and potentially nefarious past. It is from yesterday."

Philip couldn't believe she could make a joke about Clarissa's boorish insults. He would add it to the list of things he appreciated about Anna and hope that it indicated her mood was lifting. "Malachi?"

"No, something much more ridiculous." She glanced up at him and turned her face away. "Have you seen an iguana lizard?" she whispered.

Philip could not help the laugh that erupted from him. After the strain and horrible circumstances of the past few days, he'd forgotten that he had an innocent young woman in his care. He tried to conceal his mirth, holding in his laughter until his stomach hurt, and he ended up making a snorting noise through his nose. He turned toward her. "I am sorry, Anna. I just—" He snorted again.

"I know it is silly."

"It is not silly." He cleared his throat to ensure that another snort would not creep out. "The first time I saw one of those demons staring at me with its beady little eyes, I seriously contemplated running back to the boat in Kingston."

"They look like dragons."

He nodded. "But they are completely harmless. They only eat fruit and plants." He didn't mention that they would see hundreds of the large reptiles the next day in the mountains.

"I am still afraid of them," Anna said in a small voice and moved closer to him.

Philip wondered what it was about being outside in the dark of night that made people express their true feelings so freely. He looked at Anna's face, her eyes darting around at the darkness beyond the lantern light. The knowledge that she was afraid and trusted him to keep her safe caused a swell in his chest. The way she clung to his arm made him feel as if there was nothing in the world more important than her protection. Was there another man somewhere who felt the same? Did she already have a protector?

When they arrived at the small hospital building, Philip opened the door, and they stepped inside, following the sound of voices into the back room.

Dr. Bevan stood at a worktable, wiping off instruments with a cloth. Betty sat on a chair between two hospital cots—Malachi in one, his eyes open and watching them, and Ezekiel in the other.

The boy looked to be sleeping, but when the pair entered, he opened his eyes. "Miss Anna. My lord." He shifted his shoulders as if he would sit up.

"Rest easy," Dr. Bevan said to Ezekiel.

He crossed the room looking curious. "What brings you to the hospital at this late hour?" he asked. "Miss Anna, are you well?"

"Yes. We came to inquire after Ezekiel," Anna said.

Dr. Bevan looked to Philip, and when he saw his nod, pulled his head back quickly, his eyes widening. He was obviously unused to the master checking on the welfare of an injured slave.

Ezekiel moved again as if to rise.

Betty put her hand on his shoulder, and the boy lay back. Philip could see that his wound had been stitched.

Anna stepped closer, sitting on the edge of Ezekiel's bed. She took his hand and leaned to the side to get a better look at his injury. "How are you feeling, Ezekiel?" Anna touched a finger to his cheek. Her voice was so soft and the scene so tender that Philip didn't notice for a moment that Dr. Bevan had spoken to him.

The doctor cleared his throat.

"Pardon me. What did you say?" Philip was irritated the doctor was distracting him. He almost wished he could trade places with the boy.

"I said that Malachi is awake, my lord. If you still wished to speak with him . . ."

Philip turned toward the large man, noticing how he filled the small cot in each direction. Even bandaged and with eyes unfocused due to the laudanum, Malachi still looked formidable. He wore no shirt, and uneven, raised scars ran in stripes over his shoulder and chest. Philip imagined his back was covered as well. The sight sickened him when he thought of the lashings that had caused it.

Philip walked to the other end of the room and returned with a wooden chair. He did not want to speak to Malachi while looming over him like a minister at a pulpit. He sat, leaning forward and hanging his hands between his knees. "How is your injury?"

"Bettah, my lord."

"Is that the truth? I imagine it hurts like the devil himself stuck it with a hot poker."

Anna gasped.

"Pardon me, Miss Anna, Betty." Philip grimaced. Betty leveled a look at him, but he saw her lips lifted the slightest bit.

Anna raised a brow. He felt duly chastened. He would need to remember to keep his language in check with a young lady present.

"It hurts, sah," Malachi said.

Philip turned his attention back to Malachi. "From the look of it, you fought bravely, and I must thank you. I am deeply sorry for the loss of your gang. If I had known . . ." He pinched the bridge of his nose. "No blasted sugar is worth such a sacrifice."

He darted a glance to Anna, but she did not react to his profanity again. Her face was softened into a gentle smile, and her eyes shined as she regarded him. He wished his own eyes didn't sting. The last thing he needed was to weep in front of his servants and Anna.

Betty touched Malachi's arm, and he glanced toward her. They shared a look that made Philip curious as to the nature of their relationship. But it was none of his affair. He cleared his throat. "If you feel up to it, can you tell me what happened?"

Malachi nodded. "We drive de carts, sah, when men jump from de trees wit' guns and knives. Even when we don' fight anymo', dey just want to kill all de people."

"And you said you recognized their leader?" Philip wanted to be completely certain that they had not accused the wrong man.

"He de ol' *busha*. Massa Braithwaite." Malachi's eyes narrowed. He glanced at Betty again and then back to Philip. "He shoot me wit' his gun. I crawl into de weeds to hide. When dey take de carts away, all de people dead. I walk back to Oakely Park, but I's losin' blood, sah, and can walk no mo'."

Philip nodded, rubbing his palm over his cheek and chin. The man's story was consistent with what they'd found at the site where the shipment had been attacked.

Malachi turned his head to the side on his pillow. He reached his hand toward Anna. "Miss, you save my life. I t'ank you."

Anna's cheeks turned pink. "I hardly did anything. But you are quite welcome, Malachi." She laid Ezekiel's hand on the cot and stood.

"I think Ezekiel should sleep." Her gaze moved to Malachi, and she took a slow step toward him. She reached her hand toward his and hesitated briefly before she clasped it. "I am glad you are healing," she said and then hurried from the room.

Philip smiled. Anna tried to put on a brave face, but Malachi still frightened her. Philip stood.

Ezekiel opened his eyes and moved to sit up. Betty placed a hand on his chest to stop him.

"Ezekiel, I insist you remain here until Dr. Bevan and Betty think you are well enough to resume your duties," Philip said.

"But, my lord," the boy said in a voice devoid of its typical cheer, "I need to blacken yo' boots, and I've no' laid out yo' nightclothes."

"I shall have to fend for myself for a day or two. It will be difficult indeed as I am used to such fine care, but I insist that my valet should be in the best of health."

Ezekiel closed his eyes. "Tomorrow, my lord."

"I will not hear of it," Philip said. He let a sigh, much louder than the situation called for, but he wanted to make sure the boy heard. "Although I shall certainly miss having a well-tied cravat."

Ezekiel did not open his eyes, but he smiled, and blast if it didn't tug at Philip's heart. He nodded to Betty and Malachi, excusing himself to join Anna.

"My lord," Malachi said in a low voice. His dark eyes locked on Philip, and he was once again reminded how terrified he would be of this man if they were enemies. "You look after my family." He motioned toward Betty and Ezekiel with his finger. Then his eyes darted toward the door to the outer room. "She saved my life. I do no' forget. I will protect yo' family."

Philip thought for an instant about setting the record straight, explaining that Anna wasn't his family—she was simply a houseguest—but Malachi closed his eyes and nodded his head once. Philip knew the conversation was over.

He joined Anna in the other room, lifting the lantern and opening the outer door.

She walked through the doorway and glanced up at him, blinking once. "I am sorry for leaving so quickly," she said. Her voice was nearly a whisper. "He still frightens me."

"You have no need to fear him," Philip said. "Malachi will never hurt you. Or allow any harm to come to you."

Anna looked up at him, and her finger touched her necklace. She glanced back at the hospital. "We are safe at Oakely Park, aren't we?"

"I hope so, Anna."

She slipped her hand into his as they walked back to the Great House.

He studied her profile for a moment. Anna had pronounced cheekbones, and her lips were plump, the top one every bit as thick as the bottom. The effect fascinated him and heated his blood. An attractive and contradicting blend of woman and girl. As he watched her, he suddenly remembered her pensive expression at dinner. "Anna, tonight you remembered something. Am I right?"

"Yes."

"Do you want to tell me?"

She shook her head. "No."

Philip's stomach grew heavy. What had she remembered? Someone mistreating her? The death of a person she cared about? Something frightening? His mind turned over the possibilities. "Is it so terrible?" The thought of someone hurting her churned his stomach.

"It is not terrible, just incomplete. A snippet. I do not understand it."

He rubbed his thumbnail on the lantern rope. Curiosity burned inside him and made him impatient to hear her problem so he could solve it. "Perhaps I could help?"

Anna glanced at him and then away. "I remember a man."

Philip felt as if someone had hit him in the gut. He had thought hearing about something dreadful from Anna's past would be difficult, but this was infinitely worse. He forced himself to continue listening to her explanation, even as he fought to breathe evenly.

"I do not know who he is. He is young and handsome. In my memory, he hands me a book and smiles. That is all."

Philip fought to keep his emotions from showing on his face. He should be happy that Anna remembered someone pleasant from her life, but he hated it. He hated every bit of it, and even more, it hurt his heart.

He'd done it again, let his defenses down. Watching Anna hold his injured servant in her arms, seeing her in the silk gown, hearing the fear in her voice when she talked about the iguana lizard. Each was a small-weapons battery against his defenses, and they'd broken through, blasting his wall to bits. He tried to push out the sting, but it was too painful.

The day he'd learned about his brother and Jacqueline, something had begun to smolder inside him—an ember that had been fanned over the past few days by Horace Braithwaite, Tom Norton, John Stapleton, and now this mysterious man who Philip was completely aware could be no more important to Anna than a merchant at the bookstore. But the flame blazed nonetheless, and his hurt only added to it, turning it to anger.

"I should tell you that I plan to marry Clarissa Stapleton," he blurted, watching her reaction, angry at himself for the hope that he would see pain in her expression. He was not disappointed and was disgusted with himself for causing it.

Anna stopped midstride and stumbled when he kept moving and tugged her forward. Even in the lantern light, he saw her face pale. "My lord, I don't understand. You . . . Why would you do that?"

"She is extremely wealthy," he said.

Anna pulled away. She pressed a hand against her stomach as she turned toward the house.

A wave of guilt washed over him. Why had he tried to hurt her? None of this was her fault. The only thing she'd done was arrive by accident in need of help. She just happened to be beautiful and charming with a gentle humor and compassionate nature. And he'd punished her for it? Philip was furious with himself and suddenly extremely tired.

He quickened his pace to match hers. "Anna, come inside. I need to tell you a story."

***

He led her to the small parlor—Philip did not want to take her into the drawing room while there was still blood on the floor. Anna didn't say anything. Her eyes didn't meet his. He would have given seventy hogshead of sugar to know what was going on inside her mind. He lit the candles and sat on the settee next to her. Then he took a deep breath, knowing there was no way to lead into the story but to start. "About nine months ago, I fancied myself in love."

"Oh," Anna said, her face reddening. She did not look at him.

"I was introduced to Jacqueline at a dinner party. She was the most sought-after debutante in London, and I was thoroughly smitten by her charms. Within a few weeks, it was obvious she preferred me to all her other suitors." He smiled wryly at the memory. "You can imagine how I thought myself the luckiest man in London and swaggered into White's with my chest puffed out."

Anna did not raise her eyes.

"We had plans to marry in the spring. I purchased a special license, and our families' attorneys set to drawing up the marriage agreements. I may have been the happiest of men but also the most oblivious. While I strutted about in a haze of bliss, Jacqueline set her allures to work on my elder brother—the future marquess—and he did not have any qualms about returning her affection."

Anna looked up then and placed her hand on his. "Lord Philip, you do not have to tell me any more."

He turned his palm up, cradling her hand. "It was more horrible than merely the two of them stealing kisses behind my back. All of London knew of it. I became a joke among my friends—a man who was so blinded by love that he could not see what was happening around him." He did not tell her about the caricature in the *Times*. Anna may have seen it herself. "When the two of them eventually confessed, I felt as though I had been struck."

He closed his eyes, remembering the awful day. "I told her I loved her. Begged her to return to me. I would do anything she wished." The dizzying feeling of humiliation had lessened slightly over the months, but his insides still clenched as he relived it. "Jacqueline batted her eyes and looked absolutely confused at my reaction. She said she had enjoyed our games and flirtations but I should have known that our relationship was never more than a playful friendship."

He glanced down at Anna's hand and rubbed his thumb over her knuckles, thinking how this woman's steadiness gave him strength. "Even when she was jilting me, she managed to make me feel as though I was the one at fault."

"My lord, I am so sorry that you—that she hurt you so." Anna closed her fingers around his hand tightly.

Philip looked up to see Anna's brows drawn together and the deepest sympathy in her eyes. He knew he must finish the story, as it was the last time he ever intended to tell it. "I left London a few weeks later and vowed that I would not allow myself to be duped again. I would thrust myself into the management of the plantation and marry the wealthiest woman I met. My father will be proud, I will be rich, and my heart will be safe."

"But *Clarissa Stapleton*? She is so—"

"Dreadful, I know." He looked down at their joined hands. "I do not fear being hurt by her. She will never hold my heart."

Anna lifted his hand and held it between both of hers. "You would rather be unhappy with a cruel person than risk caring for someone?"

Philip pushed out a breath. He raised his eyes. "I shall lose *you* soon enough, Anna, and that hurts more than I can say."

Anna's eyes went wide. Her face paled then reddened. "Perhaps not . . . maybe . . ." She looked down.

Philip crooked a finger beneath her chin to lift her gaze back to his. "Anna, I think you are the dearest friend I have known. In you, I have found another soul so like my own that it astonishes me. But, I must do the honorable thing and act as your guardian until I can return you to your family." His chest ached as he said the words.

He lowered his hand to her shoulder. Seeing her eyes fill, he wondered how it could hurt so badly to see her cry. "Once you regain your memory, you would detest me if I allowed anything to happen to make you regret our time together." He brushed a tear from her cheek. "Do you understand what I am saying, Anna?" He forced himself to think past his own feelings and consider the reality. It was impossible to believe that Anna was not married or, at the very least, engaged to another man.

She closed her eyes, spilling more tears on her cheeks, and nodded. She made a little gasping sound in her throat and looked up at him. "Lord Philip, will we remain friends?"

"Of course, Anna. We will always be the best of friends."

"And you will wait until my memory returns before you . . . decide on a wife?"

Philip raised his brows. Anna understood perfectly what he had not said. She was naive enough to hope that there was a chance for them. But Philip had long ago learned that to hope was to be a fool. "I promise."

Chapter 14

The next morning, Anna rode with Lord Philip and Tom Norton as they made their way to the mountainous regions of Oakely Park. After their conversation, she had little hope that Lord Philip would ever be more than a friend to her. He was convinced that Anna belonged to another, and she could neither confirm nor deny it. She wished she knew one way or the other. *Was* there a man somewhere who loved her? Try as she might, she could not discover any more hidden in the depths of her mind. And even if it was determined that she was unattached, Lord Philip had told her he intended to marry a wealthy woman. Anna had no idea whether she was wealthy or not.

Although she had wept in her bedchamber the night before, today she put her sorrows aside and determined to remain happy while she was with Lord Philip. She felt that their time together was growing short. During the night, two new memories had flashed into her mind at different times. Neither gave her any more information about her past. She remembered riding in a carriage next to a dark-haired woman, but the woman's identity remained a mystery. The other memory was even more vague. The image of a wooden sword—a child's toy—appeared in her head. To whom did it belong? Anna pondered on both these new memories along with the others, hoping to expand them, to hear noises or feel emotions—but they remained only brief snatches.

They had departed early enough that dew sparkled on the leaves and undergrowth. Tropical birds shrieked, warbled, and sang in the leafy forest, and Anna could hear the lowing of cattle somewhere in the distance. The group followed the yellow dirt road—Philip had told her the dirt was red on the south side of the island—through fields that were divided into portions where each of the slaves could grow their own crops to supplement their rations or to sell at market.

"This is how a slave is able to earn his freedom," Lord Philip said. "With thrift and hard work. Some, like Malachi, have purchased their free papers."

The road led around the edge of the fields. Anna noticed objects hanging from strings in the trees. She rode closer and saw small bags and bundles; some even appeared to be animal skulls. The sight was gruesome. She shivered in the bright morning.

When Mr. Norton saw what she was looking at, he turned his horse to join her. "Protective charms," he explained, sweeping his hand to the side.

Anna turned her head and saw that the charms hung all around the garden. "Protection from what?" she asked.

"A very superstitious lot, these Africans. When they aren't here tending to their gardens, they leave these . . . talismans to guard 'em."

"From . . . ?" She gazed out at the small plots and waved at the few workers who had the day free to labor for their own profit.

"Evil spirits, animals that could eat the crops." He shrugged. "Likely, they scare the other slaves enough that they'll keep to their own parcel."

Anna looked at a little skull and grimaced. "It seems macabre."

Mr. Norton flipped one of the bundles with his finger and sent it swinging. They urged the horses up the road toward where Lord Philip waited. "I've heard tales of much stranger things—Obeah rituals with beating drums and wild dancing; a white goat slit open and, while it still bleats, its blood poured on the dancers. Many on the island believe Obeah men can cast spells on their enemies."

"I think you are just trying to frighten me," Anna said in a shaky voice.

"It is why slaves gathering in any large group is forbidden. Their heathen rituals are a predecessor to rebellion."

They joined Lord Philip, and Anna slowed, allowing the men to lead the way. The sun did not seem as bright, and the bird calls had taken on an eerie tone. The story of the rituals sent a tingle of fear through her, but it seemed merely a fantastical tale. A slave revolt, however—that she knew to be real. There had been incidents of uprisings where plantation owners and their families and any white person nearby had been slaughtered, some in their own beds. It chilled her to think of the hundreds of slave men and women surrounding Oakely Park rising up and taking weapons.

Lord Philip slowed his horse to ride alongside her. "Just over this rise is the beach where I met a charming young lady, Miss Plantation-Espionage. Perhaps you know her?"

Anna shook off her frightful thoughts. She lowered her parasol so his lordship would have the full effect of her eye roll. She appreciated that he continued to tease. It seemed that Lord Philip made the same choice as she, to pass what remained of their time together in good spirits instead of dwelling on what may never be.

They crested the hill, and Lord Philip indicated the rocky beach below. Waves broke over the jagged shoreline. Anna tried to remember being here before.

"That is where we left our horses the day we found you, Miss Anna." Tom pointed toward a shady spot beneath a cluster of trees.

"Do we have time to go closer?" Anna asked.

"Only if we do not discover any unconscious ladies on the rocks," Lord Philip said. "They do tend to wreak havoc with our schedule."

Anna smiled, glad he was in good humor. She handed him her parasol as she dismounted and then took it again.

They left their horses and picked their way through long weeds and over dark rocks.

"Over here, miss." Tom offered his hand to assist her. He led her closer to the water, and Philip followed. Reddish-black crabs with pointed legs and upraised claws scuttled away as they approached, and Anna wondered if they had scuttled over her when she lay upon this beach unaware. She winced at the idea of the spiderlike creatures climbing through her hair.

"Right there is where we found ya lookin' red and bloated as a corpse." Tom pointed. "His lordship pulled you out of the water and laid you over there. Your lips were cracked, and your mouth—"

"That will do," Philip said in a loud voice as he walked toward them. "She does not need to hear the unpleasant details." He carried an oar in his hand. When he reached Anna, he held it toward her.

She ran a gloved finger over the ribbons and string wrapped around the wood. She closed her eyes, urging her mind to find some association, but there was nothing.

"Do ya remember the strings?" Mr. Norton asked. "They were the very ones from your gown. Can ya remember tying them to the oar?"

"No." Anna shook her head.

"Perhaps if you picture yourself in the water," Mr. Norton urged.

"She doesn't remember. Do not push her, Tom," Lord Philip snapped, shooting a glare at his foreman.

"I am sorry," Anna said.

"Do not apologize." Lord Philip took her arm and led her over the rocks. When they reached the horses, he set the oar carefully on the ground.

She looked at him with a question in her eyes.

He shrugged. "It reminds me that a person can do difficult things." He looked around the area. "No mounting stool," he said. He took her parasol, thrusting it at Tom, and placed his hands on Anna's waist.

Anna's breath caught, and she laid her hands on his shoulders. She knew her face must be flaming red and did not look at Lord Philip. She thought he must be able to hear her heart pounding. He lifted her onto the saddle and mounted his own horse. Tom handed up her parasol.

When Anna dared to glance at Philip, she saw that his face was flushed as well. He met her gaze, and one side of his mouth rose in his half smile. Anna was glad for the shade that hid her red cheeks. She thought if he kept it up, her heart would pound right out of her chest.

They followed the road along the beach and then turned inland toward the mountains.

"Why did we not just ride straight across?" Anna asked, pointing at the direction they had started. It seemed as though they had ridden in a large U.

"Oakely Park is an oddly shaped property," Philip said. "Another plantation nearly bisects it, and since we do not know the owner, it is safer to remain on my land."

"Surely he would not mind if you passed through to get to the other side of your property," Anna said.

Philip shrugged. "The owner is rumored to be absent, and perhaps the land is deserted. We do not know if Landon Grove functions at all, but it is best to be cautious. Some property owners command their people to shoot trespassers on sight. Besides, this section of their property is nearly all jungle anyway. And remember, if it weren't for the detour, we would never have found you on the beach."

"Then I am glad for it," Anna said. She looked up at the jagged ridges of volcanic mountain ascending from the green jungle. A mist rose over the cliffs, casting them in a purplish tinge that gave them their name: the Blue Mountains. The road ended abruptly at a grove of trees near a stream.

"We will continue on foot from here." Lord Philip looked to Anna. "Will you be all right?"

"Of course." A bubble of excitement swelled in Anna's chest as she dismounted and ensured that Smokey's reins were tied securely to a tree but loose enough that the mare could drink from the stream. They were going to have an adventure. She could not wait to see the land and hear the plans for the coffee farm.

"You will not need your umbrella, Miss Anna. The jungle is shaded, and the trees are close together," Tom said.

She left the parasol against a tree near the horses.

Lord Philip removed his top hat, and his light hair fell over his forehead. Anna particularly liked the way his hair split unevenly over his widow's peak. It was as if it refused to remain tidy. He laid the hat next to her parasol. He put a pack over his shoulder, and both he and Mr. Norton took a moment to check their pistols.

Anna felt her first pricks of unease. "Will we need weapons?" she asked, hoping her voice sounded merely curious instead of afraid.

"It is best to be safe," Lord Philip said.

"And what might we meet in the jungle?" Anna's disquiet grew as she watched Lord Philip carefully place the pistol into his pocket. Mr. Norton crammed his weapon into the waistband of his trousers.

"If we are lucky, nothing worse than a snake or an iguana." Mr. Norton unsheathed a large machete.

Lord Philip's gaze darted to Anna. Anna's knees started to tremble. She took a step back.

"We'll not be close enough to any rivers to fear crocodiles." Mr. Norton scraped his thumb on the blade to test its sharpness. "The most dangerous thing in the jungle is men."

Lord Philip glared at his overseer, appearing as though he wished he could seal the man's mouth shut. He stepped close to Anna, blocking her view of Mr. Norton, and reached for her hand. "I will not allow anything to harm you."

Anna looked past him at the thick leaves. Her eyes moved over the branches, searching for any reptiles lying in wait.

Lord Philip tugged on her hand, pulling her gaze back to his. "Do you trust me to keep you safe?" His eyes were earnest, his forehead creased.

Anna knew he would never put her in harm's way. She tried to push down the fear, squeezing his hand tighter. "I am being silly, my lord. I am sorry."

"It is not silly," he said in a quiet voice, still holding her gaze. His mouth pulled to the side "But I am a bit displeased," he spoke in a louder voice. "Did we not decide that we are dear friends?"

Anna nodded. She wondered what had irritated him.

"Then, why is it that you do not call me by my name? I am Philip." His mouth pulled further and wrinkled his cheek in his half smile.

Anna could not help but smile in return. "I would, sir, but it deprives me of my chance to assign you a name, and I have still not come up with the perfect thing. I was considering Lord Placates-Ladies-Who-Fear-Reptiles, but as you can see, it needs some work."

His smile spread to the other cheek. "You are right. It does not suit at all. But until you think of something better . . ."

"I will call you Philip." Anna blushed at referring to him so intimately. Her gaze remained locked on the deep blue of his eyes.

"And you should call me Tom, Miss Anna." Mr. Norton's head popped into view over Philip's shoulder.

Anna startled.

Philip closed his eyes and pushed out a breath.

She smiled at the two men. "Very well then, as we are all friends embarking on an expedition into the deepest, darkest jungle, we shall no longer stand on ceremony. Are we all agreed?"

Tom nodded his head enthusiastically and grinned at being part of the teasing conversation. "Off we go then." He sliced at the plants, hacking his way into the dense jungle. "We'll eventually need to clear a road," he said over his shoulder.

Lord Philip maintained his hold on Anna's hand until they stepped beneath the trees, but the path was too narrow to walk side by side, and he released his grip, motioning for her to precede him. He touched the small of her back, giving a little push when she stopped.

Anna took a tentative step into the jungle, but in an instant she discovered it was nothing like she had feared. The sight took her breath away. Flowers in every imaginable variety and color surrounded her, vivid against the backdrop of leaves. She wanted to gather them all, to study every strange shape and dazzling hue. Fruit hung from trees and vines. The light filtering through the trees was soft and beautiful. The air was still damp and heavy, but in the shade it was cooler, and the jungle was so green it nearly hurt her eyes.

The birds she'd heard and caught glimpses of in the gardens surrounding the Great House seemed sparse in comparison to the droves in the jungle canopy. Tiny, bright-green birds with red throats flitted around, chasing each other or bobbing from branch to branch. Parrots squawked from high trees as the trio passed. Anna clasped her hands together when a bird with a black head and tail that looked like two long black streamers landed on a branch near her.

"A doctor bird," Philip said, coming up close behind her.

She tipped her head as she studied the bird and then looked at Philip wondering what he could possibly mean.

He shrugged. "Maybe because the tail looks like a doctor's coat. Or the flat head resembles a hat. I do not know how it acquired the name."

Anna noticed he spoke quietly and wondered why she felt she should do the same. The dense foliage muted any outside noise, and it seemed like they were in a separate world.

"It is so beautiful," Anna said in a soft voice. "Not only the bird, the entire jungle. Like the Garden of Eden."

"Even with the reptiles?" Philip teased.

"I have not seen any yet, and if *you* do, please be so kind as to refrain from pointing them out."

Philip laughed, and they continued, finally stepping into a less dense, flat area.

Tom stood at the edge of the semi-clearing, panting as he swept his arm in front of him. "It will only take a little effort to cultivate the first five acres." He pointed toward the far side of the space. "There in the shade we can plant seeds and start our own shoots until we have more acreage prepared." Tom's eyes were bright with excitement as he hurried forward.

Philip walked with him.

Anna took quick steps to keep up with the men's strides. "And how long does it take from when a seed is planted until you can harvest?"

"From seed it takes three to four years to grow a fully developed coffee plant, but we can purchase mature plants to begin with." Tom spoke quickly, unable to contain the excitement in his voice. He indicated a flat area in the sun, and they walked in that direction. "Here, we can dry the coffee cherries and mill the beans. And we shall need a storage building." Tom pointed toward another part of the clearing and then turned. His brows were raised, and he chewed on his lip eagerly. "It will take some work, but the location is perfect, and in a few short weeks, we could begin planting."

"I can see you have put a lot of thought into this, Tom."

"Yes, I know it does not look very promising now, and we will not turn a profit in the beginning—" Philip's mouth turned down in a frown. Tom pushed ahead. "But many people think emancipation is approaching quickly, and without free labor, sugar will become less profitable. If we could supplement Oakely Park's earnings with a less labor-intensive crop . . ." He gesticulated with his hands—and the machete—excitedly as he spoke.

Anna and Philip both leaned out of the path of the waving blade.

Tom lowered the weapon sheepishly, scratching his hand through his hair. "It is a risk, my lord, but I have thought it through, and I know I can make it work." He stopped talking and folded his arms as he watched for Philip's response.

Anna was tempted to take the machete from him before he forgot it was in his hand and hurt someone.

"It *is* a risk," Philip said. He pinched his chin as he gazed at the land around them.

The silence stretched, and the air felt heavy as tension grew. Tom fidgeted as he waited for Philip's answer.

Anna looked between the men, one with his eyes wide and shining with hope and the other with his brows pulled tightly together, staring at nothing while he contemplated the future of his holdings.

Finally, Philip lowered his hand. "What do you think, Anna?"

"I?" Anna had not anticipated that she would be any part of this conversation.

He turned toward her. "Yes. You have shown yourself to possess a level head. That is one of the reasons I brought you with us. What do you think about Tom's proposal?"

Anna clasped her hands together behind her back. She paced a few steps and turned. She did not know what answer he expected. Why would an educated member of the aristocracy ask for her advice on business matters? She had no experience in such things—that she knew of. She paced another few steps, contemplating. Would Philip take her advice seriously? Or was he stalling, hoping to avoid answering Tom? Or was he teasing her again?

She stopped and faced the men. If his lordship wanted her opinion, he would have it. "While it seems that Tom has given his idea a significant amount of thought and research, I do not think he has anticipated every eventuality. There are endless things that could go wrong: a hurricane, a trade embargo, some type of insect infestation. You could lose your entire investment."

Tom's face fell. "But, Anna—"

She held up her hand. "I am not finished. On the other hand, this land is just lying here unused and is turning no profit whatsoever. If sugar indeed becomes more expensive to produce, the idea of something else to supplement Oakely Park's income is brilliant. Especially if it means the plantation will not have to depend so heavily on slaves." She turned to Philip and tapped her fingers together in front of her waist. "You will likely not see the return on your investment for years if everything goes to plan—or ever, if it does not. But if you truly want my opinion"—Anna took a breath and blew it out—"I think a coffee farm at Oakely Park is a marvelous idea." Anna felt her blush spread across her cheeks. What had possessed her to speak so boldly?

"Well, there you have it. I will trust in the counsel of my advisor; Tom, we will start plans for the coffee farm immediately."

Tom grinned. He strode forward and shook Philip's hand. "Thank you, sir. You will not be sorry."

"But, Philip," Anna said, "do you think you should give the idea more thought? After all . . ."

Philip released his hand from Tom's grip and moved toward Anna. His expression was pleasant, as if he had not just wagered his future on the advice of a young woman with no experience. "Shall we have a picnic?" He offered his arm.

Tom walked around the area talking to himself as he planned his endeavor.

Anna placed her hand on Philip's arm. "I cannot believe you—"

"Asked for your advice? Or heeded it?"

"Both, I suppose."

"Why is that?" He glanced sidelong at her.

"Well, because I do not think my advice matters. I am not an expert on such affairs, and it is the future of your plantation—of your very livelihood."

Philip stopped and turned to her. He took both her hands in his. "Anna, you may not realize it, but you are exceptionally intelligent, with or without your memory. You consider things carefully, strive to understand every side of an argument, and do not jump into things rashly, a quality I strive for myself." He lowered his forehead, his eyes serious. "I trust your judgment." He held her gaze a moment longer and returned her hand to his arm, strolling toward a group of rocks. "That looks like just the spot."

They sat on the rocks, and Anna watched a group of hummingbirds flitting among the flowers. Their rapid, jerky movements were a perfect description of what was happening inside her chest. She was still overwhelmed by Philip's trust in her. And he considered her to be intelligent? He confided in her, trusted her opinion. She glanced to where he was unpacking the bread and fruit that Betty had prepared for their journey.

Philip's eyes met hers, and her chest filled again with jerky, darting hummingbirds.

Anna sighed. A friendship with Philip might be more than her heart could bear.

Chapter 15

PHILIP PULLED HIS EYES AWAY from Anna and concentrated on setting out their picnic. He couldn't even explain to *himself* why the young woman's opinions on the affairs of Oakely Park were so important to him. Was it because she expressed such an interest in the running of the plantation? Or that she gave him confidence in his own ability to manage the place? Whatever the reason, he needed to stop thinking about Anna as if she were a permanent fixture in his life. She would leave soon enough, and Philip would move on, making a practical marriage that would benefit his holdings and his family.

Into his mind flashed the image of Anna embracing Ezekiel, and Clarissa carrying on and pretending to weep after she'd struck the boy hard enough for him to require stitches. Which woman would he prefer as the mother of his children? He shook his head. Why did he allow these thoughts to take shape when he knew there was no hope for a deeper relationship with Anna?

He should be grateful she'd come into his life at all, even if it was for a short time. He glanced at her again, studying her profile as she watched hummingbirds zipping between flowers. Her eyes were wide and filled with interest, as they always were when she observed something new.

She glanced toward him and smiled. His chest warmed. In Anna he felt as if he'd found his perfect match—a woman who was strong where he came up lacking, a woman who completed him—but he'd found her too late. If only they had met years earlier in London. He had no doubt they would have fallen in love. And not the infatuated, mooncalf love he'd felt for Jacqueline, but a real connection with a woman who brought him happiness, who made his life better, who surprised him every day.

He looked back at the food he was unpacking. Why *hadn't* they met in London? It couldn't have been more than a year or two since Anna was presented at court. Why had he not made her acquaintance at a ball or garden party? Was she from America or another colony? He didn't think so, based on her accent. Had she married young? That would explain why he'd not encountered her on the marriage mart.

And it would also explain why he shouldn't be having these thoughts. He shored up the battlements inside him that had again started to crumble. *I am Anna's guardian and know nothing of her life and the commitments and entailments she may already have.* She could very well already be a mother for all he knew. With Anna's memory returning, he could not think she would simply pick up and start a new life. Her past would take her from him.

He looked around for Tom and saw the man standing motionless in the middle of the clearing. His hand shaded his eyes, and he appeared to be watching something over the canopy of trees.

Philip needed to put some distance between himself and Anna if she was to continue looking so bright-eyed and enchanting. He stood and walked away from the overhanging branches to get a better view of what Tom was looking at.

When he approached, Tom pointed. "Smoke."

He looked in the direction the overseer indicated. "Are you certain it's not just steam from the mountains? Or perhaps a cloud."

Tom nodded. "It's black, rising in a column. Something is burning."

Philip squinted. Now that Tom pointed it out, he wondered why he hadn't noticed it before. He guessed that the fire was on the Landon Grove property, and if it spread in any direction, it would reach Oakely Park.

"Is there a sugar works at Landon Grove?" Philip asked.

"I do not think they have planted cane for the past few years, but I don't know for sure—nobody does. It is thought to be deserted. Besides, this deep in the jungle? It seems impractical."

Philip was growing alarmed. A fire in a tropical jungle was unusual, and on a deserted plantation, it seemed even more suspicious. "Should we investigate?" he asked.

"Definitely." Tom nodded. They started toward the rocks where Anna waited with their luncheon.

For a moment Philip considered sending her back to the Great House, but she couldn't travel alone, not with pirates, highwaymen, and of course, iguana lizards roaming the country. The fire could prove to be nothing at all, but if they did not investigate now, when they were close, they could lose the opportunity without the smoke to direct them.

Once Anna heard about the fire, she walked to the middle of the clearing and looked toward the source, shadowing her eyes as Tom had."What do you think could be causing it?" she asked when she returned.

"It is probably nothing," Philip said. He darted a look at Tom, hoping the man had enough sense not to comment, for once. He didn't want Anna to be any more worried than necessary.

They ate a hurried luncheon then began to trek back through the jungle in a different direction. Tom led the way, hacking with the machete, and Philip followed Anna. He worried about what they would find. His thoughts were a mass of questions. Did people still live and work at Landon Grove? Were escaped slaves or buccaneers using the property as a hideout?

Anna stopped in front of him and gasped.

Philip's heart jolted. He pulled out his pistol and shouldered his way around to stand between her and whatever threatened her. His gaze darted around as he searched for the danger.

She laid a hand on his arm, giggling as she peered around him. "Philip, please do not shoot the butterfly."

He looked up and saw that the colorful insect had alighted on a leaf ahead of them. His shoulders sagged in relief.

Anna giggled again, pressing her fingers against her mouth. "It is large to be sure, but I do not think it is any cause for alarm."

Philip returned the weapon to his pocket and allowed himself a smile. He felt foolish at his overreaction. He peered closer at the butterfly. It was truly enormous, with a wingspan of at least six inches.

"It is beautiful, isn't it?" Anna said, watching as the wings moved slowly up and down like a hinge.

He noticed that Anna's hand was still on his arm, and she leaned around him in the narrow tunnel of vegetation in order to see the butterfly. He turned to the side to allow her to pass. "It is beautiful," he said. "And there is no need to fear. I have determined it to be completely harmless."

"You are very gallant, Philip." She patted his chest as she stepped past. "I am lucky to have such a brave protector when my life is thus threatened by such a malevolent creature." She winked and continued to follow Tom.

Philip's heart did a slow roll. She obviously had no idea of the effect her teasing had on him. He followed, shaking his head and muttering to himself, *I am Anna's guardian.*

The jungle grew thicker as they delved deeper into the mountains, and even with Tom cutting a path, each step became nearly a swim through the vegetation. They ducked beneath vines and low-hanging branches, stepped over roots, and circumvented trunks. Branches snapped in their faces and caught on their clothing. The wet, hot air was difficult to breathe, and drops of sweat rolled down Philip's back. After nearly an hour, they emerged onto a rocky mound, and Philip looked up, finding the thick column of smoke just in front of them over a small rise.

Tom held up his hand as a signal for them to wait and pushed ahead. He returned a moment later, motioning them forward but placing a finger over his mouth.

Philip's stomach quivered.

They followed him up a hill and then down a slope to the edge of a riverbank. Tom pointed to a clump of trees and long grass, and they scooted down the sandy incline, crouching and pulling aside the undergrowth to peer through the foliage.

The sight before them turned Philip's blood to ice. In a wide clearing on the other side of the river, he saw what appeared to be a makeshift work camp. Horace Braithwaite strode back and forth barking orders and yelling profanities that could be heard across the noisy river. He and a band of seven men directed a group of slaves as they transferred rum, treacle, and sugar into smaller barrels and sealed them with hot pitch. The dark-skinned laborers were gaunt, and their clothing hung on their bones, making them appear like scarecrows. Philip wondered where Horace had found them. Were they forgotten workers from Landon

Grove? They must be nearly starved. He was surprised the ill-looking people found the energy to lift the heavy barrels.

On one side of the clearing was an entire storage shed's worth of hogshead barrels in a haphazard pile. They had obviously held the sugar and other goods from the plantations that had been robbed. Though he couldn't see it from this distance, Philip knew Oakely Park's barrels must be among them. He thought he recognized his stolen carts and mules.

Once the goods had been transferred, another group took the empty barrels and burned them to remove any symbols that identified the original owners.

Philip clenched his jaw in rage.

Anna laid a hand on his arm, and he turned to see her wide eyes filled with horror.

"Horace Braithwaite," he whispered.

The men supervising the operation shoved and berated the slaves, but Horace was by far the cruelest. He kicked one man as he passed, sending him sprawling in the dirt and then thrashing him with a whip.

Anna pressed her hands to her mouth, and Philip's stomach lurched. He pulled Anna toward him, turning her face from the sight. When Horace stopped his tirade, the man lay motionless.

Philip released Anna and looked at his companions grimly.

"What do we do, Philip?" Anna's eyes were wet, and her lips trembled.

"We must go for the constable in Port Antonio," Tom whispered. "We have proof now, and—" His gaze darted across the river, and he sucked in a breath through his teeth.

Philip glanced back through the grass to see what had alarmed his overseer.

Philip pressed Anna against his chest once more, cupping her head with his hand as the report of a gunshot echoed through the jungle. Anna clung to his jacket. Her body was stiff, and she shook. Philip wrapped his other arm around her shoulders and didn't loosen his hold.

She cringed again as another shot rang out.

The man was a maniac who took pleasure in inflicting pain and causing terror. Philip had seen it the first day he'd met Horace. The man had murdered an entire gang of workers just to exact revenge on Philip, and there was no doubt that he'd have no qualms about killing the three of them too.

Horace screamed at the slaves, who hurried about their duties with renewed energy.

Philip did not release his hold on Anna; he didn't want her to see what was taking place across the river. The other slaves hurried to their tasks, not glancing at the overseer again.

Every instinct directed that Philip should charge across the river and avenge his people and his property. His heart pommeled against his ribs. His vision clouded with red, and his muscles tightened. He judged the distance and how many men he and Tom could overpower. They'd have the advantage of surprise—

A silent sob from Anna pulled his mind from its fury and back to the young woman. He could not abandon her and allow his anger to dictate his actions. There must be another way to see that justice—and vengeance—was delivered on his enemy.

Philip lowered his head so his mouth was next to her ear. "If we are seen, they will kill us." He looked down at the head of blonde hair that lay against him. "Anna, we must flee."

She raised her head. Her face was pale, and her eyes filled with panic.

Philip thought she might scream. He placed his fingers over her lips. "Can you follow Tom?"

Anna glanced at Tom and nodded. She shifted around on her knees and positioned herself to run. Her hand was fisted in front of her mouth, and she breathed heavily. Her body still shook, and Philip hoped she would be able to maintain her calm until they were safely away from Horace and his men. He did not harbor any doubts that the villains would kill them without a second thought.

"Lead the way, Tom," Philip said. He scooted closer to Anna, crouching behind her.

Tom nodded, glancing back up the bank in the direction they'd come. He moved away from the patch of grass toward a dead log and started up the sandy bank.

Too late, Philip realized the log was, in actuality, a large crocodile sunning itself on the sand.

Without warning, the crocodile swung toward Tom, clamped its enormous jaws around his foot, and began pulling him down the bank to the river.

Chapter 16

Anna pressed her hands to her mouth to muffle the sound of her scream. Her pulse banged in her ears. She darted a glance across the river. Because of the patches of thick vegetation and the noise of the river, Horace and his men were still unaware of their presence.

Tom's jaw clenched, and his eyes bulged in pain and terror as he slid down the embankment. He jabbed at the beast with his machete, but it had no effect.

Philip darted forward and grasped his arm. His strength was no match for the crocodile, which continued to pull Tom toward the water. Philip drew the pistol. He glanced across the river, then up behind them to the edge of the forest, then back to Tom.

Anna ran, hunched over, toward him. She could see the battle in Philip's mind displayed on his face. If they were discovered, the men would most certainly pursue them, but he couldn't leave his friend to be killed by this monster.

He pulled back the hammer and turned to her. "We must run, Anna." He darted a glance across the river one more time and took aim at the crocodile.

Anna scampered up the sandy riverbank, catching herself with her hands when she lost her balance. She was shaking so badly she could hardly focus; her mind was a whirl of terror. Was it merely a few hours ago that Philip had called her brave?

The blast of the pistol sent her to her knees, clapping her hands over her ears. She turned back and saw Philip shrug out of his jacket and then lift Tom's arm over his shoulder. Tom balanced on one leg and hopped with Philip's help up the bank.

Shouts drew her attention, and she looked back.

Horace pointed toward them, bellowing for his men to give chase. They ran toward the river. When Horace saw Anna, he froze and locked his gaze on her. His mouth twisted in a smile that made her heart turn cold.

She pulled her eyes away and reached to help Philip. The cords on his neck stood out as he strained to pull Tom up the hill. "Anna, lead the way. But do not follow the path." His words were tense and breathless.

She glanced back one last time as Horace's men neared the flowing river. She hoped it would detain them. She turned into the jungle, pushing her way between the tall fronds and wide leaves. She paused at the tree line and pulled aside the branches as well as she was able to allow Philip and Tom to pass unhindered. For her effort, she received scrapes and slices on her arms. Her kid gloves offered little protection from the sharp ferns. The men followed her, though she had no idea which direction she was leading them.

Anna estimated they had gone no more than a hundred yards when she heard the crashing and yells of Horace's band in the jungle. The sounds were muted, but she knew they would increase as the men got closer. It was only a matter of time before they were discovered. She turned to Philip, panic stealing her thoughts. She was unable to even put words to her fear.

"You must leave me," Tom ground out between clenched teeth. Sweat stood out on his forehead, and his face looked like chalk.

"We will not," Philip said. He breathed heavily as he adjusted his hold on Tom. "Anna, we need to hide."

She nodded and turned, scanning the area, wondering which way to go. It was impossible to see through the dense foliage, but now that she wasn't moving, she listened closely. Above the sounds of birds and insects, she thought she could hear flowing water in front of them. Perhaps there was another river and a place to hide. She led the men in the direction of the sound at a quicker pace. Twigs and branches scraped her skin. The ground was becoming moist, and the leaves on the ground smelled rotten. Speckles of light fought through the thick canopy as the jungle grew darker. She worried she was leading them to a swamp, but she pressed forward as the rushing sound of water grew louder and she had no other indication of what direction they should follow.

Moments later, Anna pushed free of the vines, emerging into a clearing bordered on one side by a sheer black cliff rising in front of them. A large waterfall blasted into a pool at the rocky base. Streams led away from the pond; mangroves with tangles of thick roots grew along the marshy banks.

Anna's heart leapt into her throat when she saw countless iguana lizards climbing over the rocks, the ground, and the roots and trunks of the trees. She shrank back, glancing at Philip as he and Tom stepped from the jungle.

He lifted his chin and held her gaze steadily. "You can be brave, Anna. I know it." Sweat ran in droplets from his forehead, and he breathed heavily. He must be utterly exhausted from supporting Tom and every bit as terrified as she, but somehow he had faith in her.

Anna took the machete from Tom's hand, surprised by the large knife's weight. The way Tom had held it and waved it around, she'd imagined it to be much lighter.

She grasped it in both hands and moved around the pool. She didn't think she would be able to slice one of the terrifying lizards with the knife, but its weight in her hand gave her courage. When she stepped closer to the mangroves, her foot sank in the swampy ground. She pulled it out, but her boot was covered in sticky mud. Anna wrinkled her nose, lifted the hems of her skirts, and walked in the other direction, away from the mangroves and closer to the rocky area near the pond. She kept a wary eye on the great lizards that hung from the cliff or lay on the rocks and branches, but except for an occasional raise of their heads, they did not seem overly concerned with her presence.

She glanced back at Philip. He had lowered Tom to the ground and was reloading his pistol, his gaze moving along the tree line surrounding them. The crashing of the waterfall covered the noise made by their pursuers in the jungle. They could burst out of the trees any second. She knew she had to hurry and find cover.

A cool mist drifted over her as she neared the waterfall. On the other side of the pond, Anna followed the wet cliff, searching for a hiding place but staying clear of the iguanas. She rounded a clump of rocks near the tree line and found just what she was looking for. Where the wall of the cliff met with the jungle trees, there was a gap in the stone. She stepped gingerly over the loose rocks and used the machete to push aside hanging vines, worried that a family of iguana lizards might have made the fissure their home. The crack was wide enough for one person to pass comfortably through and deep enough for the three of them. There was no overhang, and if it rained or one of the iguanas decided to jump, they would have no cover, but it would have to do. She stepped back around the rocks and waved to Philip.

He half dragged a nearly unconscious Tom to join her. He rounded the rock, and when she held aside the vegetation, Philip gave her a look that melted her heart into her toes. "Perfect, Anna."

The nook was large enough that Tom could lie down fully, but with him in that position, Anna and Philip were forced to remain at the entrance, practically against the foliage. The vines covered their hiding spot. The opening faced away from the clearing, and Anna strained her ears to listen above the sound of the waterfall for the noises of Horace's men.

They sat uncomfortably on the damp ground in the eerie shadows, unable to see beyond a few feet outside of their hideaway. They had to hope nobody came close enough or moved aside the leafy branches concealing them. The leaves rustled, birds jabbered, and something scampered in the undergrowth.

Philip laid both his and Tom's weapons on the ground next to him.

Tom's labored breathing echoed through the small space. His muscles were rigid, and his fists were clenched. Anna turned and moved onto her knees to examine Tom's foot. She could see blood inside his boot.

Anna worried his wounds would become infected in the moist jungle air. "Tom," she whispered, "I am going to remove your boot."

Tom made a hissing noise as he breathed through his teeth. He nodded, pushing himself up onto his elbows to brace for the pain.

Philip picked his way carefully to the far end of the cavity near Tom's shoulder. He crouched down, lifted Tom into a sitting position, then nodded to Anna.

Anna lifted Tom's foot carefully from the ground, and he gasped, inhaling a shaky breath. Tom cried out when she pulled on his boot, and Philip clapped a hand over the man's mouth, stifling the noise.

The boot wouldn't come free. As she examined it closer, she could feel that his ankle was swollen inside.

Tom collapsed onto the earth, his breath still coming in gasps and stutters.

"I am sorry," Anna whispered. "I do not think we can get it off."

"I think Dr. Bevan will need to cut it off," Philip said. He helped Tom lay back then moved back around to join Anna. "It will probably do more harm than good to attempt it ourselves. We do not have the supplies, and I for one do not know how to treat an injury like this." From the pack, he removed the napkins Betty had packed around their luncheon. Handing them to Anna, he lifted Tom's leg and slid his pack beneath the foot to keep it raised.

Anna pressed the napkins to the slices in Tom's boot. The bleeding seemed to have slowed, so she did not apply any pressure. The slightest touch was agony to Tom. His eyes rolled in his head, and his breathing sounded more like growling. Finally, mercifully, his head dropped onto the ground as he slipped into unconsciousness.

Anna resumed her place next to Philip at the mouth of the cavity, where the vines hung in front of them like curtains.

For an instant, a memory drifted into her mind. *Hiding under a table . . . peeking out from beneath a long tablecloth. I am laughing.* The memory fluttered out of reach, and she couldn't discover any more. She wrapped her arms around her legs, pulling her knees to her chest. "I do not know what else to do for him," she whispered. "At least he is sleeping now."

Philip nodded. He sat with his arms resting on his knees, the pistols and machete nearby. "He needs a doctor," he said quietly. A rustling sounded nearby. He tipped his head to the side, his hand creeping toward the pistols.

Anna listened closely. The rustling stopped, and she decided it must have been a bird or another small jungle animal.

They sat in silence for what seemed like hours. The fear that had coursed painfully through her veins had begun to abate, leaving behind an exhaustion that was only intensified by the warm air and dimly lit cave. She closed her eyes, just for a moment, and tried to recapture the memory and discover more. *Was it a memory of my childhood? Was I playing with my parents? Or was I the adult, hiding from a child? Whose child?* She nodded and jerked her head up when she started to doze.

Philip pulled her head to rest on his shoulder.

"What do we do now, Philip?" Anna said, noticing how very comfortable his shoulder felt beneath her cheek.

"I have been contemplating that very question for the better part of an hour," he said in a low voice. "Horace and his men have no doubt found our trail and the horses."

Anna lifted her head. "Smokey—"

"Horses are valuable. They will not hurt Smokey."

She laid her head back down.

"Horace knows I saw him. He will do all he can to prevent me from returning to Oakely Park or Port Antonio." He rubbed a hand over his face. "With Tom injured, we do not have many options. They will undoubtedly watch the road."

"Perhaps you or I could stay with Tom while the other goes for help?" The very thought of making her way through the jungle alone or of hiding with an injured man while enemies searched for them sent jolts of fear through her.

"Out of the question."

"But if it is the only choice . . ."

"We will find another way."

"I am glad. I do not want to leave you," Anna said.

Philip didn't respond. He rested his head on hers, and for a moment, Anna forgot that they were being pursued by thieves and murderers through a reptile-infested jungle. Aside from eminent danger and their injured friend and the hundreds of lizards, the moment was nearly perfect. But before long, her mind was pulled to the memory of Horace attacking the slave with a whip, then to the sound of his pistol . . . She squeezed her eyes shut, willing the thoughts away. "Why do men hurt each other, Philip? Men like Horace Braithwaite. Why do they take such pleasure in inflicting harm?"

"I do not know." He took her hand in his. "I wish you had not witnessed such an atrocity. The first day I met Horace, he beat a woman with no provocation, and I saw something so merciless in his eyes that it made me ill. Some men are innately cruel. I do not understand it."

"You do not understand it because you are kindhearted and generous."

"I hardly think that is the case."

Anna lifted her head and scooted around to face him, leaning her back against the damp cliff. "My lord, you saved a man's life today at risk to your own. You retain a valet who is vastly ill-suited to a man of your standing only because you are fond of him. You have not once mentioned the loss of hundreds of pounds worth of sugar because the deaths of your slaves have so distressed yo—"

Philip turned his head, motioning with his hand for her to be silent.

Anna listened, at first believing the sounds outside their hideaway to be no more than animals moving through the jungle. But the rustling grew louder and turned into a crashing accompanied by men's voices. Her heart pounded. She clapped a hand over her mouth to prevent a sound from escaping.

Philip lifted the two pistols, shifting onto one knee, ready to spring forward if their hiding place was discovered.

The men's words were distorted by the waterfall. Judging by their tones, Anna thought they were complaining.

Philip leaned forward, slowly moving the tall grass and heavy branches aside. He crept out from the cover of the vines but remained behind the screen of grass, hiding in the shadows beneath an outcropping of rock.

Anna waved her hand, motioning for him to return, but he shook his head, wanting to keep an eye on their enemies. Anna didn't dare to move any farther back into the fissure for fear of disturbing Tom by bumping his injured foot. She clenched her hands together in front of her mouth, praying that the men would not see Philip.

An explosion shattered the silence, and Anna jerked, hitting her head on the rock. She bit her knuckles to keep from crying out and squeezed her eyes shut against her tears. Another shot rang out, and something landed on the ground with a thump near their hiding place. The men cheered. Her breath came in short gasps.

Philip glanced at the cliff above them and then to Anna. "They are shooting the iguanas." He mouthed the words silently and turned back to watch through the grass.

Another shot was fired, and Anna heard scampering through the undergrowth. She imagined the lizards running over the rocks and cliff face into the jungle. She shuddered as she thought of their small legs and long, writhing bodies darting around the clearing.

Another shot sounded, and small rocks scattered on the ground near Anna. Directly afterward, a giant iguana lizard fell from above. It twisted around until it was upright and, in its panic, ran toward their hiding place. Through the vines, Anna saw the reptile running at her, its body bending strangely from side to side as it moved, and a scream swelled in her lungs. She clutched at her face. The gray-green animal drew close enough that she saw its dark eyes and sharp teeth in a lipless mouth.

Her fingers went numb, and her vision blurred as the lizard climbed over the vines in front of her to reach the cliff above. Its spiky toes scratched her legs and arms. Cool scales brushed against her, and Anna drew her limbs in, pressing her forehead against her knees and curling into a ball. She held back her shrieks but could not stop the tremors that shook her body. The lizard scampered up the cliff side, and Anna's stomach tightened. She thought she would vomit.

She was shaking so badly she didn't notice when Philip moved the vines aside and crouched next to her, pulling her into his arms. "Anna, they are gone. And the iguana, it is gone."

She continued shaking, pressing her eyes closed against the horror of the things they'd witnessed since entering the jungle. And the scales, the claws . . . Her stomach clenched again.

Philip cupped his hand beneath her chin, lifting her face. "Anna." He searched her expression. "Anna, it is all right now."

"The iguana . . ." Her voice was no more than a squeak.

"Your scaled nemesis has fled." The side of his mouth lifted in a smile. "I'd call that a victory, Miss Lizard-Survivor—to face one's darkest fear and endure it without retreat. And now, you know for certain that there is no reason to be afraid of those beady-eyed devils." He brushed his thumb over her cheek, sending chills through her nerves. "And incidentally, the villains pursuing us are also gone." The other side of his mouth spread into a slow smile. He held her gaze a moment longer before he blinked and shook his head slightly, pulling back and releasing her. She thought he muttered something about a guardian.

He glanced at Tom and then back at her. He scratched his hand through his hair. "I am trying to determine whether the wisest course is to remain here or to press on to Oakely Park. I do not know how far the men have gone or whether they will return, but with Tom's injury, the journey will not be easy and is probably best attempted before dark."

He started to rise, but Anna put her hand on his arm, stopping him. "It is not my worst fear."

His brows raised in question.

"My worst fear is not the iguana lizards like you said. I fear that something bad would happen to someone I care for. To you. That is infinitely worse." Anna realized what she had said. She felt her cheeks redden and slid her gaze away, then she hurried to add, "If any of you—Betty, Tom, or Ezekiel—were to come to harm, I could not bear it." She lifted her gaze back to his.

Philip's head was tilted to the side as he regarded her. In the dim light, his expression changed from teasing friendliness to something warm that both excited and scared her. He held her gaze and brushed a finger over her cheek. He opened his mouth, closed it, and then moved deeper into the crevice to help Tom rise to a sitting position.

Anna's face burned where he'd touched it. The combination of the panic and terror she'd felt moments ago were weak compared to the intensity of emotions that the simple action and the heat in Philip's eyes produced. She moved the foliage aside, needing to breathe, to have a moment alone to compose herself.

She stepped out of the rocks and shook her damp gown then hurried away from the crevice, pressing through the tall grass and leafy stalks. Emerging into the clearing, she lifted her gaze, and her heart lurched into her throat. A group of men surrounded her with muskets, pistols, and swords drawn.

Anna drew back toward the jungle.

A tall man with broad shoulders and dark eyes stepped forward, motioning for the others to lower their weapons.

"I hardly think this is how to greet a lady." He removed his hat and bowed deeply, sweeping his hand in front of him. "Alastair Courtney, miss. Cap'n of this 'ere band. Brethren of the Coast."

Chapter 17

Philip heard men's voices and sprang from the crevice. He should not have allowed Anna to leave the hiding place alone. Why had he become so flustered by her words? He'd ignored caution as his emotions had thrown his mind into a whirl. Images of what the evil men would do assaulted him in the instant it took for him to push his way through the grass, surge through the vegetation, and emerge into the clearing. His mind raced as he cast his eyes around, waving his pistols toward the men surrounding Anna.

The men lifted their weapons.

Anna hurried to his side, laying a hand on his arm.

A tall man in a tricorn hat folded his arms across his chest, grinning. "And she has a protector." The man's eyes moved between the two of them. "Sir, you interrupted us just as the young lady and I were becoming acquainted. Cap'n Alastair Courtney." He bowed ceremoniously. The captain was an Englishman, but his speech was not refined. His face was hard, and the lines around his mouth and eyes spoke of a hard life and years of exposure to the elements.

Philip regained enough of his composure to realize these were not the same men who had followed them through the jungle. Their appearance was rough, as if they went for long periods between bathing, and their clothes were mismatched and weathered. Articles from fashion long past—ruffled shirts, loose breeches, colorful scarves—combined to an effect that was somehow rather flamboyant. But in spite of their strange fashion, the men were not to be dismissed. Each man had at least one musket. Not to mention the sabers, daggers, swords, and other firearms that protruded from their belts and scabbards. The sound of musket fire must have alerted these scoundrels to their position. Why had Philip not insisted Anna remain hidden? He ground his teeth; frustration that he had not foreseen such an eventuality churned in his gut.

Captain Courtney cleared his throat, and Philip realized he was waiting for a reply. "Lord Philip Hamilton." He hoped his title would hold some sway with these men, whoever they were.

The captain's scratched his darkly shadowed jaw. "The new master of Oakely Park, I presume. I'd heard rumors you were a nobleman." He grinned, revealing straight white teeth. "Better and better, my lord." His gaze turned to Anna. "And this lovely young lady is . . . ?"

"Lady Anna, my sister." Philip did not glance at Anna, hoping that her expression did not give away his deception. He feared that this band were highwaymen or, worse, buccaneers. And he did not dare to think of what they might do to a beautiful woman in their clutches.

Captain Courtney's lips twisted in a smirk, and he lifted a brow. Philip got the distinct impression that the man didn't believe for a moment that Anna was his sister.

"Charmed, my lady." He looked behind her and motioned with a flick of his head. Some of the men hurried through the vegetation Anna and Philip had emerged from. "And perhaps, my lord, now that we are acquainted, you wouldn't mind lowering your weapons? It doesn't appear that you are self-possessed at the moment, and I wouldn't want any unpleasantness to occur." His words were amiable, but there was a glint in his eye. Philip knew he was being threatened.

He dropped his arms, and Anna scooted closer to his side.

"One more, Cap'n," a man said as he stepped from the jungle. "And 'is one's wounded."

Captain Courtney glanced at the man and nodded.

"Who are you, sir?" Philip stood straight. He attempted to speak calmly and put every ounce of authority he could muster into his words.

"Apologies, my lord." Captain Courtney inclined his head. "We're merely a band of privateers, just finished up the rainy season here on this lovely island while our ship is repaired."

Philip's muscles clenched, and his stomach dropped. *Pirates.*

He had never seen such an odd mixture of men: old, young, dark-skinned Africans, light-skinned Danes, and every color in between. The oldest had a white beard, and the skin around his eyes was so wrinkled and weathered that it looked like a dried apple. The youngest was probably near seventeen, gangly with red hair and freckles. Some of the men moved closer to listen to their captain. Others stood in groups, leaning on their muskets and conversing quietly. It seemed some had been assigned as sentries and stood near the tree line with weapons ready, their attention focused on the surrounding jungle.

Philip turned his head as Tom was carried from the jungle and lowered to the ground near them. He was awake, but his face was gray and his expression a grimace of pain. He leaned back against a rock, his gaze moving around the clearing.

Captain Courtney raised his chin as he studied the three of them. "Now that the niceties are out of the way, shall we speak of business matters? You are undoubtedly aware of the shortage of merchant ships this time of year. And as men of fortune we must make a living somehow." He shrugged one shoulder and his smile—complete with its threatening glint—returned. "Shall we discuss the terms of your ransom?"

Anna sucked in a quick breath.

Philip gawked at the man, amazed that he could speak so genially even as he was robbing him. "Our ransom, sir?"

"Yes, of course. I am first and foremost a capitalist, and my men would elect another leader should I not use this chance meeting to our advantage." He lifted a hand in front of him as if to stop from getting too far ahead of himself. "But I should clarify. I meant *your* ransom, my lord. Since your companion is injured, and there is no one else, Lady Anna shall return to Oakely Park to procure the funding for your freedom. I should think five hundred pounds a fair price for a man of your position."

Anna's fingers tightened on his arm.

Philip's chest was so tight that he had difficulty drawing a breath. "You cannot intend for my sister to travel through the jungle alone."

Captain Courtney drew his chin back as if it was the most preposterous idea he could imagine. "Of course not. I shall send a man to accompany her." He glanced around the gathered group, and his eyes landed on a tall man nearby. Based on his copper-colored skin and long, straight hair, Philip thought he might be an Indian brave from the Americas. "Mr. Blackbird, would you be so kind?"

Mr. Blackbird nodded once and took a step toward Anna.

Philip turned in time to see the color drain from her face. She pressed against Philip's side, and he shifted to move her behind him.

Philip tried to speak rationally, even as his vision clouded with fury, hoping he sounded like a concerned brother. "Captain, that is completely unacceptable. Not only does it compromise my sister's safety, but her reputation—"

The captain's face lost its smile, and his expression hardened. "We are gentlemen, my lord, bound by honor and oaths. When a buccaneer gives his word, you can be guaranteed of his promise. Be assured no harm will come to your . . . *sister*." He spoke the last word with a hint of sarcasm.

Philip pushed Anna farther behind him. "Forgive me for not trusting in the word of thieves." His heart pounded as the combination of fear and anger sent energy coursing through his limbs.

"Thieves?" Captain Alastair Courtney's eyes took on a steely glint. "You may want to reconsider your words, my lord." He casually fingered the firearm in his belt. Though he spoke in a low voice, there was no mistaking the anger that glowed in his eyes.

"I will not." Philip raised his arms, brandishing his pistols. Before he could even aim, men seized him, yanked the weapons from his grasp, and jerked his arms behind his back.

Philip strained against them. The only thought in his head was that he could not leave Anna at their mercy. He twisted and wrenched, kicking back. His foot made contact with someone, but before he had the satisfaction of seeing the result of his blow, his arms were pulled so tightly that he thought his shoulders were in danger of snapping. His legs were kicked out from beneath him, and he landed hard on his knees, straining his shoulders the more.

"I shall report you to the constable, sir," he spat, knowing it was a pathetic threat, but it was all he had. "Attacking a member of the aristocracy carries a heavy penalty and—"

"Stop!" Anna yelled as she moved toward Captain Courtney. She stepped in front of Philip, standing between the men with her hands held out toward each of them. "Please, stop." She spoke in a softer voice as she looked, tears shimmering in her eyes, to the buccaneers who held Philip. She turned to face Captain Courtney. "Captain, surely you can show leniency." She clasped her hands together in front of her. Her voice pleaded. "As you can see, our companion is injured, and we simply want to return home to Oakely Park before his wounds grow worse."

The captain's face remained rigid, but his eyes softened slightly. "I understand, my lady. The journey through the jungle will be but a few short hours, and once Mr. Blackbird returns with the funding, your companions will be free to go."

"Sir, I am not equipped to trek through the jungle for hours. Please allow us to remain together."

Captain Courtney's face softened further. Philip thought he would have to be made of stone for Anna's pleas not to touch his heart. He put a fist against his waist and lifted a hand to scratch his jaw. "It has been a very long time since we've had the pleasure of a lady's company." He spoke slowly. "I'm afraid I forgot my manners."

He stood up taller and widened his stance. "You may take any provisions you need." He spread his hands to indicate the other men around the clearing. "Anything at all—food, weapons, whatever will help you to feel safe in the jungle. I assume some of the men carry dried meat in their packs, or we could even find you a pair of sturdier boots." He squinted his eyes as his gaze roamed over his men's feet. "I do not think any would fit, but still, you are welcome to them."

Anna turned her head slowly, studying the men throughout the area. Philip saw that her hands shook, and she balled them into fists, pressing them against her sides. She looked at the ground for a long moment then raised her chin. "I may take anything with me?"

"As I said, Lady Anna. Though we've not much to offer."

"And you give your word?"

The captain extended his hand. "A buccaneer's oath is worth its weight in gold." He smiled, and his eyes twinkled. The expression was a little too charming for Philip's liking.

Anna stepped forward. One step. Pause. Then another. She took the man's large hand in her small gloved one. "Thank you, Captain." She released her grip and stepped backward. "Then I should like your trousers."

The captain's mouth dropped, and his eyes grew round. "My *trousers*?"

"You told me I could take anything, Captain, and I ask for your trousers."

He continued to stare. "But, my lady, we have weapons, equipment, food . . ." His lips drew tight, and his dark eyes narrowed. Any bit of gallantry had fled from his demeanor, and he glared at the men around him, who had started to laugh. "I cannot imagine that they are well suited to you, my lady, but I suppose it's not easy wearing a gown in the jungle." He let out a breath, certainly regretting his promise and began to unfasten his belt.

Anna's voice stopped him. "Captain, I should clarify. I did not mean only *your* trousers. I meant *all* of your trousers." She spread her hands in front of her, moving them outward. From Philip's viewpoint, he could see her neck redden and her fingers tremble, but she held her head up.

Aside from the sound of the waterfall and the birds in the trees, the clearing was completely silent for a long moment.

Captain Courtney glanced around at his men. A few shook their heads. One folded his arms defiantly in front of his chest. They muttered among themselves, casting wary glances between their leader and Anna.

Philip clenched his muscles. What was she doing? She was angering the pirates, and he couldn't imagine the result would be favorable. "Anna," he said, but she did not turn around.

"I ain't removin' my trousers, Cap'n," a man said. "These 'ere's the only ones I've got."

"I'm not wearing any smallclothes, Cap'n," said another in a worried voice.

The grumbling around the clearing grew louder, and the looks the pirates directed at their captain grew murderous.

He bared his teeth and pulled his pistols from his belt. "Men, you'll abide by the oath and give this woman your trousers or suffer a traitor's death."

"Perhaps you could renegotiate, Cap'n?" the man with no small clothes offered timidly.

Captain Courtney did not lower his pistols but kept them aimed at his men. He turned his gaze toward Anna. "My lady, if you don't mind my askin', for what purpose could you possibly need our trousers?"

Anna clasped her hands behind her back. "Why to ransom them back to you for the release of my brother, Captain. I think fifty pounds a piece is a fair price, don't you?" She paced a few steps to the side and raised her voice to include the other men in the conversation. "And since there are twelve of you and I assume you all would like to keep your trousers . . . Captain, your band is indebted to me one hundred pounds."

If Anna had scampered up the cliff to play with the iguanas, Philip could not have been more stunned.

Captain Courtney obviously shared the sentiment. His mouth dropped, and his forehead tipped toward her as he gaped at her. His expression changed from surprise when his eyes flashed in anger.

Philip tensed.

The captain's face reddened. He let out a heavy breath through his nose. He glanced at his men and returned his gaze to Anna. He studied her for a moment. His lips twitched, and then without warning, he threw his head back and roared with laughter.

Anna jerked at the sudden noise then relaxed. She glanced toward Philip, and a smile ticked her lips.

Captain Alastair Courtney grinned. "Ya outfoxed us, my lady," he said, refastening his belt. "I let down my guard and was out-pirated. But I can't say as the event was entirely unpleasant." He shook his head. "Trousers indeed. Lady Anna, we nearly had a mutiny on our hands." He reached out his hand, and after a slight hesitation, Anna placed hers inside it.

The other buccaneers looked relieved. A few even joined their leader in his laughter. Most appeared thankful just to retain their trousers.

Captain Courtney clapped his other hand over Anna's. He leaned toward her. "If we didn't have a strict 'no women' policy, I'd wager my men would nominate you to lead this band of ruffians. For my gallantry, I'm out one hundred pounds."

Anna offered a shy smile. "Captain, you may retain your gold if you would but see to Mr. Nortons's wounds. And, sir, if you don't mind, we are in need of a guide back to Oakely Park."

He smacked an extremely inappropriate kiss on the back of Anna's hand that sent full color to her face and had Philip exerting himself again to escape his captors. "'Tis gracious of you, Lady Anna. My band wouldn't be pleased if we'd lost money today." He smiled, and the lines on the sides of his eyes deepened. He retained his hold on her hand. "I'd not planned to do good deeds when I led the band into the jungle, but an unpredictable life is what we signed on for when we took our oath. Is it not, men?"

"Aye," they cried, and some raised their muskets to add emphasis to their cheer.

He turned fully toward the other buccaneers. He pointed to Philip and flicked a finger indicating for him to be released.

Philip stood and winced at the pain in his knees. He kneaded his fingers on his shoulder as he glanced down at his torn buckskins.

Anna pulled her hand from Captain Courtney's and, obviously attempting to soften the sting of the action, gave him a smile that caused the captain's own smile to return and Philip to step between them.

She moved to kneel next to Tom.

"Listen, ye scurvy dogs, we've guests this afternoon. Let us show them true buccaneer hospitality." The captain began to dole out assignments. Some men tended to Tom's foot with Anna keeping a close watch on the proceedings. Others collected dry wood to make a fire. A group was sent into the jungle in search of fruit. One man filled a water skin at the pond and took it around to the men on sentry duty.

Philip watched the men efficiently performing their duties, turning the clearing into an orderly campsite.

Captain Courtney stepped next to him and motioned with a jerk of his head for Philip to follow him to the edge of the clearing. When they were out of earshot, the captain turned to him. His expression carried none of the charming good humor he'd shown earlier. The captain's eyes were intelligent and serious. "If we're to be accompanying you and your companions, I'll ask ya to be honest with me. What trouble are you in that has a wounded man and a gentlewoman hiding from musket fire in a jungle cave? And no more lies, my lord. That young woman isn't your sister any more than I'm your Aunt Sally." His brow rose.

Philip narrowed his eyes, wondering at the man's intentions. He didn't like the familiar way the man had acted toward Anna, and he certainly did not want him to take any more liberties where she was concerned. He considered how much to tell the captain. Was the man in league with Horace? Philip wouldn't put it past him. "We were inspecting a parcel of land in the mountains when we saw smoke and took a detour through the jungle to investigate."

Captain Courtney's eyes didn't give away anything but continued to watch Philip steadily.

"We saw . . . highwaymen and their ill-gotten gains," Philip continued in a low voice. "Tom was attacked by a crocodile, and the scuffle alerted the men, who gave chase."

"And the musket fire? Were you discovered?"

Philip shook his head. "They shot at the iguanas on the cliffs but did not find us."

The captain watched his face, and Philip tried to discern whether he was a collaborator in Horace's scheme.

"And this is why you need an escort through the jungle? If the highwaymen recognized you, they will surely be waiting at your plantation."

"Yes, Captain. That is my fear."

"Then we will take our time with the meal, rest here, and approach the plantation after dark. I believe it is our best course to avoid anyone who might lie in wait."

"Thank you."

The pirate folded his arms and raised his chin as he looked at Philip. "I'm not one for doing charity work. 'Tisn't our way of life to protect traveling noblemen out of the kindness of our hearts."

"I understand, Captain. When we reach Oakely Park, I intend to compensate you for your assistance."

Captain Courtney shook his head. "I'd not hear of it. The lady and I have a bargain. One that she should be extremely proud of, as I am not often outmaneuvered." He scratched his jaw. "I told you we're not thieves, my lord." He looked toward where Anna had moved to help a man peel and prepare fruit for their meal. "It's been far too long since I had a conversation as diverting as I did today with your 'sister.' She's a remarkable young lady. And so pretty." His voice was low. His eyes softened as he watched her, and he reminded Philip of a lovesick youth, though he was surely near his fourtieth year. "I can see why you protect her the way you do, my lord. In your position, I'd do the same."

Chapter 18

Anna knelt on the ground next to a group of the pirates. A sack of fruit sat in front of them, and one of the men had produced a cooking pot. She had determined to help as best she could and not do anything else that might put them in danger. She glanced around the clearing and saw Philip and Captain Courtney conversing quietly near the trees. She wondered what they were discussing but knew she'd overstepped her position enough for one day. The men were undoubtedly planning the expedition, and she could not wait to return home to Oakely Park and sleep in her own bed. She ignored the nagging reminder that it was not truly her bed or her home, and she turned her mind back to the group.

Mr. Blackbird crouched near her. Anna looked up at him and shrunk away. His appearance was just how she envisioned a savage warrior—long, straight hair that hung over his shoulders, high cheekbones, copper-colored skin—but it was his expressionless face and flint-black eyes that caused her to recoil.

He didn't appear to notice her reaction. "Ackee fruit," he said, handing her a red pod that was split open on one side. He lifted one himself and indicated the tears with his finger. "Open when it is ripe, but when not, it is poison. Do not eat a closed ackee."

Anna watched him peel back the red skin and discard it, exposing sections of white flesh surrounding large black seeds. He discarded the seeds, tossed the flesh into the pot, and indicated for her to do the same. They settled into a routine, working quietly with the others until the pot was full.

Captain Courtney walked to the group. "No need to rush the meal. We'll be here until dark. Now we've time to cook some meat."

The plan was to wait for the cover of darkness? The idea of walking through the thick jungle when she couldn't see sent a chill over her skin. She rubbed her arms.

Mr. Blackbird stood and pulled a dagger from his belt as he walked toward the pool. Anna's mind barely had time to register his intent before the weapon shot through the air and impaled a large lizard on the rocks. The animal hung limp as Mr. Blackbird lifted it by the tail and walked back toward them.

Anna turned with her hands over her face, her stomach rolling.

Captain Courtney caught her arms. "Apologies, my lady." He pulled her by the elbow, leading her away from the food preparation. "I'm sure even your protector won't object to a walk around the clearing while the men tend to the more unpleasant parts of preparing the meal."

Anna glanced toward Philip sitting on the ground next to Tom. He was speaking to the overseer, but his eyes followed her. He raised his brows in question.

She shook her head and smiled. She did not mind taking a walk with Captain Courtney, especially if it meant she would be away from the bleeding iguana lizard. And now that she no longer feared the man, she wanted to know everything she could about his band and their lifestyle. She could not believe that she was among a group of buccaneers. And not only were the men courteous, she found that she actually trusted their leader.

The captain tucked her hand beneath his arm and led her around the edge of the clearing. A memory teetered on the edge of her consciousness. *A man—her father—walks with her in precisely this way. They stop to admire a rose garden.* Like the others, the memory was merely a fragment, and she wanted to cry out in frustration.

She glanced at Captain Courtney from the corner of her eye and saw that he was watching her. "Captain, I hope I am not being impolite, but I wonder about your history. How did you come to choose your particular . . . profession?"

"You are wondering how such a charming and refined man as myself found himself as the leader of a band of pirates." He laid his hand on his chest as he spoke.

Anna laughed at his humor. "Yes, I suppose I am."

He was silent for a moment before he answered. His eyes took on a faraway look as he walked. "Being a genteel lady, you don't know what life is like in the poor districts of London, but it ain't for the fainthearted. Wapping is plopped right between London Bridge and the naval yards on a marshland filled with disease. I lived with fifteen people to a room in a stinking, crumbling building that, as an orphan, I was lucky to have. The smell when it rained is something I can't even begin to describe. The churchyard had a mass pauper grave that remained open until fully occupied. Corpses of animals rotted on the roads, and people daily died of fevers or measles. Abandoned children filled the streets, starving to death, thieving, and begging. Most prayed to be bought by a chimney sweep or sent to a workhouse." He glanced at Anna and swallowed. "I myself went to sea."

Anna was horrified at his description. Her heart ached as she imagined such poverty, and her stomach twisted at his description. She shook her head to rid the thoughts of starving children and sickness. "It was a very good decision," Anna said. "I imagine it was—"

"I was not a gentleman or an officer, Lady Anna. Life at sea was very similar to the life I'd left behind; the only difference was the added fear of drowning." His lips were set in a tight line for a moment before he continued. "We were wakened at all hours and set to work—climbing slippery ropes during rolling storms; firing cannons and being fired upon; all the time, half awake and usually half drunk. My shipmates fell from riggings, were blown apart by cannons, or died after long bouts of dysentery. Heat, cold, scurvy, disease, lice, rats, cockroaches. And add to that a captain who understocks the food supplies to pad his own pockets and flogs for minor mistakes, and yer ripe for a rebellion."

Anna's chest was tight as she thought of the harsh life Captain Courtney had endured. No wonder he had chosen the life of a buccaneer. She studied him. He stood straight with his head held tall and held her gaze without wavering. She did not think a common sailor on a naval ship would have the same bearing. The man who stood before her was a confident leader. "And are you happy now, Captain?"

He smiled and tucked her hand back into his elbow crook, continuing their stroll. "Happier than I'd ever have imagined. My band is my family. We divide our spoils equally, elect our leader by popular vote, and fight for no king." He lifted his face to the sun. "I've seen the beautiful places of the world and been the master of my own destiny." His eyes slid to the side. "And now I'm in a flowered paradise with the prettiest lady I've seen in years. Aye, I'm a happy man, Lady Anna."

"I am glad for it."

"And, my lady, if you don't mind me asking, from whence do ye hail?"

Anna grimaced. She should have anticipated the question and did not know how to answer. If she did not want to reveal that Philip had fabricated the story of their relation, she needed to continue with his untruth, but she didn't want to say something that contradicted him. She squirmed inside. Even drawing on the truth wouldn't work as she had no idea of her real past.

"His lordship already confessed to his deception. Yer not his sister." He turned to face her, holding onto her hand. "So who are you, Lady Anna?"

Anna studied his expression, grateful that he did not seem angry at being lied to. His expression contained no more than friendly curiosity. She shrugged her shoulders. "I do not know who I am." Seeing the confusion in his face, she continued. "Lord Philip told me I washed ashore on his beach, but I have no memory of anything before awaking in his guestchamber." She watched him, waiting for his reaction.

He scratched his jaw. "That explains it." His eyes twinkled, and the creases around them deepened. "I lost a wife named Anna. I thought you seemed familiar. Let us return to the boat, my dear." He attempted to maintain a straight face but failed, and a large grin spread onto his cheeks.

"Captain Courtney, you are teasing me."

He shook his head, making a *tsk* sound. "Didn't fool ya, did I? But it was worth a try."

She swatted at him, laughing at his jest.

His smile waned as he studied her. "I'd imagine it makes matters a bit complicated between the two of ye." His gaze darted across the clearing to Philip. "Not knowing yer past. You could be . . ."

Anna nodded, surprised how quickly a lump rose into her throat.

Captain Courtney patted her hand where it rested on his arm. He sniffed the air. "I'd say our supper is nearly ready. Shall we return?"

Anna turned her glance to the other side of the clearing where the buccaneers, Philip, and Tom had gathered near the fire.

When she and the captain joined the group, Anna was given a large leaf with cooked ackee and shredded meat. She discovered the ackee turned bright yellow when it was cooked. She could not bring herself to eat the meat.

***

It was nearly dark when they left the clearing. The men had fashioned torches from branches and cloth, but those did little to illuminate the area beneath the jungle canopy. The pirates had also made a crutch for Tom, and the combination of a medicinal tea and the splint on his leg made walking bearable though slow. Anna followed Captain Courtney. Philip walked directly behind her.

A few buccaneers were sent ahead to scout. Others chopped a path through the trees. They moved efficiently. The quiet was broken only by the crackling of the flames, the slashing of the machetes, and the rustling of the foliage around them. Even the birds were silent. Periodically, the entourage would stop to listen.

The air was nearly chilly. Anna wrapped her arms around herself, wishing for a shawl. She hoped it would not cool much more before they reached Oakely Park. She ran her hands up and down her arms.

Captain Courtney halted. One of the scouts had returned—Mr Blackbird. Anna didn't know how he had approached without her hearing. She stepped closer and overheard him tell the captain that the highwaymen waited on the road near the beach.

She glanced behind to see Philip's expression. In the flickering torch light, she saw his mouth set in a grim line. He moved closer to the buccaneers' discussion, and his hand bumped Anna's arm.

"Your skin is cold as ice." He pulled her in front of him to lean back against his chest as he rubbed her arms.

Anna felt like butter on a warm piece of bread. She wanted to rest her head back and relax against him—but it was completely out of the question. Her heart sped up, her cheeks warmed, and she was most definitely no longer chilled.

More of their group gathered around to hear Mr. Blackbeard's report.

"Will you be all right?" His breath was warm against her cheek.

Anna nodded. Her voice had somehow stopped working.

A man bumped into her in the space between the leafy stalks. In the torchlight, she recognized him as the pirate who did not wear underclothing. He was short and very hairy and wore the most beautiful Oriental silk scarf around his neck. The fabric, however, was torn and filthy. She'd seen him use it to wipe his mouth during supper. He glanced at her and removed his cape, holding it out toward her. "I'd not want ya to be cold, m'lady," he said, his smile revealing missing and yellowed teeth.

"Thank you, Mr. . . . ?"

"Teach, m'lady."

Philip took the cape and draped it around her shoulders.

An odor rose from the wool, which had obviously not been laundered for quite some time, if ever. The combined scent of food, sweat, and wool in a tropical climate had her eyes running and tickled the back of her throat. She coughed to disguise her gag. "Oh, my." Anna gasped and coughed again as she looked at Mr. Teach's smiling face. "What a thoughtful gesture, Mr. Teach," she said between clenched teeth.

She felt more than heard Philip's chuckle.

"Course, 'an yer welcome to it." He nodded, obviously pleased that his offer had been so well received.

Anna smiled, not allowing herself to breathe through her nose. Mr. Teach's personal smell reminded her strongly of livestock. She prayed that no fleas or other creatures lived in the cape.

Captain Courtney informed the company that they would alter their route. Anna was relieved to hear that the detour should not take them much longer than they had planned.

Anna walked with one hand beneath her nose to block the smell and the other holding onto the grimy cape. She was certainly warm now, but she much preferred Philip's method. Her pulse jumped at the memory of his touch. *Philip*. Merely his name had the power to make her heart trip. Why did she allow herself to care so deeply when her situation was unknown? Why had she become so involved in this life that she could not imagine any other, even though she knew it was temporary?

Philip's touch had left trails of heat on her skin. His voice sent a thrill through her core. Was there another man somewhere who made her name sound as if it were the most precious word ever uttered? From her brief scraps of memory, she knew there were other people in her life. Being unable to attach any emotion to those quick glimpses left her feeling anxious and frustrated. She both longed for her memories to return and feared what she would find once they did.

When Anna stepped out of the trees into the moonlight, she found that Mr. Blackbird's detour brought them to the clearing with the slaves' gardens. An enormous weight lifted off her chest. They were at Oakely Park, and they were safe! She breathed a prayer of thanks, and when her eyes met Philip's, she saw the same relief reflected in his face.

He took her hand and squeezed it, letting out a heavy breath. "We are home, Anna," he muttered.

He couldn't have any idea the effect his words had on her. Her throat constricted. Oakely Park wasn't her home. She wished she could burrow her face into her cape to keep from looking into his eyes, but her gag reflex would have none of it. She turned away, hoping to school her expression so he couldn't see her lip quivering.

Captain Courtney bowed and began to take his leave.

Philip held up his hand. "You are my guests, sir. Please come with us to the house; we will see that you and your men have a suitable place to sleep and a hearty breakfast in the morning."

"'Tisn't necessary, my lord." Captain Courtney scratched his cheek. He looked extremely uncomfortable with the idea.

"I insist, Captain. If you will not accept payment for your services, you must at least consent to our hospitality."

"Please do, Captain Courtney," Anna said. Philip continued to hold her hand, and it didn't escape her notice that he had said *our* although he surely referred to the household staff and not her.

She and Philip walked across the plantation hand in hand. The night was beautiful. Bats flitted through the sky, and insects trilled and chirped in the trees. Anna loved the feel of her hand in Philip's and stole glances at his profile in the moonlight. If she tried very hard, she could almost forget the unspeakable things they'd seen—their injured friend, the men looking for them, their pirate escorts, and her foul cloak—and imagine it was just the two of them, out for a late stroll.

When they neared the house, Betty ran to meet them. Ezekiel followed behind as quickly as he was able.

"Where in de worl' have ya been?" Betty said. She grasped Anna in an embrace then stepped back quickly, wrinkling her nose. Her gaze moved around the company nervously.

"My lord!" Ezekiel panted. "Where is yo' horse?"

Philip released Anna's hand. He turned to his servants and began to give orders, and the illusion was over. He was the master once again, and she—she was simply Anna. "Send for Dr. Bevan. Tom is injured. Betty, please see to the accommodations for our guests." He indicated the band of buccaneers, and Betty's eyes grew wide.

"No accommodations necessary, my lord," Captain Courtney said. "We're accustomed to sleepin' outside. If ya don't mind, we'll camp here on yer lawn. We'll not be any trouble, and soon as we've broken our fast tomorrow, you'll not even know we were here."

"Very well, Captain." Philip nodded once and shook the pirate's hand. "I am indebted to you, sir. If you need anything, you have but to ask."

"I thank ye. And we'll not be needin' anything a'tall." Captain Courtney turned to Anna. He took her hand and bowed but did not kiss it again, for which she was grateful. "Good night, Lady Anna."

"Good night, Captain. And thank you for seeing us safely home." She unwrapped the cape from her shoulders, grimacing as a fresh wave of odor hit her nose. She thanked Mr. Teach for his care, and as it seemed there was no further need for her, she climbed the stairs to the Great House.

Anna was exhausted. She glanced behind her and saw that Dr. Bevan had arrived and was taking Tom away on his horse. The band of men spread out, sitting in groups on the ground. Some lay, wrapped in their cloaks, and she wondered if they were already sleeping.

She felt immensely grateful for the pirates. If not for the unlikely heroes, she had no doubt they would have been discovered in the jungle or waylaid on the road. The thought of Horace's red face, twisted with cruelty and sneering at her, and the men chasing them through the jungle, intent on their destruction, caused a new wave of fear to wash over Anna, jolting in her chest and leaving her cold and shaking. She walked into the house and crossed the main hall.

They were safe for now, but what of the workers in the fields? Would Horace enact revenge on them? Would they attack another shipment?

The road to Port Antonio wasn't safe, especially for Philip and his workers. If only there was a way to protect them.

The idea came so suddenly that Anna stopped with her foot in the air. It was obvious, but could she convince Philip? She had been extremely bold today, first with her endorsement of Tom's coffee farm and then in her negotiations with the pirates. Neither was something a woman in her position—or in any position—should have presumed to do, and she *should* just keep walking right up to her bedchamber and leave these matters to those in authority. She ran her finger along the crease in the wooden handrail, knowing she wouldn't be able to stop thinking about it if she didn't at least make the suggestion. She would always wonder if her idea could have helped. She turned and sat on the steps to wait for Philip.

It was not long before he entered with Ezekiel trailing, offering to assist him in preparing for bed.

His brows rose when he saw her on the stairs. "Anna, you are still awake?"

She rose and stepped down the steps to stand before him. She smiled at Ezekiel, who moved to stand against the wall, precisely as a perfect footman would do. She clasped her hands in front of her. "I wanted to speak to you for a moment."

"Of course." He held his hand toward the parlour.

Anna shook her head. "It will only be a moment. I have an idea. I know I am too often sticking my nose where it does not belong, and you may not agree with me, but—"

"I consider your opinions very carefully, Anna. What is your idea?"

His sureness boosted her confidence. She lifted her chin and raised her eyes to his. "I think you should employ the pirates."

Chapter 19

PHILIP DRUMMED HIS FINGERS ON the arm of his chair. His gaze moved around the drawing room, and he observed each of the individuals he'd summoned to participate in the conference: Tom sat on the settee with his foot splinted and bound, a crutch lying on the floor next to him. He had apparently not slept well; smudges shone dark beneath his eyes, and his face seemed pale. Captain Courtney and Mr. Blackbird sat in armchairs, looking unsure of how to behave and why they were in the drawing room at all. Malachi stood against the wall on the far side of the room, even though Philip had offered him a seat. His one arm was bandaged and the other in a sling. Philip studied him, wishing he had that man's calm. Malachi seemed to possess self-assurance in every situation, though Philip could see a bit of confusion in *his* eyes as he no doubt wondered why he had been asked to attend the meeting.

The men stood as Anna entered.

She looked around with her brows drawn together and gave a small smile to the gathering. She rubbed a hand on her arm as though she were nervous. But this was her idea, and he had insisted that she propose it to the group. The pirates, at least, seemed to listen to her. And since the proposition heavily involved them, it couldn't hurt to appeal to their—especially their captain's—tender feelings for Anna.

Philip had observed the way Mr. Blackbird slipped into the jungle and returned with reconnaissance without alerting their enemies, the sure way Captain Courtney led his men, and the arsenal of weapons the buccaneers carried. All of this had made him think that just maybe . . . But it wasn't until Anna suggested it that the notion became an idea and then a full-fledged plan; he'd thought of little else the entire night.

Anna greeted each of the men, and Philip indicated for them to be seated.

He remained standing. "Thank you for meeting with us," he said, speaking specifically to the pirates and then turning his head to nod at Tom and Malachi. "Oakely Park is under threat, and we—well, I shall allow Miss Anna to explain." He gave Anna a smile, holding out his hand in an invitation for her to join him, nodding his head in encouragement.

She moved her gaze around the room, opening her mouth and then closing it; then she stood and moved next to him, speaking softly. "I do not know if—"

He leaned closer to speak in her ear. "This was your idea, Miss Trouser-Bargainer."

She clasped her hands behind her back and darted another look to him. Anna took a deep breath. "Gentlemen, you know that highwaymen have made the road to Port Antonio impassable. The only other route from Oakely Park to a seaport leads through the Blue Mountains, and it is obviously too dangerous to transport goods by that road because of bands of Maroons and buccaneers living in the hills." She smiled at Captain Courtney and Mr. Blackbird apologetically.

Both men nodded their agreement. They obviously knew the perilous state of the road as they were likely responsible in part for making it so.

"Lord Philip and all of us at Oakely Park would therefore like to ask for your assistance, sirs. With your band and weapons, we should be able to apprehend the"—Captain Courtney leaned forward, shaking his head. Anna furrowed her brow and continued in a less-confident voice—"highwaymen who threaten—"

She was interrupted again when the captain cleared his throat and held up a hand to stop her words. He stood. "I am truly sorry, but it is impossible." He glanced at Mr. Blackbird, whose expression had remained unchanged since the moment he entered the room. The Indian brave sat straight-backed and still, watching his captain. "If it were up to me, I'd do anythin' you asked, Lady Anna. But the Brethren of the Coast operate as a democracy. I already lost a good ransom yesterday because I was blinded by yer charms. The men, they'll not be convinced to offer assistance again." He bowed, his eyes and nose wrinkled in an apology. "I'm sorry, but I can tell ya now, 'twould result in a mutiny, and I've no desire to lose my position—or my life." He jerked his head to the side, motioning for Mr. Blackbird to rise. "I thank ye for the breakfast, and the libations, and 'twas a delight meetin' ya, my lady, but we'll take our leave now."

"Captain, please, if only you would ask—" Anna began.

"We believe they have a boat," Philip interrupted. "They've taken fifty hogshead from me, and according to the bookkeepers, at least another three plantations have lost goods on their journey to Port Antonio. All of that cargo needs to be transported somehow. Braithwaite wouldn't risk taking it through the Blue Mountains with his small band. The army in Port Antonio is unable to assist us, and as I have no crew to sail a ship loaded with sugar, treacle and"—he glanced at Captain Courtney and saw he had the man's undivided attention. He played his final card—"rum." He drew the word out slowly, not missing the gleam in the pirate's eye.

The captain leaned forward in his chair. "You assume there is a vessel, but you have no proof?"

Philip nodded his head once. "We have none. That is the wager. There are most certainly hundreds of pounds worth of goods hidden on the Landon Grove property. Once the band is abolished, you will profit with or without the boat. Either way, once the highwaymen are conquered, you'll have the stolen goods. I would, however, appreciate it if my mules and horses were returned."

"But if there *is* a boat . . ." Captain Courtney stared at a spot on the carpet, tapping his finger on his lip. "Plenty o' hidden coves to conceal it," he muttered. After a long moment, he raised his gaze. "And what of the other plantation owners? Have they attempted to apprehend the highwaymen?"

"I do not know," Philip confessed. "Dr. Bevan told me this morning that they have taken the same measures as I, speaking with the constable and the colonel at the fort, but were met with the same reply. The local law enforcement does not have the strength to confront the band, and the army is guarding the fort from an attack they fear could come from French forces at Hispaniola at any moment." He watched as the captain shrewdly internalized each of these facts. He may have told too much information to the wrong person—enemies of the crown, and he had just told them that law enforcement on this side of the island was practically nonexistent. But he was asking for their assistance, and they would need to understand that they had his trust.

"I will consult with my men if you don't mind, my lord," Captain Courtney said.

Philip's hopes rose in a wave of anxious energy. "Of course. I would not ask you to enter into any sort of agreement without their consent."

Captain Courtney excused himself and exited the room with Mr. Blackbird following behind.

Anna sank into a chair once they'd left. "I do not know if they will help us. And if not, then whatever will we do?"

The battering ram struck Philip's armaments again. He was touched beyond measure by her disheartened expression and the knowledge that Anna considered his problems to be her own. If only they were. If only the two of them were partners caring for Oakely Park together. If only . . . It seemed that where Anna was concerned, "If only" was his most commonly used phrase.

He sat in the chair next to her. "I think the possibility of a ship and barrels of goods, not to mention the rum, will convince them. What do you think, Tom?" He'd nearly forgotten that Tom and Malachi were in the room. Both had remained silent during the meeting.

"I do not know, my lord. I . . ." Tom rubbed the back of his neck, looking away from Anna's direction.

"Speak, sir. If you have a concern, please do not keep it to yourself."

Tom glanced back at Anna before he spoke. His eyes were tight. "I know Miss Anna trusts the pirates, and I mean no disrespect, but as one with *experience* on the island, I think we should be wary. There is a reason buccaneers are hung at the ports and their bodies left as warnings to others who might dare to imitate their methods. They are villains who would betray us at the first chance."

Philip was surprised. He'd not known Tom to speak so forcefully about anything—aside from coffee. He was surprised not only at the words but their tone. He seemed not only worried but indignant, and the overseer seemed to be directing the majority of his anger toward

Anna. He wondered if Tom felt betrayed that Philip had consulted with Anna instead of him.

"I understand your concern, but try as I might, I cannot think of another plan. And while I myself do not mind avoiding Port Antonio, if we are to turn a profit, we must sell our harvest. I agree that we could be in danger from the pirates—"

"No, they would never—" Anna began.

Philip kept speaking, "But, we did all sleep safe in our beds last night and were not murdered in our sleep. None of our sugar was stolen, and . . . I agree with Anna. The Brethren do not seem averse to using illegal means to achieve their ends, but they seem to be honorable and loyal once they've given their word."

"I still think it is a mistake," Tom said.

"Please tell me if you can think of another way. I am open to propositions. If we do not sell the rest of our harvest, Oakely Park will be lost."

Tom grumbled something and turned away.

Philip was concerned about Tom's reaction. He had already lost one overseer. Tom's main objection seemed to be to the companions and not the plan, and Philip had some of the same worries. Could he trust the pirates? Did he have a choice? He turned to the remaining person in the room. "Malachi, what is your thought?"

The large man studied him with his dark eyes. "I do no' wan' anymo' people to die, sah. The ol' *busha*, he shou' be stopped."

A simple answer, Philip thought, but it had gotten directly to the heart of the matter. "While Horace Braithwaite roams free, each of us is in danger, as is the property. The man is purely evil and has a personal vendetta to settle with me. He did not hesitate to needlessly kill an entire gang of my workers to enact his revenge; he will certainly not stop waylaying our supplies until Oakely Park sinks. He seems to have somehow found others who share his thirst for violence, and Malachi is correct—they must be stopped."

Malachi nodded his head once, but that was the only answer he made to Philip's speech. Tom looked resigned, which Philip guessed to be a victory. He turned to Anna.

Her lips were set in a line, and her brow furrowed. He wondered if she had understood the direness of the circumstances before now.

"Do not worry, Anna," Philip said, wishing he had not spoken so boldly, yet in the same instant knowing that Anna was not the type of woman to be sheltered from the truth.

She nodded and looked as though she would reply when Betty opened the drawing room door and admitted Captain Courtney and Mr. Blackbird.

"We will do it," the captain said before he'd even reached his chair.

"Oh, thank you, Captain," Anna breathed. She pressed her hands to her heart, a gesture that made the captain's eyes turn wistful once again.

Philip felt the exact sentiment but maintained his expression. It was not the time to become overly emotional. "I thank you, sirs."

The captain stepped closer and sat facing Philip. Mr. Blackbird sat next to him. "We will apprehend the highwaymen on the road to Port Antonio and make sure they're not able to continue waylaying shipments from the plantations—either by dispatching them or delivering them to the authorities—your choice, my lord."

Philip nodded.

"In return, we will take the hidden barrels near the river in Landon Grove, and with luck, a ship that is hidden in a cove on the northwest shore. I would ask you not to tell the constable nor the other plantation owners the location of the stolen barrels for at least two days to give us time to relocate our fee. And you will not mention the possibility of a ship to anyone."

Philip stood and held out his hand. "We have an agreement, sir."

Captain Courtney stood and shook his hand. The pirate's eyes were solemn, and Philip knew they had just made a buccaneer's oath.

The captain stepped back and resumed his seat. "Have ya a plan then, my lord?"

Philip sat and then leaned forward in his chair, rubbing his palms together. "I have never undertaken an operation such as this, as you very likely can tell, but I believe it is logical to assume that the highwaymen will attack a group of slaves with a caravan of merchandise since they have done so at least four times."

"And ya want us to follow, out of sight, and when the band is attacked—" Captain Courtney clapped his hands together with a loud smack, grinning.

Philip saw Anna jump at the sound. "Yes and no. My workers are not warriors, Captain. They have no training, no weapons, no experience. To send them unarmed would be signing their death warrants, and I'll not do that." He glanced at Malachi and saw the man was watching him thoughtfully, but no other expression crossed his face.

"So ya want us to wait and hope a group of slaves from another plantation happens to pass?" The pirate furrowed his brow. "We could be waiting for a week, my lord. Even longer."

Philip shook his head. "You and your band will be the slaves." Captain Courtney's brows shot up, but Philip continued before he could speak. He'd formulated the plan in the early hours of the morning and hoped the others would not think it foolish. "Undoubtedly, some will need to follow behind in secret, but I'd like your men to drive the wagonloads toward Port Antonio."

"You do not think the bandits are so daft they'd believe we were slaves?"

"You would need disguises, of course. Hats pulled low, a change of clothing. But the road is lined by trees and shadowed, and I noticed many of your men have very sun-darkened skin. I think the bandits will be fooled, if only briefly, which is all we need. And with weapons hidden among the barrels, we will be ready for an ambush."

"*We*, my lord?" Tom said.

From the corner of his eye, Philip saw Anna's face snap toward him and her mouth open. He didn't give her a chance to speak. "I will accompany you. I would not ask men to risk their lives for my interests if I myself am not willing to do so."

"But, Philip." Anna's voice was soft. "Horace Braithwaite, he will single you out. You cannot . . ." She pressed her lips together and blinked quickly.

He knew she did not want to say more in front of the others. And truthfully he had the same fears. But it was his responsibility to see it through. He was not the same man who'd left London. Working on the plantation had strengthened him. His jackets were tight around his arms and shoulders. And it was not just physically that he'd changed. He knew he could not depend on others to do the job just because he was the master of the plantation. He felt a duty and an obligation to Oakely Park as well as to the men who would defend it.

He forced a teasing smile to his lips. "Miss, you have so little faith in my combat abilities? I'll have you know that not every gentleman in London worries only about fashionable waistcoats or drinking tea at garden parties. My sword master was quite proud of my skills, and I did study pugilism under Gentleman John Jackson. I am not completely useless in a fight." He hoped she couldn't see his real fear. He had never fought in an actual battle where his life was on the line.

"I did not mean to imply—I am sorry, my lord. I just . . ."

He tipped his head and winked. "You just forgot that yesterday I killed a crocodile? I thought that was quite heroic. And I did protect you from the butterfly."

"No, of course, sir. I apologize." Anna turned her gaze to her hands in her lap. Her jaw was clenched, and she swallowed hard. His teasing had not allayed her fears.

Philip felt guilty for making light of her concerns. Horace no doubt had designs on him as she feared, but he had a deeper worry—he had seen the expression on his former overseer's face when he stared at Anna. As Malachi said, the man needed to be stopped. If his reign of terror was not ended, Philip had no doubt that Horace had designs on Anna, and the very idea sent panic through his chest. He would see to it once and for all that this was ended. His plantation, his workers, and his Anna—*Anna*, he corrected himself—would be safe.

"We'll need a strategy. Tell me what ya know about this band then. How do they fight?" Captain Courtney asked. "What weapons 'ave they?"

Philip waved Malachi closer. "Malachi survived their last attack."

Anna stood quickly, and the men rose as well, Tom with an enormous grunt. "I apologize. If you'll excuse me, I shall assist Betty with the noon meal." She hurried from the room without looking back.

Philip knew she was upset, and his chest was warmed to know it was because she was worried about him. Aside from his mother fretting when he left London, he didn't believe anyone had shown such concern for his welfare, and in spite of the discussion of battle strategies and his eminent danger, the knowledge made his chest light.

The meeting took much longer than Philip had imagined. He was amazed by Captain Courtney's thoroughness when it came to stratagem. He knew each of his men's strengths, their particular weapons, and the best position for them in the campaign. He discussed weather, laid out the road, and devised different scenarios and their ability to react to every eventuality imaginable. Tom and Malachi participated in the planning even though their injuries would prevent them from joining the party.

Philip glanced out the window at the front lawn and saw the other buccaneers mingling in groups or resting. He was surprised how well behaved the men were. In fact, so far everything about the pirates had surprised him. He'd imagined them to be undisciplined savages—attacking, plundering, killing without a second thought—but the last two days had shown them to be organized, careful, and, judging by their captain, quite intelligent.

The door opened, and Betty and Anna delivered a luncheon.

Anna did not meet his gaze as she placed a tray of fruit and meat on the low table. Her lips were pursed, but somehow it did nothing to diminish her beauty. He was extremely proud of the way she had presented their case to the pirates and how she cared for Oakely Park. Her concern for the mission touched his heart. He would need to speak to her before he left. He couldn't leave things unsaid when there was a chance that he'd not have another opportunity.

Finally, in the late afternoon, they adjourned to begin their preparations. With any luck, they'd be ready to leave the next morning. Philip stood and shook every man's hand as they exited the room.

Malachi was the last to depart. He clasped Philip's offered hand. "I will protect her," he said in his deep voice.

Philip raised his brows.

"Miss Anna. I know you worry, sah. I watch over yo' house while you are gone."

"Thank you," Philip said. The immense relief at having this man protect the people he cared for washed over him like a cool wave. "I do worry. You, of all people, know what Horace Braithwaite is capable of."

Malachi nodded. "I know dis too well, sah. De ol' *busha*, he a wicked man."

"I am lucky to have you at Oakely Park, Malachi. Perhaps when I return, we can discuss your position? I hoped you would perhaps consider assisting Mr. Norton in the overseer duties while he establishes a coffee farm."

Malachi's eyes squinted the smallest bit. He lifted his chin slightly, and his lips spread in a smile. "Perhaps, sah," he said before he strode out the door.

Chapter 20

ANNA ROSE EARLY THE NEXT morning to bid farewell to the men as they set off on their journey. The previous day had been filled with preparations. Ezekiel had run back and forth from the slave's village, delivering coarsely woven, thin clothing for the pirates to wear. He even managed to procure a variety of broad-rimmed hats to complete their disguises.

Men had loaded wagons, discussed strategies, and prepared weapons late into the evening. Anna spent the majority of the day assisting Betty in the kitchen building, as feeding twelve extra men took quite a bit more work. She'd only seen Philip a handful of times after the meeting, and each was merely in passing. She still didn't know what to say to him. The idea of him participating in the trap—in the battle filled her insides with lead. She didn't think she could speak to him without her emotions getting away from her.

Philip was a gentleman, not a combatant, no matter what training he'd had in London. As the day had progressed, so had her dread. Guilt that the entire mission had been her idea overwhelmed her. If something were to happen to him—to any of them . . . She couldn't bear to allow her mind to travel that path.

Anna swallowed back her tears as she hurriedly dressed and left her bedchamber. She stepped through the front doors and in the faint, predawn light saw the men preparing the mules and carts. She could feel the excitement in the air, but it only increased her dread. A chill ran over her skin as she spied swords, sabers, muskets, and even axes hidden beneath the canvas covering the barrels. Her stomach turned from heavy to sour. As she scanned the scene, looking for the plantation owner, Captain Courtney approached.

"Good morning, Lady Anna. Fine day, is it not?" He strode toward her with his white smile flashing.

She forced a smile to her own face. "Yes, Captain. And again, I must thank you for what you are doing for us—I mean for Oakely Park."

He offered his arm and led her down the stairs and along the pathway. They walked in silence, passing by the groups of men loading the carts and then strolling a bit farther. Once they were out of earshot, he stopped and turned to her, taking her hand from his arm and holding it in his. "I'll not allow any harm to come to Lord Philip. You have my word."

Anna was startled by the intensity in his gaze and the directness of his statement. She felt her cheeks flush. "I do not know what to say, Captain. I obviously desire all of you to return safely . . ."

He placed his other hand over hers. "My lady, I have, ah . . . known women all over this world. As ya may have realized, I've a soft heart for ladies. But if any one of them had ever looked at me the way you look at 'is lordship, I'd've left the sea in an instant. I confess I'm mighty jealous."

Anna's flush deepened, but she did not sense any judgment in his words, only kindness. They turned back toward the group, who had finished loading the wagons and appeared to be nearly ready to depart.

Philip was still nowhere to be seen.

When they arrived at the Great House steps, Mr. Blackbird motioned to Captain Courtney.

"I bid you farewell, my lady, and don't forget my pledge. Set your mind at ease." He bowed and turned to go.

The lump in Anna's throat grew as she looked at the group of men. She did not know which of them would return. She placed her hand on his arm. "I care about all of you, Captain. Even though you attempt to convince me that you and your band are blackhearted scoundrels, I have found you to be quite the opposite." She stood on tiptoe and kissed his cheek. "I wish you well, Captain Alastair Courtney."

The grin returned accompanied by increased color in his sun-darkened cheeks. He cleared his throat, bowed his head again, and left to join Mr. Blackbird.

Anna turned and found Philip standing in the doorway. A sword was strapped to his belt, and two muskets protruded from the waist of his trousers. He wore only his shirtsleeves with no cravat, jacket, or waistcoat. His hair was tied back in a string, but without a hat, it blew over his forehead. Even though he was not filthy, unshaven, and scarred like the rest of the group, he appeared every bit the swashbuckling adventurer.

Anna could not help but stare at the dashing gentleman-turned-pirate, and a flush of heat surged over her, leaving her slightly breathless.

Philip's gaze was on her as he stepped down the stairs and strode toward her. "I noticed Captain Courtney received a kiss. Do you reserve your affection for true buccaneers, or might I ask for the same treatment?" He touched a finger to his cheek, and one side of his mouth lifted in a smile.

"You look like a buccaneer, my lord." Anna's throat tightened, and she fought to keep back the tears she could feel stinging the backs of her eyes. Would Philip return from the mission?

"Good," he said, waggling his brows up and down and turning his cheek toward her.

How could he possibly tease at a time like this? Anna wondered. She didn't know how he remained so easy when her insides were tied into knots. She leaned forward and pressed a kiss to his cheek, closing her eyes and breathing in his spicy smell. When she pulled away, tears filled her eyes. She blinked, and they escaped to roll down her cheeks.

All traces of playfulness fell from his face in an instant. He slid a hand beneath her ear and wiped his thumb over her wet cheek. "Do not fear, Anna. In a few hours, all will be well." His gaze held hers, and for just an instant, his confidence slipped, revealing vulnerability in his eyes. And something else as well—fear?

The sight brought a fresh wave of tears. "I am sorry, Philip. I did not mean to act like a ninny this morning."

"I will return, Anna."

Her throat closed, and her tears blinded her until she closed her eyes. "How can you know for sure?" she whispered and immediately wished she hadn't. She didn't want Philip to think she had any doubts that he would succeed.

"I will because I must." He lifted her chin, and she raised her eyes to his. "I will because I know you are here." He brushed the back of his fingers over her cheek and departed.

Anna wanted to run away and hide or to strap on a saber of her own and join them, but she knew now what Philip needed. He needed her confidence.

She climbed the steps and watched as the group set off. She forced a smile to her face and waved until Philip caught her eye one last time. As soon as they were out of sight, Anna's shoulders slumped, and she brushed away the tears from her cheeks.

Ezekiel appeared on the step next to her and offered a handkerchief. Even he had lost his smile.

"Thank you," she said, wanting to embrace the boy but knowing it would only embarrass him.

"His lordship will come back, Miss Anna."

Anna nodded.

Ezekiel opened the door and held it for her, but she didn't want to enter the empty house. "I think I will take a walk, Ezekiel. Would you join me?"

"Sorry, miss. I must press my lord's cravats."

"Of course."

Ezekiel bowed and entered the house, leaving her alone.

Anna walked slowly down the steps. She didn't want to continue in the direction the men had gone, so she strolled around the side of the house and made a point of admiring the colorful flowers.

An image flashed into her mind. *I am on a dock, held in my father's arms, waving a handkerchief toward a ship.* Who was she waving at? Was the ship arriving or departing? She tried but could not see her father's face. Still, somehow she knew that was who it was. The surety that she had a father, that he held her in his arms, comforted her.

Her tears slowed, and she no longer felt desperate and frantic. She was resigned, as was Philip, that this was the best course. Captain Courtney and his men were fighters. She remembered the sure way they had handled their weapons, and it comforted her a bit more. Remembering the pirate captain's promise helped as well. He would protect Philip, and a pirate's oath is worth its weight in gold.

She knew Philip was grateful to be *doing* something instead of looking over his shoulder every moment in trepidation, worrying about what Horace might do. This time they had the element of surprise, which gave them an advantage. That knowledge eased the fear but did not completely abolish it.

Anna rounded the corner of the house and came face to face with Malachi. She gasped. "Oh my. You startled me."

He stepped back. "Excuse me. I did no' mean to scare you."

Anna's heartbeat sped up as it did each time she'd saw the man. But she did not feel the shiver of fear accompanying it. Malachi didn't seem as intimidating as he had before. "I am not scared."

He smiled slightly, watching her. He pointed to the scars on his forehead and cheeks. "Dis is frighten you befo'."

"Yes." Anna blushed as she admitted it. "But it does not frighten me now."

His eyes squinted, and he nodded once. He pointed at her bare arm. "De firs' time I see men wit' white skin, I t'ought dey was devils. Dey climb over de wall of my village and take me and my sister away from our home. I was frighten' of de strange talk and hairy faces."

"They *were* devils, Malachi." She studied his face. Beneath the mask of scars, his eyes were kind, sad even, and she found that she was not frightened at all. "I was going to see if Betty needed help in the kitchen building. Would you like to walk with me?"

He dipped his head and walked next to her toward the back of the Great House.

Anna glanced at him from the side of her eye. Malachi was still the largest man she had ever seen, but in his low voice and soft tones she perceived a gentle giant instead of the menacing hulk she had assumed him to be. "What happened to your sister?" she asked, hoping that she wouldn't offend him by prying into his personal life. "Is she here in Oakley Park?"

"When we come to Jamaica, the ol' *busha* take me, but I will not leave wit' ou' her. So he take her too. When he wan' to punish me, he punish her. And one time, he sen' her far away"—Malachi's expression did not change, but his eyes were pained—"to punish me," he finished softly.

"Do you know where she is now?"

"She is dead."

"I am so sorry. What was her name?"

"Aminata," he said in a quiet voice. "I call her Ami."

Anna thought of a frightened brother and sister taken from their homes and forced into slavery. The only family Malachi had was gone, and her heart ached for him.

"I work hard. Buy my free papers. Seven years. Den I work to buy hers. But when I get to Whitehouse, she is already dead."

"Whitehouse?" Anna said slowly. The story sounded familiar. Betty had said her friend went to Whitehouse. "Is Ezekiel Ami's son?"

"Yes." Malachi raised his brows and turned to her.

Anna turned over the information in her head. The pieces of the puzzle tumbled around, and her mind worked to put them together. "And you purchased *his* freedom instead."

He nodded again.

"And Ezekiel's leg—the injury happened while he was at Whitehouse?" Anna could not imagine Malachi would have allowed the boy to be harmed under his care. It must have happened before.

"De doctor say his leg was broke and not put right. It healed badly."

Poor Ezekiel. A child with a broken leg seemed such a simple thing for a doctor to mend. Anna's chest ached. They rounded the back corner of the house and neared the kitchen building.

"Why would you return to Oakely Park and its cruel overseer when you and Ezekiel were free to go anywhere you like?" Anna asked. *Betty.* The last piece clicked into place, and she spoke before he could answer her. "You returned for Betty."

He said nothing, but Anna saw the truth in his eyes. And along with it, fear. She realized why his feelings for Betty were kept secret. Malachi knew if they were discovered, the relationship could be used against him as his sister's life had been.

Anna stopped walking and turned to him. "I'll not reveal your private affairs, Malachi. You can trust me."

He was quiet as he watched her, and finally he raised his chin. "T'ank you." His gaze moved to the kitchen building and then back to her. "When yo' life is no' yo' own, you hold those t'ings dat are yours close to yo' heart."

Anna felt a rush of compassion for this man. For Betty. For Ezekiel. For all the slaves in Jamaica. People who suffered physical and emotional pain and found their only strength in concealing the things that made them human.

They walked the remainder of the distance in silence, and when they reached the kitchen building, Anna opened the door and peeked inside. Betty was not there.

"Maybe she is in the house," Anna said.

They crossed the small court to the outer dining room door. Malachi held it for her, but before she stepped inside, they both paused, hearing a sound from the front yard.

"Horses," Anna said, rushing past Malachi into the house. She hurried through the dining room, down the hallway, and into the drawing room to watch from the large windows. Had the company returned so soon? Had everything gone to plan? Was it really over? She stepped into the bay of the windows and peered up the lane.

A grand carriage—an open landau—pulled by four horses approached. Anna's stomach hardened as she recognized the lone passenger. Clarissa Stapleton.

Chapter 21

PHILIP FOLLOWED MR. BLACKBIRD THROUGH the jungle on the side of the road. It didn't matter how carefully he tried; he could not make his footsteps and movements as silent as his companion's. He had learned—through very few words on Mr. Blackbird's part—that the man was an Iroquois of the Mohawk tribe. His people were driven from their land in New York after the Americans revolted against the Crown. The tribe settled in Canada, where they joined with the British to fight against the American colonists.

Mr. Blackbird had been a crew member of a ship Captain Courtney had captured and had joined the buccaneers without question. His former captain was "not fond of Indians." The statement was the only clue Mr. Blackbird gave as to his experience in the navy, but the way in which he said it gave Philip reason to believe he had been treated cruelly.

They pushed through the vegetation without the benefit of a machete to clear a path, trying to keep the wagons in view while they themselves remained hidden. Mostly it was the noise of horses and the creaks of the wooden wheels that kept them apprised of the caravan's position. They lagged behind—trying to keep fifty meters between them and the wagons. When the highwaymen attacked, they would be surrounded and caught unawares.

He thought of how different this journey was than the one of the day before. When he'd walked with Anna, he'd not even noticed the heat and the insects and the scratching branches. Their outing had started out pleasant, enjoyable even. He'd watched Anna study every flower, bird, even insect with interest, and even now, his mind turned to her, wondering how she fared after they'd left Oakely Park. Though she had put on a brave face, he had seen apprehension in her eyes.

Philip's cheek tingled where Anna had kissed him. He pressed his fingers to the spot, remembering the softness of her touch. Her eyes had been wet and frightened, and the sight of her lip trembling made his heart twinge. He would do almost anything to keep her from tears.

But this mission, it was the only way to keep Oakely Park—and Anna—free from the threat of Horace Braithwaite, and her safety had moved to the top of his list of priorities.

How had he allowed this to happen? He grimaced. He had promised himself that his heart would not be hurt again. And now he was in precisely the positon he had vowed never to allow himself to fall into. He was in love with Anna.

The thought took him by surprise, and he released a branch with a snap, earning a backward look from Mr. Blackbird. Why did Philip insist on setting himself along paths that ultimately ended in pain?

He glanced at the road through a gap in the trees, wondering how close they were to the ambush point. It couldn't be much farther. They'd been walking for well over an hour. He strained his ears, but the sound of the wagons was all he heard.

They continued on, and Philip thought for sure the wagons must have passed the spot where the road turned. What if the highwaymen didn't take the bait? Would he be able to persuade Captain Courtney to make another attempt? He thought it would take quite a bit of rum and Anna's sweet talking to convince them again. What if the bandits had filled up their ship and were preparing, even now, to sail away from the island? Philip did not think the pirates would be very understanding if that was the case.

He strained his ears. His gut told him that Horace was after more than merely sugar and rum. Horace was a man blinded by revenge, and Philip didn't think he would be satisfied until Oakely Park was ruined and his former employer destroyed.

He was so intent on his thoughts he didn't notice that Mr. Blackbird had halted until he nearly collided with him.

The pirate held a finger in front of his lips and pulled a dagger from his belt. His head was cocked, and he motioned with his eyes toward the road ahead of them. Philip didn't notice anything different, but Mr. Blackbird lifted his dagger and dipped his head once.

Philip's muscles clenched, and energy shot through his veins, making his pulse race. He wondered if his companion could hear Philip's heart banging on his ribs and in his eardrums.

A shot sounded, and Mr. Blackbird burst from the trees and ran up the road toward the wagons.

Philip drew his sword and followed. More shots. Shouts. Clangs of swords. Mr. Blackbird plunged into the fray.

The scene before him was chaos. Philip squinted through the smoke and dust, trying to make sense of what was happening. A man with a sword rushed toward him. Philip barely had time to raise his blade in defense before the other crashed against it with such force that it threw him off balance. His hours of training took over, and he shifted his weight, twisting to throw his attacker backward, responding with a blow of his own that knocked the man off his feet.

The man rolled, grabbed a handful of sand from the road, and threw it into Philip's face.

Philip's eyes burned, and he rubbed at them frantically, trying to see through the tears.

His opponent's foot swept around, striking Philip's knees, causing them to buckle. He fell forward and rolled out of the way as the man lunged at him. The sword sliced into his arm. Philip jumped to his feet, his eyes streaming. His arm felt like it was on fire.

The man dove toward him, taking the offensive, and Philip twisted out of the path of his blade, looking for an advantage as he favored his wounded arm. Luckily, the cut was not deep. He had never faced an opponent who did not honor the rules of swordsmanship, and he realized that if he were to gain the upper hand, he would have to fight underhanded as well.

He blocked another swing then stepped forward quickly, planting his fist in the man's jaw. While the man blinked and shook his head, Philip shoved him backward and thrust with his sword. The man blocked weakly, and his weapon flew from his hand.

When the man was disarmed, a member of the pirate band grabbed him, tying the highwayman's hands with rope.

Philip stepped back, breathing heavily. He lowered his sword to the ground, staring at the man. It was unnerving to look into the eyes of a person who had, a moment earlier, tried to kill him, and the calm way the man watched him sent a chill over his skin. He turned away and saw that the confusion of a few moments ago had settled. The highwaymen were outnumbered and overpowered. He let out a relieved breath. From the corner of his eye, Philip saw a man spring from behind the cart next to him, weapon raised.

Philip's heart froze. There was no time to think or lift his weapon in defense. He could only watch, knowing that in an instant the blade would cleave into him.

But before the man's sword made contact, it was deflected with a loud clang by another. Captain Courtney had leaped between them, blocking the strike. But in doing so, he left his side open, and the man swung around, plunging his sword into the captain's torso.

Philip whirled around to help the captain.

Captain Courtney swung an elbow into the man's face and kicked forward, but his strength failed and he sank to his knees.

Philip felt a swell of rage course through him. He dove at the attacker, driving him away from the pirate captain with renewed energy. His strikes were not well planned, but they were forceful, one after another until the man weakened from blocking them and was disarmed and taken to join his friends.

Philip hurried toward Captain Courtney. He sat on the ground, his back against a wagon wheel. Mr. Blackbird and another man had lifted his shirt and were examining his wound.

The captain ground his teeth. "'Tis no worse than any blows I've taken before. Tend to the others." His voice didn't carry its usual note of command, and his face was chalk white.

Philip knelt next to him. "Captain Courtney, sir, I—"

"Don't thank me, yer lordship. I'll not have it. I came to fight and managed some blasted good blows if I do say so myself. Besides, what would that young lady say should I bring ya home in a sack?" He winced as Mr. Blackbird pressed a cloth against his side. "I acted for her alone, and don't ya be forgettin' it."

"I understand, Captain."

Captain Courtney closed his eyes, leaning his head back.

Philip stood. He dusted off his trousers as he looked around. A few skirmishes continued, but they were quickly ended and the highwaymen subdued. At least three men lay in the road, unmoving, and others moaned and held their wounds.

He resheathed his sword, and the sting of the gash on his arm burned fresh. His shirt was torn, and blood was spreading down his sleeve.

Dizziness overtook him as the energy left his system and the terror of what had just occurred hit him. He leaned a hand against the wagon, breathing hard.

He looked toward the group of prisoners, fiercely relieved to see Horace Braithwaite sitting among them with his hands tied. The former overseer's eyes were merely slits, and his lip curled, exposing his teeth in a snarl. The glare he fixed on Philip was so full of hatred that Philip could have sworn the man's eyes glowed red.

Philip could not wait to see Braithwaite behind bars.

He turned away and saw that, with their captain injured, the other pirates now looked to Mr. Blackbird for leadership. It was determined that even though they were closer to Oakely Park than Port Antonio, all able-bodied men were needed to both transport the injured and keep the prisoners under guard. Each side had suffered one casualty.

The empty barrels were left on the side of the road to retrieve later. The injured pirates rode in one wagon, and the prisoners sat next to the bodies in another.

"We should 'ave known they wasn't Negroes when we saw their boots," one of the highwaymen grumbled.

Philip walked ahead with Mr. Blackbird. He wanted to explain to the constable what had happened before the remainder of the group arrived. The constable would more readily take a nobleman's word over a band of pirates who had fought with a band of highwaymen.

Philip also needed to find a doctor for his friends. As the thought crossed his mind, he could not help the wry smile that pulled at his mouth. Who would have thought when he left London merely a few months ago he would come to consider a band of buccaneers to be as loyal friends as any he'd known? His life was so different than he would have ever imagined, and he found he liked it. He was proud of the man he had become in Jamaica. He realized that if he'd stayed in England

and married Jacqueline, he would have remained a spoiled, arrogant fool, all his goals in life revolving around status and diversion.

When he reached the town, he hurried directly to the constabulary.

The constable raised his brows when he saw Philip's clothing, but the lawman said nothing.

Philip spoke quickly, explaining as thoroughly as possible so as to leave no doubt as to the identity of the true villains when the two bands arrived.

The constable listened, astonished, to Philip's story. He had received various complaints about the highwaymen, and he was relieved that the menace was eradicated—and with very little effort on his part. "Well done, my lord," he said, shaking Philip's hand.

They stepped out into the main square to await the caravan, and Philip sent a boy for a doctor.

When the wagons arrived, the constable took the bound men into the gaol, and Philip accompanied the buccaneers to the hospital, ensuring that they were properly treated and that the expense for their care was paid in full.

The doctor stopped him as he was leaving, reminding Philip of his own injury. The doctor stitched the gash closed before he attended to the buccaneers.

Philip accompanied the remainder of the pirates to the small tavern, purchasing enough rum to keep them occupied until their crewmembers were ready to travel. Then he walked back to the constabulary to deliver his statement against Horace Braithwaite and his men.

The colonel from the fort had joined the constable, and Philip told them the entire story of their adventure the previous day, including the murder of two slaves at Landon Grove, and the slaughter of his own workers prior to that. He recounted each detail to the best of his memory, his account lasting well over an hour.

When he was finished, the constable asked him to sign a statement. "With your testimony, my lord, we've enough evidence for Horace Braithwaite to hang."

Philip nodded. He thought that the news would have made him cheer, but the idea of a man losing his life—even a vile man such as Horace—left him feeling somber. He signed the document and accompanied the constable to the cells in order to identify Horace.

The gaol was a stone building with iron bars. The cells were small and damp and hardly large enough for seven men.

The constable lifted his lantern, illuminating the scowling faces of the men in one cell.

Philip shook his head.

They moved to the next, and by the flickering light, Philip studied each man's face. Horace was not among them. He looked at the constable. "Sir, he is not among these men. Where are the remainder of the prisoners?"

"There are no other prisoners, my lord."

"Ye'll not find 'im 'ere," a man said. He glowered at his captors.

Philip felt the beginnings of panic. "Speak up, man. Where is your leader?"

"Gone and left us, 'e 'as. Escaped 'isself and left us to hang."

Full-blown terror exploded in Philip's chest. He ran through the door of the gaol, knowing exactly where Horace had gone. *Anna!*

Chapter 22

ANNA SAT IN THE SMALL parlour, listening as Betty answered the front door and admitted the visitor. She and Betty had both agreed that Ezekiel was not to appear at all while the woman was in the house. Clarissa's voice rang through the hall as she complained about the absence of a proper butler or footman to taker her hat and gloves.

Betty opened the parlour door, and Clarissa pushed past her into the room. "Miss Clarissa Stapleton," Betty announced the visitor, catching Anna's gaze and raising her brows behind Clarissa before dipping in a curtsy and exiting the room.

"Miss Stapleton." Anna rose and attempted what she hoped was a pleasant smile even though the last time she had seen the woman, she had hoped never to have the misfortune of encountering her again. "I am afraid Lord Philip is not home today."

"Obviously, as I am a *lady*, I did not come to call on the gentleman," Clarissa said, sniffing and glancing around the room. She located the softest seat and sat with a flounce that set her ringlets springing.

Please have a seat, Anna thought as she sat on the chair across from her. "So have you come to call on me then?"

"Yes, of course," Clarissa said, glancing toward the doorway and then out the window. "When will Lord Philip return?" She opened a fan and began to wave it in front of her face.

"I do not know. His lordship naturally does not explain his schedule to me." Anna was deliberately vague about Philip's whereabouts. She didn't know how much he wanted to share with the other plantation owners concerning his deal with the buccaneers, especially since their stolen goods were part of the promised reward. Besides, she didn't want to speak with Clarissa any longer than necessary.

"Of course he does not. And how is the trouble with your . . ." Clarissa made a swirling motion with her finger and pointed to her forehead.

"I appreciate your very kind concern, but I am afraid my memory is still missing."

"I have sent inquiries myself to everyone I can think of. We must get this mess sorted out," Clarissa said. "Obviously we cannot have you living at Oakely Park forever. His lordship has expressed an interest in marriage, and I am certain having an indefinite houseguest is the only thing that could be detaining his offer to me." She fixed Anna with a look that expressed exactly how much she loathed Anna's presence. "I, of course, will not tolerate the imposition when I am mistress. There must be a church man or someone who will take you."

Anna's vision clouded, and heat rose from her chest to her head. She actually thought her skull might burst from the pressure of her rage. She did not believe it would be possible for her to completely abhor another human being as much as she detested Clarissa Stapleton. She couldn't even think of a reply and knew that anything she could say would spurt from her mouth in a torrent of fury. The idea of that woman in her beloved Oakely Park, abusing the servants, changing the furnishings, demanding to be treated as a spoiled princess. And married to Philip. The thought sickened her stomach and left her light-headed.

Anna breathed in and out to calm herself and stood, balling her fists. "I am sorry that Lord Philip is not here. And what a pity that you must be leaving after so short a visit." She walked to the door and opened it.

"Do not presume to send me away, miss. It is *I* who should dismiss *you*. I do not believe for one moment that you are an innocent victim. I am not so easily taken in. You are a charlatan, and I intend to inform his lordship of your deception. Loss of memory, indeed."

Anna called to Betty. "Please fetch Miss Stapleton's things." Her hands trembled, and she clasped them behind her back.

Clarissa stood slowly and sauntered toward her. "I will depart when I am wholly ready."

"Very well, Miss Stapleton. If you will excuse me then." Anna left the room and marched into the hallway.

Clarissa followed. "How jealous the ladies at the Governor's Ball will be when *I* am Lady Philip, a member of the nobility and wife to the son of a marquess. I shall have my own title and shall outrank nearly every other woman on this island aside from Lady Lockwood, of course."

Lady Lockwood. The name repeated in her mind, and Anna froze with her hand on the stair railing. "What did you say?"

Clarissa snatched her gloves from Betty and pulled them on. She lifted her shoulders in a shrug. "Amelia Becket of Spanish Town, a woman of no consequence, sailed away three years ago and married an earl. Society has talked of little else, but before long . . ."

Anna did not hear the rest of her words. She hardly noticed when Betty led her to a chair. *Lady Lockwood, Amelia . . .* Anna's mind churned as images assailed her. *Captain Fletcher held the book to her; Nico's sword was lost on deck.* The bits of recollection spread, forming complete sections in her mind and then connecting with others. *The ship. The storm.* It was all there. Every bit. She closed her eyes and put her hand to her forehead. She remembered her parents, her childhood. *Laughter, riding her pony, country dances . . . the dark day her father learned his business partners had cheated him, moving to a cold, damp house in London, her parents growing ill and dying . . . the vicar finding Anna a situation as a chamber maid.*

She had sailed on a ship and fallen into the sea. Gasping for breath as the waves buried her . . . She remembered it all. She even remembered her name. *Anna Wheeler.*

No blank spots remained, and Anna gasped at the intensity of the emotions associated with memories she had forgotten. They returned with such force that she felt as though she relived each of them. Anna Wheeler—she was not married, not engaged. Her chest was light as she realized she was free from any other attachments. But the reality crashed in, dashing her hopes to bits. She was also not wealthy. Not even a small bit. She had nothing. She was a maid, a servant, and should not have feelings for a nobleman in the first place. Philip . . . they could never . . .

Anna breathed heavily and noticed she had broken out in a sweat. She lifted her eyes to find Betty's face in front of her. Her friend's expression was pulled with worry. "Betty, I remem—"

The crack of a gunshot stopped her words. Anna jumped to her feet as the front door flew open and hit the wall with a crash.

Horace Braithwaite stood in the opening.

Clarissa screamed, and Horace struck her with the back of his hand, sending her into the wall. She crumpled to the ground.

Fear flowed cold through Anna's stomach as her own situation paled in regard to the fact that if Horace Braithwaite was here and Philip was not . . . *Philip!* What had happened? "Run, Betty!"

Betty ran from the hall, and Anna followed but was pulled back when Horace grabbed her. His large hand squeezed around her arm painfully, and she jerked, trying to pull it from his grasp. A primal scream forced its way from her throat.

The pistol in his hand still smoked, and he tossed it aside. It landed with a clatter on the wooden floor. Anna pulled and twisted, trying to free herself from his iron grip. Her breathing came fast and sounded loud in her ears.

"Struggling will do ya no good. But if it makes ya feel better, by all means, have at it."

Anna kicked at his legs. She pulled at his fingers with her other hand but couldn't loosen them. *Where is Malachi?*

Horace picked at his teeth, watching with an indifferent expression as Anna became more desperate to escape. He seemed to be waiting for her to tire.

Anna was determined to flee. She lunged forward, digging her fingernails into his face and scratching at his eyes.

He howled and released his grip, pressing his hands against his face.

Anna bolted for the stairs. She scrambled upward, resisting the impulse to turn around. Her vision was spotted, and her mind felt sluggish. She grasped onto the only thought she could manage. *Escape.*

Horace grasped her ankles, and Anna fell forward, banging her arms and knees on the stairs. She didn't even register the pain and continued to climb.

He seized her around the waist and carried her up the stairs, struggling and kicking and screaming, into a bedchamber. He threw her on the floor and locked the door behind them.

Anna tried to run to the veranda door, but Horace took hold of her arms and pulled her away.

He turned her toward him, pressing his face so close she could smell his foul breath. One arm was wrapped around her waist, and the other held her wrists together. The scratches around his eye were bright red and inflamed. "I told ya it would do no good." His gaze dropped to her pendant, and he pulled it, snapping the chain. He held it up, tipped it, then grinned at her. "Hello, Anna."

She did not think she had ever truly seen evil in a person's eyes as she did now. Anna strained in his grip but could not budge. Her gaze darted to the door, wishing that someone would enter, but at the same time her heart tightened as she imagined Ezekiel or Betty coming in. She knew Horace wouldn't hesitate to harm them.

"And now, where to begin . . ." He bared his yellowing teeth in a malevolent grin.

"Where is Philip?" Anna's voice was a sob.

Horace's eyes narrowed, and his lip curled in a sneer. "Do not fear. His lordship is at this very moment escorting my band of fools to the gallows."

Anna felt a small bloom of relief. At least Philip was alive.

"That blasted nobleman has taken everything from me, and I have decided to repay the favor." He thrust Anna into a chair and stood, towering over her.

Anna clutched the armrests, shaking her head. "Please, do not hurt him."

Horace slid a thin blade from his belt. The hiss it made caused Anna to tremble.

He studied the blade, turning it back and forth. "There are better ways to destroy a man than killing him. I intend to take away everything he cares about. Starting with you."

"Please, no."

"Do not worry. I'll not kill you right away. I want his lordship to know I took my time with ya."

Anna couldn't take her eyes from the blade in his hand. Her heart beat so forcefully that it hurt her chest.

"And don't be holding out hope for rescue. With the big Negro bleeding out on the front steps and the pathetic band of buccaneers in Port Royal, all of your protectors are gone. No one will disturb us for hours."

He lowered the blade.

Anna jerked, pulling away from him. He held her shoulder against the back of the chair and pressed the cold metal to her collarbone. He applied pressure, and she felt it pierce her skin. A warmth trickled beneath her neck.

She closed her eyes, determined not to scream. She should be coming up with a plan to escape, but terror stole her ability to think.

Another cut stole her breath, and against her will, she whimpered.

"I was hoping for a bit more screaming," Horace leaned his face close until she could feel his hot breath on her face. "Do you know how long it takes a person to bleed to death? We have hours to—"

A banging sounded on the door, and Anna's heart dropped when she heard Ezekiel's voice on the other side calling her name.

Horace's face twisted into a grin. He left her and strode toward the door.

"Run, Ezekiel!" Anna yelled. She pressed her hand to her bleeding neck. Sobs clogged her throat. "Run away!"

Horace pulled the door open, but it was not Ezekiel outside.

Malachi stepped into the room and yanked the blade away, dropping it to the floor. He grabbed Horace's head in his large hands and jerked it to the side so fast and sharp that it took a moment for Anna to realize what he'd done.

Anna covered her eyes as a sickening thump vibrated through the room.

Malachi pulled her hands from her face and crouched down in front of her. She saw that blood seeped from a wound on his side, near his waist. He tipped her head and looked at her bleeding neck. Ezekiel and Betty stood behind him.

Betty held her hands pressed against her mouth, her eyes wide as she looked back and forth between Horace and Anna. She blinked and shook her head. "Ezekiel, fetch de doctor," she said.

Ezekiel's face was ashen, and he stared as if shocked. Her words roused him, and he hurried from the room.

Anna couldn't contain her sobs. She collapsed forward into Malachi's arms, clinging to his shirt and weeping.

"It is all done now, Miss Anna. De man will no' hurt you anymo'." He patted her back.

Anna sat on the floor with her cheek resting against his chest. The emotions of the past hour were more than she could bear. The pain and horror of Horace Braithwaite, the rage she'd felt at Clarissa Stapleton, and the return of her memories all combined to a flood of tears that she couldn't have held back if she'd wanted to.

Betty knelt next to them. She used a wet cloth to wipe the blood from Anna's neck and collarbone, then she pressed it to the cuts. "Hol' still, miss," she said, placing a hand on Anna's cheek and smiling gently.

Anna tried, but she couldn't stop shaking.

Betty guided Anna's hand to press against the cloth while she turned to inspect Malachi's wound. The large man kept his arm around Anna. Betty pressed a cloth to the bloody hole in his side and spoke to him in the pidgin language.

Anna thought she must be imagining it when she heard Philip's voice calling her name, but a moment later, he rushed into the bedchamber followed by the doctor.

His eyes took in the scene. He looked from Horace's body to the trio on the floor. "Anna!" He rushed forward. "What happened? There is blood all over the house. I thought . . ." Malachi lifted her gently away from his chest.

"Thank you," Philip said to the man. Anna thought she heard his voice hitch.

Anna's tears returned in full. She pulled her knees to her chest, rubbed her hand over her cheeks, and sniffled. "I am sorry," she managed to say with her catching voice. "I don't mean to cry. I was just so scared."

Philip moved closer, putting his arms around her shoulders. "Do not apologize." He studied her face and lifted her chin, pulling down her hand and the bloody cloth. His jaw tightened, and his nostrils flared. He moved his hand to cup the back of her neck and brushed his thumb over her jawbone. "How could he hurt you like this?" he said in a low voice. He turned his head slightly to speak over his shoulder. "Dr. Bevan."

"No," Anna said. Exhaustion was quickly stealing her energy. "Tend to Malachi first. He has been shot."

Philip looked at Malachi, perhaps for the first time noticing the blood as Dr. Bevan and Betty helped him toward the bed and cared for his wound.

Anna stood, but her head felt dizzy. Philip tried to assist her, but she drew away and sat in the chair behind her. She could not even manage to sit up straight and fold her hands properly in her lap. Black spots burst in front of her eyes, and she pitched forward, hearing the faraway sounds of people saying her name as she sank into darkness.

Chapter 23

Anna woke and opened her eyes slowly, looking through the gauzy mosquito netting that hung around the bed in the guestchamber. The bright sun shone through the shuttered windows, making yellow lines on the wooden floor.

She pushed herself into a sitting position. Her neck stung and . . .

The events of the day crashed down on her. She trembled as she remembered Horace Braithwaite's attack and—Philip. He was alive, he was safe . . . and he was lost to her. She gasped at the pain in her chest. An ache squeezed her heart.

She had so badly wanted her memories to return, wanted to remember who she was, but if she'd known it would mean losing everything she cared for—losing *him*—she would have gladly remained in ignorant bliss forever.

A knock sounded at the door, and Anna slid off the bed as Betty entered. "Miss Anna, you should no' be up."

Anna pressed a hand to the bedpost, worried she would have another dizzy spell. But her mind was clear. "Malachi, is he . . . ?"

Betty hurried to her, taking her arm. "He is sleepin'. He'll be well." Her eyes moved to Anna's neck and then rose to her face. "I'm glad you well also, miss." She laid a hand on Anna's cheek.

Anna leaned against her palm. Her throat constricted, and fresh tears sprang to her eyes as she thought about leaving Oakely Park and the people she had come to love. "And where is—"

"Lord Philip left. Wit' Miss Stapleton."

Anna pressed her hand to her mouth. Of course he had gone with Clarissa. She had no right to expect anything different. She squeezed her eyes shut, willing the tears to stay where they belonged. He had told her that was his plan all along, to marry Clarissa Stapleton for her dowry.

The ache in her chest grew until she thought her heart would surely crack open. Anna loved Philip, she loved Oakely Park, and she would not want its owner to settle for less just because he had mistakenly allowed himself to care for a poor servant girl.

Anna insisted she was well and that she was perfectly capable of preparing herself something to eat, so the housekeeper left to care for Malachi without argument.

As she walked down the staircase, Anna ran her hand over the polished wooden railing, wanting to remember every last bit of Oakely Park when she was gone.

She was nearly at the bottom of the steps when Philip stepped through the main door. Her heart tripped at the sight of him, and it made what she had to do all the more difficult.

"Anna, are you all right?" He rushed across the entry hall and clasped her elbow, putting his arm around her and leading her into the parlour. "You need to rest." He helped her to a seat. "Do you need a drink?"

She shook her head. "Is Miss Stapleton well?"

"As well as you might imagine." Philip pulled the stopper from a decanter and poured her a drink anyway. "The way she carried on, you'd have thought she lost a limb instead of simply receiving a blackened eye." He sat next to her and held out the glass.

Anna folded her arms in front of her, pulling away from Philip, although she wanted nothing more than to be held in his arms.

His gaze rested on her neck. "Oh, Anna. I . . . I am so sorry." He reached his hand toward her, but she shook her head, putting out a hand to stop him.

"I remember, Philip."

His brows pulled together. "You do not need to be afraid now. Do not think of him anymore."

Her throat was tight. "No, not Horace. I remember everything. All my memories have returned."

Philip's face blanched. He opened his mouth and took a jerky breath. "And are they . . . Are you . . . Are you married, Anna?" He raised his shoulders, and the skin around his eyes tightened as if bracing himself for her answer.

She had never seen his expression so exposed—so vulnerable and unguarded. Yet she knew she would have to tell him the truth, and it would hurt them both. "I am not married, nor am I engaged."

Philip closed his eyes and let out a breath. His face relaxed into a smile, and his shoulders dropped. He leaned toward her.

She put out her hand again. Her stomach ached, and she could not raise her eyes to his. "But I am not a lady. I am only a maid."

"Anna, I don't—"

"I am a *maid*, Philip—my lord. A servant. And I am sorry." Anna stood and pushed past him, feeling as though her body was collapsing in on itself. Her cheeks and eyes were hot with humiliation, and she wanted nothing more than to escape before she saw the disdain in Philip's face when he looked at her as a person so decidedly below his class.

He called her name, but she didn't look back.

Anna stumbled out of the dining room door toward the kitchen building. She didn't know where to go, but she knew she couldn't remain as a guest in Philip's—*Lord* Philip's—home. Her chest ached so badly that she wrapped her arms around herself, hoping to ease the pain.

She needed to leave. Her mind traveled over the past weeks, and her stomach burned with humiliation when she remembered speaking boldly to his lordship, telling him to invest in a coffee farm, recommending that he hire pirates. Philip must at this very moment be remembering the same things with contempt as he realized he'd allowed a servant to direct him. He must be disgusted that he had even brought her to his guestchamber, that he had invited her to dine in a silk gown . . . She gasped at the memory and what he must think of it now.

Philip was undoubtedly embarrassed as well. Mortified that he had been taken in by a servant girl. Anna thought she would be ill when she imagined encountering him again. Especially after all that had transpired between them.

She must escape. She would find Lady Lockwood at her plantation near Spanish Town and return to her position in that household, provided the countess had not found a new lady's maid.

A sob escaped as she realized she would never see Oakely Park again. Never stand on the veranda and listen to the low sound of the workers singing in the cane fields. Never meet Ezekiel and his large grin in the hallway. Never ride Smokey over the yellow dirt roads. These weeks had been nothing but playacting in a life that didn't belong to her.

She hurried toward the stable, thinking maybe she could borrow a horse. Lord Lockwood would certainly make sure the animal was returned to Oakely Park. She could remember the map in her head and realized it would take days to reach Spanish Town. Perhaps if she found a boat leaving Port Antonio, she could travel by sea. If Captain Courtney was still there, he would help her, she was certain.

Anna entered the gloom of the stables and considered her options. With the two riding horses still missing, only the carriage horses remained, and she couldn't ride one of them. Frustrated and discouraged, she sat on a barrel of grain.

She could not make the journey on foot alone. By the time she arrived in the town, it would certainly be dark, and she had no money to pay for a room at an inn. The idea of encountering a crocodile or a bandit on the road made her shiver. She could, perhaps, ask Betty for help. She would know what to do. And perhaps Betty could recommend someone to accompany her . . .

"Are you leaving me, Anna?" Philip stepped into the doorway.

She stood and curtsied but kept her gaze upon the ground. "I'm afraid I must, my lord," she said in a quiet voice.

"And where will you go?"

"To Port Antonio. I must get to Spanish Town. My employer has a plantation there."

Philip was silent, and she stole a glance at him. Finally he spoke. "It is a long journey."

"I understand, my lord. If you will direct me to the servant's quarters, I will start in the morning—"

"And do you miss your former life so much that you must leave immediately?"

Anna didn't know what to say. She didn't dare look into his face and see what she feared was there. "I must, sir. I thank you for caring for me, and I am certain that Lord Lockwood will compensate you for the cost of my accommodations."

"Blast Lord Lockwood! Blast the compensation! Blast all of it!" Philip's raised voice shocked her, and Anna gasped. He stepped closer. "Anna, why will you not stay? Has the return of your memories changed you? Do you not feel the same as you did?"

She looked up at him. His face was pale, and his brows pulled tightly together. "My lord, nothing has changed, and yet everything has. I am not who you thought I was—who *I* thought I was. I am not a lady; I am a servant. I have nothing. I am nobody. It has all been a mistake, my lord. If I had known . . ." She couldn't continue. She put her hand over her mouth, holding back her weeping.

Philip rested his hands on her shoulders. "If you had known, would you have trekked through the jungle and bargained with pirates? Would you have protected Ezekiel? Would you have bumped my leg at dinner while I attempted to keep a straight face?" He paused, but she did not look up at him. "Would you have allowed me to fall in love with you?" He spoke in a low voice.

"I did not mean to—I am so sorry I deceived you." Anna's shoulders shook beneath his hands, and her voice was little more than a whisper broken by gasps.

Philip crooked a finger beneath her chin and lifted her face. His eyes were warm, and the sight made her pulse jump. "If you had known, you would have done none of this. You would have acted like a servant, treated me as an aristocrat." He ran his thumb over her lips.

A shiver skittered across Anna's skin.

"I would have missed the most wonderful thing to happen to my life. The day you washed ashore on my beach, I changed. And each day since, I have become a better man—because of you. I am not the person I was before either." He brushed a strand of hair from her forehead. "Anna, I feared each moment since I saw you on my veranda that it would be the last, that you would find your memories and leave me. And now it has happened, and I cannot bear it." He leaned forward until his forehead touched hers. "Please stay."

"How can I? I have nothing to offer. I am simply . . . Anna."

He pushed his hand into her hair and lowered his lips to meet hers, pressing gently and then more forcefully as his other arm slid around her waist and held her tightly. Anna wrapped her arms around him. The world around them faded away, and she forgot all the many objections she should be making as her knees went limp. The heat from his kiss spread through her body, making her feel weak and, at the same time, pulsing with life. She pressed closer against him.

Philip pulled away until his lips were just a breath from hers. "You are not simply Anna," he whispered. "You are *my* Anna."

Epilogue

PHILIP HELD HIS NEW BRIDE's hand as he led her up the stairs to the master's bedchamber. He'd deemed the day a success every time he'd seen Anna's smile.

The wedding had been an event the island would be talking about for years to come. Anna refused to be married in a church when she learned her dark-skinned friends were not allowed inside, and so the vicar had agreed to perform the ceremony at Oakely Park. Philip thought his mother would have swooned had she been in attendance, but this wasn't London; it was Jamaica, and he only cared what one person thought.

As Philip had looked down from the Great House steps that morning, he considered that there had likely never been a gathering quite like this. An earl and his family, a ship's captain, a band of pirates, local landowners—though the Stapletons were conspicuously absent and had been ever since Philip returned a wailing Clarissa to her home a few weeks earlier and told her he planned to marry for love not money—and hundreds of newly freed, former slaves.

Full emancipation at Oakely Park had been his wedding gift to Anna. When he saw her smile and tears of gratitude as she threw herself into his arms and covered him with kisses, he did not spare one thought to the cost that would be the result of what the other plantation owners had called "ridiculous philanthropy."

When the ceremony had ended, the doors to the Great House were thrown open. All were welcome to celebrate at a grand party with food, dancing, and laughter that lasted late into the night.

Philip had been unable to take his eyes from Anna the entire evening. It was nearly impossible to believe she was his wife. She'd danced with Captain Courtney, Malachi, Ezekiel, Captain Fletcher, and Lord Lockwood; finally, Philip decided that enough was enough and kept her at his side for the remainder of the night. She didn't seem to mind at all.

He watched Anna and her former employer, Lady Lockwood, talking and laughing and then embracing when it was time to part. His heart swelled as he thought of all the lives Anna touched. He could not be luckier in his choice of a wife.

The last guests departed or were shown to their rooms, and he finally had Anna to himself.

He set the candelabra on the dressing table and turned to see her staring at the oar mounted to the wall above the bed.

"It does not complement the room at all."

Philip stood next to her and studied the piece of wood with weathered scraps of fabric and string still wrapped around it. "That oar brought to me the thing I love most in the world. Normally, I would defer to my wife in matters of home decor, but in this instance, I must insist." He slipped his arm around her waist.

Anna turned into his embrace, sliding her hands up his chest to rest on his shoulders. "Your wife." She sighed. "Today was perfect, Philip. Everything . . . completely perfect." She fingered his cravat. "I cannot believe you freed all the workers. Are you certain we can maintain Oakely Park without the unpaid labor?"

He kissed the tip of her nose. "Let us just hope that Tom's coffee farm turns a profit. And we shall not be wealthy, my love."

"I do not care one bit because we will be happy. Thank you, Philip. I am lucky to be married to such a kindhearted man."

A knock sounded on the door, and Ezekiel poked his head inside. "Can I assist you in preparing for bed, my lord?"

Anna hurriedly jumped out of his arms.

"Thank you but no. I am in good hands. Good night, Ezekiel." Philip closed the door and turned the key in the lock. At the moment, his thoughts were the farthest thing from kindhearted.

Anna giggled; her cheeks had turned a lovely shade of pink.

Philip pulled her back into his embrace. "And what are you laughing about, Miss—" He opened his eyes wide. "'Pon my word, I just had a realization."

Anna raised her brows, and her lips twitched in the way that drove his heart wild.

"The reason I was never able to find a name that suits you is because only one would do—mine." He pressed his lips to hers and feathered kisses over her cheek.

Anna sighed, and the sound made his heart lurch again. "I like it very much," she said. She pulled back and placed her hands on the sides of his face. Deep in her eyes something smoldered. "I love you, Philip."

She kissed him, and he held her closer. He adored the way she melted into his arms and decided that there was nothing in the world as perfect as loving Anna.

"Do not ever forget it," he whispered.

Author's Notes

Researching and writing a book about slavery was more difficult than I could have imagined. I found that I couldn't bear to work on this story for days at a time. The topic became so heavy and painful that I thought I wouldn't be able to finish. But I felt such a need to tell Malachi and Betty's story. Reading old plantation journals, I found some of the most beautiful stories of survival and endurance and love: owners that cared for their slaves like family, and workers that protected their white masters at risk to their own lives. Learning that the world in the nineteenth century was not strictly divided by color was a comfort.

This book was intended to be a happy story, a romance, not a dissertation about the evils of the transatlantic slave trade. I hope my failure to delve into the more gritty details does not portray a lack of caring or understanding on my part for what real people suffered. It was a hard line to walk, telling enough to feel as if I was being true to those who were there and not being so extreme that I would change the tone of the story.

As much as we would like to believe that human slavery is a thing of the past, human rights organizations estimate that 21 million victims of human trafficking exist at the time of this book's publication. To find out how you can be a voice for those who cannot speak for themselves, visit ourrescue.org

About the Author

Jennifer Moore is a passionate reader and writer of all things romance due to the need to balance the rest of her world, which includes a perpetually traveling husband and four active sons, who create heaps of laundry that are anything but romantic. Jennifer has a B.A. in linguistics from the University of Utah and is a Guitar Hero champion. She lives in northern Utah with her family. You can learn more about her at authorjmoore.com.